Death After Dark

ALEXANDER PEEL

DEDICATION

For Kavita

CONTENTS

ACKNOWLEDGMENTS

A truly sincere acknowledgment to all the people who have helped and encouraged me along the way. If I were to give full details on how much I need & appreciate all these people, then this section would likely be longer than the book itself, but while I will endeavor to be brief, I hope those listed know that my appreciation is far from that.

Lewis Warner was a wonderful sounding board for ideas (both good and bad) and helping me shoot down tired plot cliches. Dean Cormack read my first draft and told me things that stayed with me right until I finished my final edit. Alejandro Mora helped me write consistently, despite being thousands of miles away.

I must also thank Marek Mihok, Luka Vasilj and Malik Wahba for allowing their names to graduate from placeholders to permanent characters. I have too much love for their characters to change their names. Thank you in particular to Malik, whose excitement for my eternally 'upcoming novel' never waned.

To Jack Dickson, I thank you for being the inspiration behind my writing and the reason why I finished. You are a superstar, and I hope you enjoy reading it as much as I enjoyed writing it.

To my parents, my other friends, my coworkers, and anyone who encouraged me along the way, I appreciate you more than you know.

And to Kavita; I don't have enough space on this page, but the only reason I am able to grapple with the idea of writing books is because you are by my side.

CHAPTER 1

Guinness House was the latest addition to New York's sprawling metropolis, slotting in seamlessly with Midtown's nouveau architectural designs. It had cropped up just a few years ago, a hundred metres west of the major financial district, after they'd demolished one the city's remaining car parks to make space for another contemporary masterpiece.

Architectural Digest called it a "squircle." It was a short, squat building, bulging at the edges, as though struggling to contain its inhabitants. Large steel bands encircled floor to ceiling windows, tinted a dark blue to keep out the sun, which had faded a few hours ago to make way for a half-moon, just sitting shyly behind the clouds.

Despite its size, Guinness House housed a modest number of residents on a day-to-day basis. The businesses inside touted either billion-dollar portfolios, or billion-dollar clients, and with the price of rent in the offices, it was only the elite who could afford the opulent spaces. A total of six floors of post-modern office space housed companies with no promises of work-life balance. Those who worked inside, worked. Lawyers crossed paths with accountants and consultants inside polished wooden hallways from the early hours of dawn until past sunset. Even on a dark night, Guinness House perpetually sparkled, reminding those who dared to go home that it was already almost tomorrow…almost time to get back to work.

Fortunately for their families, most of the office fodder had managed to sneak out for the evening. Indeed, Pat Dickson – the night shift security guard – knew that apart from himself, the building was home to a very select group of people that evening. It was those who labelled themselves night owls, squirrelled away in their offices, their faces tanned by the blue light of their computer screens. Those who would die before they stopped working.

But what Pat didn't know was that this Tuesday would be like no other. He'd done his count before the shift started, and he knew for a fact that there were fourteen people pacing the halls of Guinness House that night.

By the morning, only thirteen would leave alive.

CHAPTER 2

Pat shoved his feet – big, booted, size ten feet – up on his desk. Netflix roared away with abandon on his tablet. One of the few perks of this job – it was why he'd been here almost twelve years. He'd slogged for ten years in the old building and had been rewarded with another two in one of the most opulent workspaces in Manhattan.

Security', they'd called it. Really, the only security he'd ever done was chasing a few skateboarders away from the front lawns. But it came with a whole host of cameras to peer down, and his own desk – just for him!

Except during the day, when it was Lionel's, of course.

Pat fondled his belly absent-mindedly, shoveling more Doritos into his mouth. The clock ticked past eleven. Rain roared outside. Comfort. Sweet, sweet comfort.

And soon, lunch time!

A fleeting glance over the cameras told Pat all he needed to know. Everything was fine. He didn't want to invade their privacy too much, so he watched over the cameras, did his rounds on time, and kept an ear out for any disturbances. But he did love a chat when he could have one, and the women seemed happy to have him around. His desk was right in front of the main doors, meaning anyone who walked in had to go through him. Pat liked to think that everyone felt safer knowing that he was the first port of call for any late night visitors.

The only interruptions to his night were when he had to let people out. Everybody had a key-card, but not everybody kept track, so often Pat would have to use his to set them free. He'd often get a slice of cake, or Chinese takeaway for his troubles.

And he was a sucker for a slice of cake.

Pat didn't have cameras in the offices, but they were everywhere else. Hell, he could see the lobby he sat in from half a dozen different angles,

3

and he had a reasonably good view of each floor, up to the double-glazed doors where people toiled away late into the night. He didn't consider himself a pervert, but he did take a little bit of pleasure in watching people who didn't know they were being watched.

He enjoyed a good chuckle as a hotshot lawyer in a pencil skirt shimmied past her co-workers with a flirty grin before digging her finger so far up her nose she was touching her brain. Once, he saw James – a virtuoso accountant – shoving a finger down the back of his pants to surreptitiously inspect his underwear. It was a nice reminder that they were all human, despite them being paid a hundred times his salary.

He was on level one. Just him, an elaborate lobby with some priceless artwork, the toilets – no cameras there, of course. From his vantage point in front of the doors, he was flanked by two reasonably steep, straight staircases that led up to the next level. He tended to dodge them as much as he could...the elevators were just a little bit faster. And they didn't leave him out of breath.

Each floor had the same vibe; soft lighting, tasteful fixtures and fittings. Anyone who entered for an interview was suddenly desperate to work in such opulence. On every floor there was a large, tastefully designed office, and they were occupied on each one but the sixth.

Level two was a doctor's surgery. It was a schmick outfit. Pat could swear they only saw about three clients a day, and the doctors – all young men – looked like models. There were maybe half a dozen of them total, all in their late twenties and early thirties, all disconcertingly friendly. Pat would often wander by the offices in the afternoon to see them with beer bottles on the desks and the TV on, which they could afford to do solely because of how much they charged for a single consult.

What a life.

Next door to them was PubStunt, a public relations company. They had big clients. Big clients. He didn't pay much attention, but he'd seen the company name enough all over the news for what -- the last ten years? They had great big blue signs with their logos on, flashing all over national TV while they spoke on behalf of sports stars at NBA games. They were a sponsor of the US Open!

Whilst the small office on three was empty, the large one was occupied by a banking outfit. Suits, ties, money. Pat had seen more than enough people come and go from Mihok & Mihok. More often than not, the newest recruits would be chased out in under a week after they couldn't hack the workload, then miss the inevitable party where music and booze raged late into the night. Pat had caught a youngster licking residual champagne off the front windows one time. He always liked stopping by to chat to the bankers. They always seemed happy to see him.

Above them, on four, the lawyers schemed in their den. They were a little quieter than the bankers, but business was booming. They worked late into the night, running past Pat in the lobby at all hours, yelling into phones, paperwork spilling out of their briefcases. Nonetheless, they too had an end of year party where everyone seemed to enjoy themselves a little too much

Work hard, party hard.

Level five was…different. Pat would even admit that it creeped him out a little. There was no fun at all, and there were no parties. It was a biopharmaceutical company, with bright white lights and opaque glass doors called Microceuticals. Unlike the doctors, they did wear lab coats, as well as sour expressions. Pat had almost come to blows with the CEO a few months back, but cooler heads had prevailed.

Yes, he had been looking through the windows, but he was security! He had to make sure that everything was safe and secure.

And beneath the skylight was level six. The quietest of all floors, with only the small office was occupied by a one-woman photography studio. And that woman…well, there was a reason that Pat always started on the sixth floor.

Netflix rolled through another batch of credits.

Time to get walking.

*   *   *

Even the elevator was luxurious.

Pat maneuvered his overwhelming bulk inside as the doors parted, and then he was stuck in a mirrored box with only his own reflection. He was going on forty-five, but his hair – a band of brown just above his ears, balding on the top – was going on sixty. His hairdresser refused to cut it any other way.

"I've got nothin' to work with, so quit complainin'!" she'd shriek in that broad Brooklyn accent, before going at his pasty white dome with the electric razor, ending the lives of any stray hairs that dared crop up on the top of his head. "This is how all the guys are doin' it these days anyway!"

Karen had told him it suited him. But then again, in one of their more recent fights, she'd called him a "fat ugly fuck," so messages were a bit mixed.

She'd taken it back, but the words still stung as Pat caught sight of his own reflection. His gut had grown so large that it rolled over the front of his pants, obscuring his belt buckle. His shirt was bursting at the seams, the buttons threatening to pop at any moment, but he had a spare in his locker, just in case. At the start of the night it was always a freshly laundered white, but by the time Pat had scoffed down a bag of Doritos, those sneaky sweat stains had started to well around his armpits and on the top of his chest.

Karen had always said he should do more walking at work to try and lose the weight, but that only made the sweat worse!

She was lovely, and only had his best interests at heart. And to tell the truth, Pat knew better than anyone else that he had to make a change...but as his wife, Karen had taken command of reminding him of that.

"You're piling it on, Pat, and it's not stopping! Get out and get to the gym, like Larry!"

Larry was their sixteen-year old. Just the one. Sex had largely stopped a few years after their marriage. Between him picking up the security job, Larry being born, and Karen piling on some baby weight, libidos had hit an all-time low. They'd gotten back into the swing of things more recently, which was yet another reason Karen was his absolute favourite person in the world. He knew it couldn't be easy for her...particularly when he was on top.

Meanwhile, Larry – his little Larry – had piled on the right sort of size. Muscles – like the ones Pat used to have – rippled beneath his T-shirts. If he wasn't doing his maths homework, he was at the gym most nights, and if he wasn't there, he was out with girls! Pat couldn't have been prouder. Karen was his childhood sweetheart, and though they'd had their ups and downs through the years, they were still rock solid. He had his fingers crossed that Larry could find his own Karen.

A hundred feet later, the elevator doors opened to the top floor. Pat checked both ways before getting out.

You have to be smart! What if there's an intruder?

It was like he was living in a fantasy world at times, but at least it made the evenings a touch more exciting.

Fortunately, the floor was empty...as always. The elevator had opened into the middle of the landing, a long stretch of wood-flooring stretching left and right away from Pat. Amber lights planted in the ceiling lit the whole place with a dull glow. Pat could practically smell the dust.

A glass balcony with a steel railing bordered a huge drop – maybe forty, fifty feet – back down to the lobby. Pat ambled right – to the left was the large office, and he had no business there – the shadows of his feet looking huge on the floor as they caught the lights on the rails. Opposite him, on the north side of the building, an array of floor to ceiling windows treated him to a phenomenal view of New York city, basking in the moonlight.

Pat plodded on, whistling in the quiet.

Lafferty Inc.

Not exactly a household name, Lafferty Inc had moved into Guinness House about a year ago. Pat was surprised that a modelling agency could even afford the rent, but had accepted his mistake when he saw the steady stream of talent moving through the front doors from the moment that they'd opened shop. Some of the models he'd seen on TV, on the runways in New York when Karen was watching Fashion Week. He'd even spotted one of the girls as a cheerleader at a basketball game when he went to watch the Knicks play. From time to time, Pat had heard them discussing what they wanted in their portfolios, and when he caught wind of the prices, how the lady behind the camera afforded the rent made a lot more sense.

Pat paused at the front door, running his finger softly over the logo etched into the glass. A bead of sweat ran down his forehead.

Settle down, Pat! She's only human!

He straightened himself to his full height, and knocked.

CHAPTER 3

The woman who answered the door was a vision. Green eyes shone radiantly in the dim light of the hall, couched in sharp cheekbones and soft lips. Light red locks fell effortlessly on her slim shoulders.

Monica Lafferty. CEO, business owner, photographer extraordinaire.

She cocked an eyebrow and threw him a flash of those dazzling pearly-whites. Casual wear hugged her tightly – yoga pants, a top that just allowed her midriff to peek through – and she was wielding a camera that was so big it could be mistaken for a weapon.

"Well, Pat," she hummed. "To what do I owe this pleasure?"

"Uh, ma'am." Pat could feel his brow sweating already. She made him nervous, and she knew it. "Just, checking in, y'know. Making sure you haven't, uh…seen anything, suspicious…y'know. Around here. Tonight."

God, get it together.

She chuckled. "My, my, Pat, I think the only thing suspicious is how many times you seem to come and check on me in one night." She winked conspiratorially. "I've got a girl in here, if you'd like to meet her…?"

Pat coughed, and wiped his brow. "Oh no, no, that…that won't be necessary, Monica. I've got, uh, other things to do – just thought I'd check in before I hit the other floors."

Monica giggled again and brushed a lock of hair back from her face. Her engagement rock flickered under the hallway lights.

She's flirting, right?

"Well, Pat – as much as I'd love to hang around with you…" she waved the camera, "….she's got half her clothes off, so…"

Pat felt his thoughts moving determinedly – and quickly – in an inappropriate direction.

"Of course, of course," he puffed. "I'll leave you to it, and if anything comes up – you know where to find me."

She winked at him again and swept back inside the office as Pat turned on his heel and hurried back in the direction of the elevators, sweat streaming down his face, his thoughts racing.

Yep. Definitely flirting.

He mashed the elevator button for down and pulled his phone out. No word from Karen yet, but she'd call any minute now. Like clockwork, she always checked in just after eleven, when she was going to bed.

The elevator doors closed with a quiet hum.

*　　*　　*

Pat popped out on the fourth floor, and was greeted by a gentle chatter somewhere in the distance. The way the floors were set out, it was like each end of the building belonged to a different company, and they met in the middle at the elevators. He wheeled out towards the left, in the direction of the law firm, a joyful jaunt in his step. The air down here had the lingering smell of someone having doused themselves in cologne; sandalwood. Pat liked it.

Collymore & Donovan, LLP.

Two people emerged from the doors, striding towards Pat.

Catherine Kim was their newest associate. She was a small Korean girl – Pat's best guess put her at twenty-five, or twenty-six – with furrowed eyebrows and a determination in her step. By her side was Mateo Brown – a culturally androgynous guy, well-seasoned, maybe in his thirties. Pat often saw him greeting high profile clients in the lobby. He was their poster boy; on the front page of their website and posters. Good looking, smart, personable. His black curls bobbed under the dim light of the hallway as the two of them beelined in Pat's direction, Catherine's head nodding furiously as Mateo gabbled on.

They looked up when they spotted him.

"Ma'am, sir." Pat doffed an imaginary cap. "Everything alright this evening?"

They didn't answer, but Catherine offered a timid smile. As they passed each other, Mateo resumed his verbiage.

He's got to earn that fancy car somehow.

Pat checked to make sure they'd gotten in the elevator, then hustled over to the front door of their office and slipped inside.

Collymore and Donovan was as gorgeous as always. He'd heard Joseph – the building manager – say that Collymore hadn't even checked the office space before moving in. More than that, they'd actually bought the office instead of leasing it. It had become the most luxurious space in the building; laminate wooden floors, a marble-topped reception desk, and even some vague efforts at greenery, with plastic plants stuffed into the corners.

Behind the reception desk, an oversized opaque door led to the bullpen. Pat had been through there once, when their fire extinguisher had fallen off the wall, and it was chaotic. Phones ringing off the hook, paper flying out of printers, maybe twenty or thirty people buzzing about, and a Congressman in with them too. Nevertheless, as busy as it usually was, Pat always knew exactly how many people were in the building, and his math told him that there could be only one other person in the bullpen that night.

"Hello?" he called out, lingering at the counter to stuff a fistful of wrapped candies into his pocket. "Security! Just…just checking in."

Something slammed in one of the back offices. Pat took a cursory step backwards.

The door to the bullpen flew open.

Johnny Ray.

He was a young, surfer-looking guy with a hell of a lot of attitude, but the firm kept him around because he was good in a tight spot. He managed to get himself in a lot of them as well. The ever-whirring rumour mill had him spotted in handcuffs after fights in bars at the Meatpacking district.

"Yeah?" His voice sharp; harsh and heavy in the quiet. Not like the usual fractious – but friendly – Johnny. Pat knew him quite well. So did everyone in the building. Lawyer, younger, good-looking, gay. It was hardly a secret. Johnny made no bones of the fact that he used the privacy of the night shift to hook up with whoever was on the local dating apps. In situations like that, it was reasonable for them to have a few drinks and come back here, singing and dancing, as happy as one could be.

But tonight, he didn't look anything like his usual self.

He looked a mess.

Johnny's mop of brown hair was slick to his forehead, his pupils dilated and darting. And despite being at the office, and not at the club, it seemed like he was still trying to enjoy himself in one way or another…

"What're you drinking?" Pat asked, jabbing a finger in the direction of the bottle swinging from Johnny's hand.

It was like Johnny didn't even hear him. He had that thousand-yard stare, like in *Saving Private Ryan*. Like he'd seen a ghost.

"Johnny?"

The vacant stare vanished, to be replaced with…rage?

"None of your business!" he hissed, before turning on his heel and vanishing back into the bullpen.

Pat stood in the doorway for a second, totally perplexed. He liked Johnny, they got along well! He was a California boy. Normally they talked about hockey, or basketball.

What's wrong with him?

Pat's phone rang.

* * *

"Well, glad to hear it's been a peaceful night my love!" Karen cooed.

Pat was pacing back and forth in front of the huge window on the fourth floor, treating himself to a view of Midtown.

"Did you ask your boss about the fourteenth? Larry's got his tournament, remember."

"Oh, uh— he isn't here tonight," Pat grunted. "Should be fine, though?"

Larry had taken up an interested in amateur boxing. Pat had guessed it wouldn't last, but as if to prove him wrong, Larry had been going almost two years now, well past the six-month stint Pat had fought in his youth.

And that meant Karen was getting more insistent on her husband finally making an appearance.

"Be sure to ask!" Karen chided. "It'll be…two weeks today. You work seven days a week, you should be able to get at least one evening off!" She lowered her voice to a whisper. "He really wants you there. He's been asking me all week if you're coming!"

"Yeah, yeah – I'll get it done," Pat sighed. "I'll talk to Joseph about swapping shifts. Just…don't make any promises for me."

"Too late!"

Pat wandered towards the staircase as Karen yawned her way to the end of the conversation.

"Goodnight my love," she whispered. "Come for a cuddle when you get home."

"Wouldn't miss it for the world. Goodnight, my angel."

Normally, it took Pat about half an hour to sweep the whole building, if he wasn't rushing to get back to the TV. His phone logged his steps nowadays, so he tried to do some laps of the fourth floor landing before heading downstairs. Karen was in the habit of checking how long he was spending walking nowadays, and this was the easiest way to get her off his back, otherwise she'd try and send him out running, which just hurt his knees.

And he wanted to stay active! He just wasn't young anymore, and working 12 hour shifts each day meant it was a bit more difficult to get to the gym after work. He'd moved on from that lifestyle.

The sleek black office of Mihok & Mihok greeted Pat as he ambled down the staircase. Ordinarily, Pat generally wandered over on a more boring night to spend some time with Nadine, defender of the reception desk. She was a bit more of a wisecrack than the people normally in her role; mid-forties, sophisticated dress sense, hell of a tan. She'd laugh at his dumb jokes and genuinely seemed happy to see him. With Monica, Pat felt like he was playing with fire. With Nadine, she was just a friendly colleague. They'd swap stories about their spouses and talk about food. She even brought him doughnuts!

Unfortunately for Pat, Nadine wasn't the person sitting in the chair at the front desk. She'd been a bit off colour over the last few weeks; maybe she'd taken the night off?

A man was hunched over a keyboard, his face illuminated by the blue light of his laptop. The other face that Pat of Mihok & Mihok that Pat knew quite well, as he was normally the only one around at this hour...unless he'd brought his bulldog associate with him.

Pat had heard stories of this man's ruthlessness. Almost every day, employees were being turfed out with their briefcases after botching a single trade. The business worked on ruthless profit margins, and anyone who wasn't earning Marek Mihok money was losing him money.

Pat knew — as well as anyone else — that the man was a snake in the grass.

And as friendly as Marek was, Pat really wasn't a fan of snakes.

CHAPTER 4

"Patrick!" Marek Mihok wasn't a large man – he would've been a few inches shorter than Pat, who stood at a stocky 6'3" – but he filled up the room. His blonde hair was cut short on the back and sides, and blue eyes peeked out from behind bespoke spectacles. His white shirt was crisp and neatly-ironed, despite the fact that there was no-one around to impress.

He was here to do business.

Some people said Marek had set up the firm all by himself, but stuck his name on the door twice to make it seem more appealing. Others were of the opinion that he thought himself twice as important as anyone else. Everyone, however, agreed that he was a goddamn viper.

Marek grinned as Pat entered, rising from his laptop behind the front desk to offer one of those vice-like handshakes.

"What can I do for you?"

"Just happy to see you, Mr. Mihok. Checking in. Am I interrupting?"

"Not at all, not at all, Patrick!" Marek motioned him over to a navy-blue sequined chair in the corner of the foyer. It was a comforting space; dark, stylish. The lighting was moody; soft oranges from small overhead lights, the glow of a lamp in the corner reflecting off the black marble of the reception desk. Everything was dark and classic, save for an absolute monolith of a printer – a light grey, plastic box that stood maybe four feet high – whirring quietly opposite the reception desk. You'd have to edge past it to get into the back room.

Perhaps that was Marek's way of reminding people they weren't supposed to go back there without an invitation.

Marek took a seat opposite, resting his feet on the coffee table. He conjured a decanter from a side table. The liquid inside shone a dark amber.

"Drink?"

"I really shouldn't…"

Marek smiled and topped him off with a generous half-glass.

"My friends back home," he sighed. "They only drink Vodka." He said it with a W. *Wodka.* "Vodka this, Vodka that. But, since I moved over here…I started trying the good stuff."

Pat's eyes fell over a small cabinet nestled behind Marek's chair, stocked with bottle after bottle of 'Johnny B Goode's Beautiful Bourbon.' Marek followed his gaze.

"Oh, don't worry," he chuckled. "That's Sal's. You wouldn't catch me drinking that if it were the last on earth. This is much better."

They clinked their glasses together, and Pat sipped, not taking his eyes off Marek. He was right – this wasn't dollar store bourbon. The warmth spread like a fireball down his gullet, wrapping its warm tendrils around his heart before slowly fading into his stomach.

Marek slugged his back in a single gulp. "Macallan '25. Not bad for the long nights, eh? But I have a rule. Never drink alone!"

"Oh no doubt," Pat hummed, weighing the drink in his hand. "No-one else to share it with today?"

Marek sighed, checking his watch. "Nadine vanished about half an hour ago. We're doing some work, like a joint venture. It's us down here and Microceuticals upstairs, so she's running documents back and forth. She's been a while, though…"

The disappointment must have been evident on Pat's face. Marek clapped him on the shoulder.

"Aw, my friend!" he guffawed. "Don't worry, Papa Mihok will keep you company. And I'll tell her you stopped by."

"No really, that's fine, Mr. Mihok. You've probably got things to do, and…well, I shouldn't be drinking on the job anyway."

"Well…" Marek hummed, gliding back to his laptop, "We all do things we probably shouldn't. Finish that up before you go, can't have it going to waste. And come back for another before you knock off. I'll be here."

It didn't sound like an invitation. It sounded like an order.

Pat dutifully finished the glass, the tendrils coiling around in his chest again, and left Marek in the company of his laptop.

Back outside, he leaned on the glass balcony to take the weight off his knees. Frankly, he was disappointed Nadine wasn't there, but it made sense. He'd seen her flitting back and forth between Mihok & Mihok, Microceuticals and even MedHealth on the second floor, but he'd never been told the reason. He'd never asked – it wasn't his business. But if he got his timing better tomorrow, maybe there'd be a chance at catching up with his friend.

Pat wasn't lonely, as such. He could always call Karen. But on nights like this, he often felt alone. There was a distinct difference – one he wasn't smart enough to be able to articulate to Karen, who insisted he should just call for a chat. Talking to someone on the phone just wasn't the same as sharing laughs – or doughnuts – in person. Plus, she would have gone to bed now, and he'd hate to wake her if she was sleeping.

No, he wouldn't call her. He'd head down to check on PubStunt, do the stairwells and check the fuse box, then double back and do Microceuticals. The nosy part of Pat liked doing the fifth floor last. It was like they were keeping secrets up there.

And Pat loved a good secret.

*   *   *

The second floor felt deserted. If a tumbleweed could get into the building, this is where it would be.

Just like the other big names in the building, Eric Van De Berg worked long hours for his business, but he was so quiet with his movements and spent so much time holed up in his office that it was often like nobody was home at all. When Pat did see him, he looked utterly exhausted; he didn't take care of himself as well as Marek did. He'd hired his daughter – Charlotte? – a few months ago. She'd come in bright and bubbly for the first few weeks, but over time the late nights had drained her as well. Pat would see her aimlessly wandering the hallways on occasion, devoid of any substance. She was as skinny as a rake – he'd offer her a doughnut, but most of the time she'd just float by, with that blank gaze that said her mind was somewhere else.

The bright blue logos of PubStunt's LED signs next to the front door were blinding as Pat pressed his eye up to their door, trying to see what was going on inside. Nothing tonight, apparently. The lights were on, but the doors were locked. Pat could see the swish lobby inside; just what he'd expect of an upmarket PR company. It was like something in the magazines – jet black leather chairs, a carefully curated collection of magazines fanned on glass coffee tables, and a water cooler straight out of Google HQ. As always, there was a door at the back of the foyer with a tiny glass window, leading into the company's more private space. But no people. It was a small business. Eric, Charlotte, and a few more fresh-faced youngsters who looked healthier in front of a camera.

Pat knocked once as a formality. "Security!" he called out. A silhouette moved across the window to the back room so quickly that Pat almost missed it.

Somebody's home, but nobody's answering.

And so Pat gave up, wandered in the direction of the elevators, then doubled back to the stairs. Better take the stairs, he thought. Got to give Karen something to work with. He checked his phone as he huffed his way down to the lobby. Nothing from Karen, or from Larry. He was probably asleep as well, given that it was a Tuesday. It was a good routine. They had never set a curfew for him – that wasn't Pat's style, although Karen would've liked it. They'd caught him out drinking once or twice, but that wasn't a big deal – at least, not to Pat. He was a good kid, and even good kids make mistakes. Pat had definitely made his fair share of them.

The stairwells were, as they were every night, completely quiet. The fire escapes were still closed, and all the fuses were fine. If anyone had opened them, then the cameras would go on the fritz and Pat's phone would be blasting alerts.

And so, in the moment of peace and tranquility, Pat dug in his pocket for his trusty vice – a pack of Marlboro Reds. Every time he lit one up, he remembered the days where he and Karen would kick back on their back patio in New Jersey, slinging insults and beers until the wee hours. That was when they had just gotten together. She didn't smoke much, but by the end of a few glasses of wine, she'd fire one up and then fall asleep on his shoulder.

The good old days.

Now, it was three of them, in a much smaller house, up in Queens. No back yard, so Pat had taken his little habit to work.

Well, it's not like there's anyone around to tell me off for it.

As he puffed away, the noxious smoke filling his lungs and pluming up the east stairwell, his phone dinged twice in quick succession. The first was from the Joseph, the building manager.

J: Busy night?

Pat flicked a quick response.

P: Nope. All good here.

That was all it took. Prompt answers were the best way to keep the boss happy, which meant less work appeasing him elsewhere. As long as nobody died in the building, and Joseph felt he had someone reliable around, Pat's job was safe.

And everyone in here was as safe as houses.

The second text was from Catherine Kim, on the building's IT chat.

C: Thinking of leaving in ten. Can't find my card, are you downstairs?

Even though they didn't talk much, even though they didn't have anything in common, Catherine was always polite and courteous. It made the job a thousand times easier.

P: Of course, Catherine. Be there in a jiffy.

He flicked the cigarette into the dusty underhang beneath the concrete stairs and watched as the butt smouldered for a few seconds, then ducked back into the lobby.

*   *   *

Pat walked Catherine out to the carpark. He had to check on the gardens anyway, so they strolled up to the main gate together. She vanished into the dark with a timid wave.

It was amusing. Here she was, a total hotshot lawyer brainbox, earning five times his salary, but at his mercy over a piece of plastic. "Good night!" he said as she hurried away from him, bundled up in her coat, and dove into her car. Not only was it almost midnight, but it was absolutely freezing. Anyone would be in a rush. She roared away in her little Lexus, and the front gate's motor kicked in, pulling the cast iron bars closed and keeping her out. See you tomorrow.

Pat turned back towards Guinness House, pulling his windbreaker up around his shoulders as the wind chill stung at his neck. Even though he'd been working here for almost two years, it still took his breath away. The lights from inside were so luminous they blocked Pat's view of the skyscrapers behind. The walls curved in a gentle scope, bounded by those steel bands that stretched for miles and miles. It was on the cover of every magazine when they'd finished building it. An icon, in its own right.

The gardens were similarly stunning. Guinness House wasn't the largest of buildings, but when they were renovating, the developers had bought the lot next door so that they could set the new building into a double block and surround it with greenery rivalled only by Central Park. Pat traipsed around the perimeter to turn off the sprinklers, eyeing the rainbow of flowers fresh from their blessings. Neatly trimmed hedges loomed above his head as he crunched across the lawn, archways covering the cobbled pathway from the car park up to the main entrance.

All in all, it was a remarkably peaceful place to work. If Pat ever found his mind wandering or his anxiety flaring up, he found like a spell outside – particularly on these colder, winter nights – relaxed him plenty.

After making sure the gardens were void of skateboarders who had the tenacity to jump the fence, Pat looped back to the hedged pathway and ducked inside. He contemplated firing Netflix back up for a second.

No, no. Better to finish work and then relax.

But Karen had cooked him up a stir fry for dinner – or was it technically lunch? – and his stomach was rumbling. Reticently, he jumped back into the elevator and hit the button for five. The fifth floor was a little bit different to the others. They never turned the lights off. They glowed a stark white, so bright that they were almost painful to look at. The office was so huge it looped corner to corner, covering the entire floor, leaving only the large floor to ceiling windows looking out onto the gardens as free space.

So who was making Microceuticals their home tonight?

Pat had a few guesses.

The CEO, Luka Vasilj, was a young man in his thirties. Good friends with Marek, apparently. Pat supposed they might call him a 'go-getter', but

Pat didn't have much time for him. He was, for lack of any other description, an angry young man. His voice would echo down to the lobby as he talked down to his employees, shouted on phone calls, and occasionally screamed into the void. Even at the Christmas party, he only spoke to his own subjects.

Pat peered over the opaque branding on Microceuticals' main doors and through the same tiny back window that all the offices had. Back there, they had their lab. Three distinct silhouettes were flitting back and forth. They were bulky, and alien; he caught a flash of a hazmat suit, and goggles. Luka – for sure. At this hour, one of the others the other was probably Gopal Tendulkar – one of the lab's leading researchers, and maybe one of his assistants, or a new lab tech. They'd hired Gopal when they were still set up in the old building, and Pat remembered he'd fired half of the office support staff in his first week. Brutal! Pat didn't even try keeping up with the employees names anymore – as long as they had a key card, they weren't his problem. Pat tested the glass doors.

Locked.

That wasn't unusual; Microceuticals liked to keep their business extremely private, even though it was plastered all over the news. But, when Pat wasn't watching Netflix, he enjoyed doing a little bit of…digging. He called it 'research.' Karen called it 'being nosy.' Luka had started Microceuticals straight out of college. It had become a national phenomenon as they powered through with their research, always working on some new drug that was supposed to revolutionize healthcare.

At the moment, all Pat could tell was that they had their fingers in business with Mihok & Mihok, and judging by the number of doctors he'd seen up here, MedHealth were likely involved too. Pat didn't quite understand the relationship, but judging by the expensive cars and immaculate clothes they all wore – and that Macallan that he'd enjoyed with Marek just before –there must be a big financial incentive to their work. Probably seven figures. Pat knocked.

Within moments, the lock snapped open.

Luka was a naturally good-looking man, with high cheekbones and bright blue eyes, but his pursed lips and haughty expression made him…unsightly. He flicked back a mop of brown hair.

"Yes?" he snapped.

"Just…uh, check—"

"We're busy," he snarled. "Come back later."

He slammed the door in Pat's face. The lock clicked back into place.

Asshole.

Pat meandered away from the office and down the hallway, whistling merrily, lunch on his mind. He was honestly thankful that their exchanges were so short and he'd have nothing more to do with Luka that evening.

Maybe he'd head back to Mihok & Mihok and grab another drink with Marek. Perhaps Nadine would be there.

Pat rounded the corner, the sights of Manhattan shining in through the large glass window, taking the long way for those extra steps. He spotted something on the floor, maybe halfway down the landing.

Pat stopped, dead in his tracks.

Nadine wouldn't be down in the offices of Mihok & Mihok.

She was collapsed in a heap next to the windows, the moonlight shining on her stillness.

Nadine...

Blood was pouring from a gash in her throat.

CHAPTER 5

Nadine!

Pat dashed over as fast as his legs would carry him.

Nadine was most certainly dead. Her face – normally a picture-perfect bronzed tan – had faded to a ghostly white. Her eyes were sunken in their sockets as they stared up at Pat, lifeless.

And...the blood.

So much blood.

Pat fumbled for his phone.

Cops. Gotta call the cops, Pat.

His fingers were sweaty and numb against the screen.

Secure the building.

He whirled to his feet and started towards the elevators – but then turned back to Nadine.

I can't leave her here.

The phone started to ring in his hand. His head was spinning. Bile rose in his throat. Call the cops, then secure the building. Come back for her later. He hurried towards the elevator.

"Emergency Telecommunications here – you need fire, medical or law enforcement?"

"L-Law enforcement."

"Patching you through."

Pat knew the procedure. Panicking and doing things wrong wasn't going to help anyone, but try as he might, he couldn't do anything about the fierce sense of dread that was completely overwhelming him.

Secure the building, get the cops here. You can get back to her afterwards.

Focus, Pat.

Focus.

The elevator dinged open and Pat dashed inside, sending it straight down to the lobby and mashing the button to close the doors.

Faintly, a male voice crackled on the other end of the phone.

"NYPD dispatch on the line. What's your address?"

"H-hello? Can you hear me?" Pat panted as the elevator doors finally closed. "Is anyone there?"

"I can hear you sir. Who am I speaking with?" The lines were delivered so flawlessly, so calmly, that it seemed almost mocking.

"My, my coworker! She's been stabbed. She's, uh, she's dead. I think she's dead...they cut her throat. Fuck..." Pat's mind whirred as he choked on his words. The image of Nadine, prone on the parquet flooring, was burned behind his eyelids. "We're at Guinness House! Guinness House – that's the address. Manhattan."

A slight pause on the line. The elevator whirred insistently as it took him downstairs.

"Is that on West 43rd Street in Manhattan, sir?"

"Yes, yes! Please, please hurry. I'm Pat, I'm security in the building. I just found her. I've got to open the front gate for you..." Pat hustled across the lobby and practically threw himself into his chair. His shirt was soaked through with sweat; whether from fear or exertion, he did not know.

"Pat, is the assailant still in the building?"

"Uh..." Pat desperately scanned the security cameras, looking for any sign of movement in the gardens or the stairwells. He whirled desperately in his wheely-chair, sending the empty bag of Doritos and its crumbs flying all over the tiles. "I – I don't know! How would I know?!"

"Okay Pat, I'm going to need you to listen to me." The voice was more urgent now, less rehearsed. "A squad car is on the way. My name is Josh, and I want you to stay on the line with me until the officers arrive. Does your building have security protocols for situations like this?"

"Yes, yeah, we do, yeah."

"Okay, Pat, I'm going to need you to do whatever you're supposed to do. Do I need to send an ambulance as well?"

"Uh, I don't know. I don't know, maybe?"

"Hold the line please." The background static behind Josh's voice vanished, to be replaced by a loud beeping while medical dispatch were patched in. Pat fumbled for the big red button under his desk. It had a reputation for being a little temperamental, but Pat prayed tonight, of all nights, it would work.

Josh's question rung in his ears.

Is the assailant still in the building?

Pat hit the button. The lobby erupted. A flashing blue-red strobe shattered the peaceful orange glow of the ceiling lights, plunging the entire building into a scene out of a horror film. A robotic voice boomed out alongside a piercing alarm from loudspeakers on each floor, deafening in the quiet.

"WARNING! WARNING! EVERYBODY TO EMERGENCY STATIONS! WARNING! WARNING! EVERYBODY TO EMERGENCY STATIONS!"

Pat tried desperately to focus on the security cameras, his heart pounding in his chest.

What if someone was still here? Should he go and get Nadine? In case they came back? Why would they come back?! She's already dead! Help the others!

Shock and fear sent Pat into autopilot. He could hear his heart in his ears as he charged over to the east stairwell – the one to the right of his desk – and checked to make sure the external door was closed before wedging the internal one open. People were meant to take the fire escape in case of an emergency, but they hadn't had one in so long he wasn't sure if they knew what to do.

He hurried back to the cameras, desperate to not miss anything. Through the din of the alarm and robotic voice, he could hear smatterings of conversation, and the ding of an elevator from the floors upstairs.

Pat rushed over to the west stairwell, on the opposite side of the building.

"EVERYBODY GET DOWNSTAIRS!" he bellowed up to the rafters as he charged across the lobby to wedge open the west door, just for anyone who did the right thing.

His phone. Cops on the phone. Get your phone, you fool!

Pat practically sprinted back to his desk, fumbling for the phone in such desperation that he slapped it off the desk and into the trash can. As he rummaged through the graveyard of empty chip packets, he could hear Josh's muffled voice.

"Pat, Pat? Are you still there?"

"I'm here, sir!" Pat shouted back over the alarm. "Building is on red alert. Employees making their way down to the lobby. The front gate is…" he clicked furiously on his computer and found the button to open the gate, "…open now!"

"Great work, Pat. Stay calm, okay? Officers will be on site in three minutes."

Help was on the way.

People started to filter into the lobby. First up was Charlotte Van De Berg, followed shortly by Eric.

"Is there a fire?" she asked, her face a mask of curiosity and confusion.

Pat had no time for questions. He was already back on his security cameras.

"Line up in front of the elevators!" he barked at the growing crowd, phone still pressed to his ear. The entire cast of Microceuticals – Luka,

Gopal and Amy – stepped out of the elevator a second later, pushing their way into the throng of people.

"You're not supposed to take the elevators!" Pat roared at them. "Get in line!"

Luka looked like he was about to argue, but Pat's face must've conveyed the fact that he had no time to suffer fools, as Luka fell in line with his colleagues.

"Pat, officers are just two minutes away." Josh's voice was quiet through the phone. "You're doing great. Is everyone okay?"

The alarm blared furiously, the robotic voice still playing the same message. *Too distracting.*

"I'm turning off the alarm," Pat panted. "I think everyone's here."

"If you're sure. One minute out."

As Sal Whiteman, a handsome twenty-something from Mihok & Mihok, fell into line with everyone else, Pat did a quick headcount.

Eleven.

Twelve, including me.

Plus Catherine – that makes thirteen.

That's everyone.

Everyone except for Nadine.

CHAPTER 6

"What's going on, Pat?!" someone called through the hubbub of conversation. It was Charlotte Van De Berg again. Pat's mind scrambled for an answer.

You're not smart enough to lie to these people, dummy. Just give it to them straight.

He took a deep breath, and did his best to stand up as straight as he could. Thirteen pairs of eyes scrutinized him, awaiting further orders.

Pat grimaced.

"There...there's been a murder," he announced. "Someone was killed, tonight. In this building."

Some of them gasped. Some stayed silent. Most of them looked around – trying their best to level a guess at who was missing. He watched their faces, desperately searching for any indication that they already knew. Gopal's brow was sweating. Monica Lafferty and her client – an ethnically ambiguous teenager with poofy hair – looked like they were about to faint.

Pat glanced at Marek, who looked as surprised as anyone else.

"Who?" Charlotte asked. "Who's dead?!"

"Nadine," Pat said. He felt his breath catch in his throat.

"Nadine Matthews." More jaws hit the floor.

"Who did it?!"

"Pat can't do his job!"

"What if they're still in the building?!"

Arguments rose to a fever pitch. Within seconds, people were practically at each other's throats – some in defense of Pat, some in fear for their own lives.

Take charge. Control the situation.

Pat stepped forward and inhaled.

"QUIET!" he bellowed...and the cacophony ceased.

While Pat had never felt more out of his depth, he had to do damage control.

Figure out who's in the building. Names, signatures.

"Everybody is going to form an orderly line behind Gopal," he said firmly, grabbing a pen and notepad from his desk. "You're all going to wait your turn and write down your names, phone numbers, email addresses, and a short description of what you were doing tonight."

"Is the killer still in the building, Patrick?" asked Marek, softly.

"I don't know," Pat admitted. "I don't know much. But I know that I have to keep you safe. Keep the rest of you safe."

He scanned the crowd again. All familiar faces. Johnny was still clutching the bottle of whisky that Pat caught him with. He looked like he'd seen a ghost. Charlotte and Eric were even whiter than usual, like they were about to faint. Sal was lurking in his boss' shadow. Mateo – the gorgeous lawyer from Collymore & Donovan – looked shellshocked.

Step two, go deal with the body.

"The cops will be here in two minutes," Pat said. "I'm…going upstairs." His eyes scanned the crowd.

Who's trustworthy?

"Malik," he said, proffering the pen and paper. The doctor's eyes flickered up to meet his. He was a huge man – maybe 6'4", or 6'5" – with massive muscles rippling under his shirt. His face was covered in a sheen of sweat, pulling his glasses down his nose. Right now, he looked just about as shocked as everyone else, but Pat figured that if anyone here was able to perform under pressure, it was him.

"I'm going upstairs," Pat said. "You're in charge until I get back. Make sure you get everyone's names. There should be eleven."

Malik nodded breathlessly and took the paper.

"Monica," Pat said. "Come with me."

Monica's eyes went wide, and she threw pleading glances to the other occupants, before reluctantly following Pat into the elevator.

*   *   *

"What happened, Pat?"

Monica didn't sound her usual self. The bubbliness from earlier in the night was gone, replaced by an overtone of fear and an anxious tremor in her hands as Pat led her along the corridor of the fifth floor.

"I don't know, Mon. I don't know."

"Why did you drag me up here?"

Pat stopped her before they rounded the corner, his voice choked up as he tried to speak. "I…needed a friend, and…I need confirmation."

Monica's eyes boggled. "You mean you haven't checked if she's dead? Jesus, Pat! You just told everyone that there's been a murder, you – you called the cops! And she might not be dead!?"

They rounded the corner, and Nadine's body came into view, pale and motionless under the moonlight. Monica gasped.

"Oh God. Oh God, Pat. Yeah, okay, yeah – she's dead. Jesus."

Pat moved forward cautiously, unable to take his eyes off the body. The blood was pooling in a huge circle, from the windows to the edge of the landing. Some of it was spilling over the edge of the balcony, now dripping down to the lobby a good fifty feet below them. As Pat got closer, Monica inching forward behind him, he could see the depth of the slash across her throat.

"Jesus…Pat. They've gone ear to ear…"

They had, indeed.

A very sharp knife. Or a very strong arm.

Ever so slowly, Pat before the body, his pants pooling in the blood.

"Pat, it's a crime scene. You can't do that!"

Pat knew she was right, but it was almost like his body was on autopilot as his shins sank into the pool of red. He wanted a clue – he wanted something, anything that could tell him who had done this.

Nadine's eyes stared up at him as he scanned her body desperately, searching for something – anything – under the red blanket covering her chest. Blood coated his hands as he reached forward and under her back, meaning to move her aside.

Can't do that. Wouldn't be right.

"Pat!"

Pat struggled to his feet, hands shaking and dripping in hot blood. He had to stop and think, but his mind was in overdrive from the adrenaline.

Was the killer still in the building? Was everyone downstairs safe? Had someone gotten in?

If not, was it…was it someone he knew?

As if she was reading his mind, Monica spoke.

"Do we know who did this Pat? Did you see anyone leaving?"

He shook his head. "No-one…no-one left the grounds. I checked the cameras."

Monica swallowed. "What…what does that mean, Pat?"

Pat didn't reply. There was no need to. She knew as well as he did; unless he'd missed something on the cameras, unless the security system had inexplicably broken down and not reported both a break-in and a break-out from one of the most secure buildings in the city, there was only one conclusion.

The killer was still in the building.

The killer was downstairs in the lobby.

*   *   *

As the elevator doors brought them back to the lobby, the police burst through the front door. Clad in full black outfits, with visors over their eyes, they skated across the lobby in front of a crowd of breathless onlookers.

And as Pat came out of the elevator, hands and pants covered in Monica's blood, all their attention turned to him. "POLICE, POLICE! GET DOWN, GET DOWN ON THE GROUND NOW!"

Pat fell to his knees, throwing his arms above his head as they raced towards him.

"I'm security!" he yelled.

Monica stood stock still by his side as two of the officers patted Pat down and then finally helped him to his feet. They kept their rifles raised, not entirely convinced of his innocence. Pat couldn't blame them.

Another lady strode through the front door. She was Hispanic, dressed to slim in a grey suit and pink blouse. A holstered gun slapped her thigh, and her square jaw clacked on a piece of gum as she beelined towards him.

"Sergeant Alvarez," she chewed, offering a handshake, then retracting it quickly as she spotted the blood. "How'd that get on your hands?"

Pat kept his hands half-raised. "Pat Dickson. I...I was checking the body."

She looked bemused. "You touched the body?"

Pat felt his cheeks burning. "Yes. Sorry, officer."

Alvarez scoffed and blew her hair off her face. "Where is it?"

"The fifth floor, ma'am."

Alvarez waved a hand at two of the cops, who shoved past Pat and Monica and disappeared into the elevators.

Monica took the opportunity to vanish back into the throng of onlookers.

Alvarez looked Pat up and down. "Why did you interfere with the crime scene?" she asked irritably.

"I was just, uh...checking for clues—"

"—not your job, Mr. Dickson. Not your job at all." She pulled a small leather notepad out of her pocket and dug a pencil out that was hidden behind her ear, in ringlets of hair, and jotted something down.

"Go wash up," she snapped. "Wash up, then get back here. I'll need to speak with everyone in the building."

His face still red with embarrassment, Pat hurried off to the bathroom and threw his hands under the tap. The water was so cold it burned the tips of his fingers as he lathered everything up to his elbows in soap and desperately tried to scrub away the red stains. They were stubborn. Finally, he gave up, wiping the sweat off his brow with some paper towels and inspecting himself in the mirror.

A close up look did him no favours. His hair was matted to his face, his mouth hanging open like a dog desperate for water, eyes bloodshot from fear.

Look at you, you mess.

With no warning, bile rose in his throat. He dashed to the toilet and let it all out, a violent eruption of Doritos and soda as his stomach cramped aggressively on repeat. Eventually, he came up for air, panting desperately. Someone walked into the bathroom.

"Hello?" Pat coughed.

"Pat?" The voice was quiet and anxious, but familiar.

Pat struggled up from the toilet, his knees leaving two bloody prints at its base, the smell of his own vomit lingering in his nose and mouth and stuck his head out of the cubicle.

Mateo Brown was sitting on the counter next to the sink, head between his hands, looking shaken.

"You okay?" Pat asked.

Mateo nodded numbly. "You?"

"Yeah, I…I'm doing okay," Pat breathed, snatching a wad of paper towels from the dispenser to wipe his mouth.

Silence filled the space. Pat could hear a ringing in his ears.

"You…you just found her like that?" Mateo asked, quietly. "Just, found her…dead?"

Pat nodded, grimacing. A stray tear dripped down Mateo's cheek. And then he was gone, back into the lobby.

Pat leaned over the sink, sucking in air as more bile rose in his throat and his heart thumped in his chest, a desperate mess of a man who wanted nothing more but to calm down.

But he wasn't calm.

The walls were closing in.

I need Karen.

CHAPTER 7

"Dear God, sweetie, are you okay?"

Pat could hardly speak. He was slouched in the chair at his desk, just thankful to hear Karen's voice.

"So the police? The police are there, right, sweetie?"

Pat mumbled a reply. He could hardly hear his own voice over the persistent ringing in his ears.

He filled Karen in on the night's events, a cruel ache welling in his chest as he recounted finding Nadine on the floor, her sunken eyes forever burned into his brain.

Karen soothed him, as best one could over a crackly phone line.

"Just talk to the police and come home, okay my darling?" she said. "Come home. I'm here for you. I'll be up when you get in. Do you want me to put the kettle on? Make some tea? What do you need?"

"I...I don't know," Pat sighed. "I just want you. Let me...let me talk to the cops. Try to get out of here."

"I love you."

"I love you too, babe."

It wasn't strictly true when he told Karen he didn't know what he wanted. He knew what he wanted.

He wanted Nadine to not be dead.

He wanted his shift to be over.

He wanted to go home.

Pat struggled out of his chair to make a beeline for Alvarez, who was flicking through the pages of the notepad and counting heads.

"Eleven names on here," she said sourly, "Only eleven. Plus Nadine...that makes twelve."

"I...I'm another," Pat said. She thrust the pad at him.

"Write."

As he wrote, in shaky handwriting, Pat surprised himself at his own attention to detail. His movements which were painstakingly accurate, chiefly due to the fact that they were the same as every other night. He included a few possibly extraneous details – what time he remembered checking the cameras, smoking a cigarette in the stairwell – and by the time he had finished, he'd taken up almost a whole page.

Flicking back on the pad as he finished, he realised some people hadn't written anywhere near as much as him. The Van De Bergs from PubStunt had written the barest of contact details, and Luka had simply written his email address – not even his full name.

Alvarez snatched the notepad back, open to Luka's email written down on an empty page, and gave him a knowing look.

"You've done alright," she said, her voice a little softer. "Apart from moving the body. That...that was really fucking dumb, if you'll pardon my French."

Idiot.

"I know", Pat sighed. "I was...I just..." He trailed off, lost for words.

Alvarez squared up to him, and lowered her head to meet his eyes.

"What do you know?" she asked quietly as she led him away from the crowd.

Pat grimaced.

"I...I'm not the best at my job," he admitted.

Alvarez looked at him, quizzically. "And?"

"I'm not the most...proactive," Pat continued, "but I keep a good eye on the cameras. And you need a swipe card to get inside the gate, unless I open it for you."

"Have you opened it tonight?"

Pat nodded. "An employee forgot her swipe card in her office. Didn't want to go back for it. Catherine Kim. She's from the lawyers – Collymore & Donovan. Fourth floor."

Alvarez's eyes flashed. "What time did she go home?"

There it is.

Pat knew this was how it normally went, from the movies. First up – find a suspect.

Who better than the woman who left right around the time of the murder?

"Maybe eleven, eleven thirty?"

Alvarez scrawled the name on the pad, and checked her watch, a huge chunk of gold on her wrist. She called over an officer.

"Catherine Kim, from the law office on the fourth floor. She left about an hour ago. Bring her in, now."

Pat's skin flushed hot.

Was it Catherine? Did she kill Nadine, then leave?

That couldn't be possible. She was in a rush – sure – but isn't everyone in a rush when it's cold and dark out?

"Alright everyone!" Alvarez strode forward to the center of the lobby, her audience on tenterhooks. "I've got all your personal contacts, but some of you seem to be a little hazy on the details." She waved the notepad. "We'll be performing full inspections on all of your personal belongings, so please empty your pockets to make this a little easier on my officers. Everything on the bench, please."

Grumbling quietly, the men and women in the lobby began turning out their pockets onto Pat's desk.

Pat watched the downpour of cell phones, wallets, and car keys from almost all the men, followed by some less conspicuous items; Altoids, grubby pieces of paper with hastily written phone numbers. Mateo even tossed some condoms into the pile, which raised some eyebrows. But no knife. No weapon.

No dirty, blood-stained blade.

Pat shouldn't have been surprised, but he was a touch disappointed.

Alvarez nodded at him, her face stern. "You too."

She was just doing her job, but Pat couldn't help be a little bitter about it. He turfed out his pockets, and it was much the same as everyone else's; pens, a pack of gum, his phone, a pack of cigarettes. He finished up with the walkie-talkie on his belt and raised his arms to be patted down.

Alvarez was thorough, if nothing else. She checked under his arms, under his tie, and as she hands up his legs.

"You're fine," she said. "Take your stuff back."

As Pat packed his things hurriedly back into his pants, a question burned on his mind.

Is the murderer here?

Meanwhile, some more interesting items were being unearthed from people's pockets.

Luka – off to the side – was fuming as they pulled a small notebook from his pants.

"That's confidential!" he hissed. "You have to give it back!"

"We don't have to do anything, sir," Alvarez snapped as the officer continued to pat him down. She rifled through his belongings.

"That's a lot of credit cards you've got there."

"I run a business."

"Yeah, and this is an active crime scene. Next time you're ordered to turn out your pockets, turn out your damn pockets."

Johnny Ray had a pocket knife which was promptly bagged up and sent away. Good to check it out, but Pat was convinced that it wasn't the murder weapon. Not only was it not sharp enough to bother swinging, but judging by what Pat had seen of Johnny that evening, he was hardly stable enough on his feet enough to swing it.

"Get him some Gatorade and a burger," Alvarez told one of the cops as he sat Johnny down in one of the lounge chairs, the bottle swinging by his side. "He needs to sober up."

Pat watched Johnny lolled in the chair. Marek stepped forward and quietly prised Johnny's hand off the bottle while nobody else was looking.

"I'll head up to the crime scene," Alvarez said to the officer nearest her. She looked Pat up and down. "You found the body, didn't you?"

Pat nodded, gulping.

"Okay. Show me."

*　　*　　*

Courtesy of the repeated elevator rides and his stomach still turning from his little episode in the bathroom, Pat was beginning to feel like a jack-in-the-box. He rode up with Alvarez to the fifth floor and led her down the hallway.

Nadine's body lay perfectly still under the moonlight.

"I was doing my 11pm round," Pat offered quietly, as Alvarez knelt by his friend's body. "I did five last. I started on six, then worked my way down to the lobby, then came back up to 5."

Alvarez knelt by Nadine. It was a harsh contrast; her pristine work suit and pink blouse bright against the ocean of blood. She hummed to herself, brushing a lock of hair off Nadine's face. Pat couldn't help but flinch.

"You always do five last?" she hummed.

Am I a suspect?

"No..." Pat admitted. "I sort of forgot. I was in a...bit of a tizzy. And then...I stopped in on third, and had a drink with Marek—"

"—you always drink on the job?" interrupted Alvarez. She had the notepad out again.

Shit.

"Oh no," Pat said hurriedly. "It was just a sip, really. He offered me some...some scotch, and I said I shouldn't and...and then I left."

Alvarez hummed again, and then – shockingly – pressed her palm to Nadine's cheek.

"She's been like this a few hours, at least."

Pat nodded, unsure what to make of that information. Alvarez had obviously formed some conclusion, which she promptly jotted down in her book. She rose to her feet.

"When was your last round before your eleven o'clock, Mr. Dickson?" she asked, pen poised.

"I start at seven," Pat said. "And work until three. I'll do a round when I start, and then nothing else until eleven, then my last one at three. I just...hang out in the lobby."

"Did you go anywhere else tonight?" The pen raced across the paper. *Anything you say can be used against you in a court of law.*

"I had a cigarette in the East Stairwell," Pat admitted, frankly. There was no point hiding it at this point. Security cameras would show him coming back a little merrier after a five-minute break if they were ever checked.

"Just the one?"

"Uh, twice. Once just before I checked five, after I got back down to the lobby. The other... maybe an hour after I started, I don't know."

"Okay. And you mentioned you let a lady go home? Catherine?"

"I walked her down to the front gate and let her out, then checked the gardens."

The questions kept coming as Alvarez walked Pat back to the elevators. As the doors opened for what felt like the umpteenth time that day, she finally tucked away her notepad and smoothed down her jacket.

"You've been very informative, Mr. Dickson," she said. "We'll be going through all this again at the station when we conduct more formal interviews, so I apologize, but I do appreciate your candor. Makes this whole process a whole lot easier."

Pat nodded, unsure what to say. "You're welcome, I guess."

She sort-of-smiled at him – probably the closest she ever came to a smile – and then walked into the center of the lobby, waving over the crowd that had spread out across the lobby.

"It's late, and this isn't easy for anyone," she announced. "Remember you can call the crisis hotline if you have any questions or if a situation like this makes you feel uncomfortable. I really don't need another dead body on my hands this evening. We'll be back in tomorrow morning with a larger team to collect statements and perhaps take some people down to the station for questioning."

Her eyes flicked over to Luka, and then the Van De Bergs.

She's smart. She knows what to do.

The crowd stood silent, awaiting instructions.

"You're free to go," she puffed, exasperated. "Go on, get out of here!"

With no need for any further encouragement, Pat and everyone else simultaneously rushed for the doors to get into the cold night.

And as they pushed past each other, shunting through the double doors, Pat couldn't help but wonder if he had perhaps just rubbed shoulders with a cold-blooded killer.

*   *   *

Karen wasn't in bed waiting for him. No, she'd set the table and prepped him his favourite; Mac & Cheese, and was waiting up way past her bedtime, her look a picture of concern.

"Honey?"

He said nothing, but threw his arms around her and let out a few heaving sobs.

It wasn't so much about Nadine – even though she was wonderful, and it was cruel, and it was unfair – but the emotions of the past hour had finally welled to such a depth that Pat could do nothing but let them out.

Karen seated him at the small round kitchen table, wiped his eyes with a stained handkerchief, and slopped a portion of mac into a bowl for him.

Pat dove in as she sat down opposite.

"Are you okay, hon?"

He nodded, slowly. There were no words.

"Well honey, when I found her body she had her eyes open and I thought she looked uncomfortable, so I messed up an active crime scene. Also, I think I might be working in the same building as a violent murderer! Anyway, how was your evening?"

Pat ate mostly in silence. The details could wait, and Karen knew that. The best – the absolute best – thing about Karen was that she knew how to read a room. Emotional intelligence, they called it. She knew when it was a good time to ask questions and when it wasn't.

And right now, it wasn't.

"Larry waited up for you," she said. "But he couldn't keep his eyes open."

"Don't wake him. Just...let him be."

As if on cue, his burly sixteen-year-old wandered into the kitchen, rubbing his eyes.

Pat's friends had always talked about how much their lives had improved after having children – something about personal satisfaction, personal growth, and they were right. Little Larry was the light of his life, even though he wasn't so little anymore. His mop of brown hair just inches away from the low kitchen ceiling, he beelined to his father and wrapped him up with his big arms.

Pat choked back his tears, and held tight as Larry whispered in his ear.

"If you wanna talk about it, Dad...I can listen."

"We can listen," Karen agreed. "We're here for you. Do you need more food?"

Pat shook his head. "Tomorrow," he said. "Tomorrow, we can talk."

Larry nodded and kissed Pat on the forehead before retreating upstairs with heavy footfalls, and Karen grabbed Pat another beer out of the fridge. She set it in front of him and ran her fingers through his hair.

"Tomorrow," she said softly. "Or...whenever you feel like it."

"Thanks, hon. Thanks."

She kissed him on the forehead as well and vanished up to their room. Retreating to normalcy.

Pat appreciated the gesture. It was like this when his Dad died. He'd vented to Karen about how everyone treated him as though he was fragile; a glass bowl, just waiting to shatter.

He knew he wasn't the sharpest knife in the drawer; he knew he processed things slightly slower than other people. Having folks fawning over him just wasn't the best way for him to understand what had happened. More than that, it just made him feel pressured into thinking or feeling a certain way, and he hated that.

He needed time, he needed space.

And he needed a good night's sleep.

He polished off the beer, headed upstairs, and crawled in beside Karen, who immediately wrapped her arms and legs around his wide body for some warm cuddles, murmuring sweet nothings in his ears.

Pat closed his eyes. He wasn't a religious man, but for a brief moment, he prayed that sleep would come.

But hours later, with Karen fast asleep by his side, it didn't.

Perhaps he'd wake up tomorrow, and it would all be just a bad dream.

Unlikely.

CHAPTER 8

It hadn't been a good night's sleep for Pat. In fact, he was so overtired, that when he finally woke the next morning, he experienced for a fleeting second that beautiful moment where he couldn't remember what day it was, or what he had to do that day.

He'd asked Karen about that on occasion.

"Do you ever wake up and not know what day it is?"

"No, honey. I think that's just you."

Then, the memories of yesterday flooded back.

Nadine, dead.

Police.

A killer, in the building.

A murder, on my watch.

Anxiety filled Pat's chest and he practically dove into the shower. The warm water sent his blood surging to his limbs. Steam plumed up his nose.

No matter what today throws at you, you can handle it. And you'll be a better person for it.

That's what he'd tell Larry before an exam. That results never mattered; only effort. And today, today was going to take a whole load of effort, Pat knew that for sure. As he shut the water off, he heard that ringing in his ears again. He pulled on a new uniform, and did his tie extra carefully as the clock ticked 7.

Larry and Karen were in the kitchen, where Larry was huffing down an obnoxious pile of scrambled eggs. Karen shot him a quizzical look as she noticed his uniform.

"Babe?"

"I know, I know. But I have to write the incident report for last night. And talk to Joseph...about what happened."

The thought of speaking to Joseph made Pat almost physically ill.

36

Joseph was the building manager, and the biggest perk of working the night shift was that Pat hardly saw the guy who wrote up his pay stubs.

"The time clock says you were late today, Pat."

"The bathroom's filthy, Pat. I know you're not the janitor, but please just do your business at home."

"This meeting isn't for you Pat. We...we just don't think you'd understand the content."

Either way, if the price of a few days of annual leave was a meeting with the boss, then it was a price that Pat would happily pay.

He clapped Larry on the back and bussed Karen's cheek before waving them farewell.

"Tonight," he said, "I'll fill you in. Promise."

They nodded in unison and Pat took his leave out the back door.

Pat's ride was a dark green Volvo 200 series, an absolute hunk of junk. They'd bought it almost twenty years ago, when it was already a few years off the market, and had never replaced it, despite Karen's protests.

And that was because Pat loved his hunk of junk. He knew every single dent in the paintwork, every rattle of the gearshift, and he was confident that he was the only person who'd be able to drive it considering the clutch was so sticky.

But more than that, he had memories with it; memories he wasn't quite ready to give up. Neither of them had owned a car when they'd gotten together, but Karen's Mom had gotten sick and they needed something more reliable than the New Jersey trains to get to Philly.

So, Pat had done all the right things; worked the late shift as a night club bouncer, letting Karen get through college and took care of her Mom, and after a few sleepless months, he'd rolled up in the driveway of their apartment block with a spring in his step and a grin on his face.

Their car was everything to him. Karen had told him they were expecting Larry in it. He'd taken Larry for his first drive by duct-taping him to the front passenger seat! Not responsible parenting of course, but fun nonetheless.

And so, on days like this, when fun was most likely nowhere to be found, the drive to work gave him a touch of comfort. Pat set down the handbrake, eased off the clutch, and rolled out of the driveway in the direction of Midtown on the river.

*   *   *

From the front parking lot of Guinness House, you could just see the large glass-fronted doors of the building.

Moreover, you could see if there was anyone standing in front of them.

Pat gulped as he spotted the stumpy figure of Joseph, arms crossed, a silhouette waiting against the doors.

Waiting for me.

Pat threw the car into park and slowly got out. He lit a cigarette in the parking lot for a few reasons.

Firstly, he was allowed to – it was only 'no smoking' inside the building, and it wasn't like anyone followed that rule anyway.

Secondly, he'd found a dead body yesterday, so he figured he'd be entitled to showing up to work with cigarette breath.

Thirdly, he wanted Joseph to wait, just a little longer.

Eventually, however, the devil could be dodged no longer, and he wandered up stretched front steps to meet with his boss.

Joseph reminded Pat of a weasel. He was about forty, forty-five, with beady eyes so deep inside his skull that you couldn't see the colour of his irises – they were just pinprick black dots. His nose was small and upturned, and his moustache was so thin that it only really qualified as whiskers.

"Patrick," he sniffed. It was just one word, but Pat heard the undertones.

Time for me to grill you.

His arm shot out for a handshake. Joseph always insisted on shaking hands, which Pat just hated.

But today, Pat shook, and they walked inside together.

Guinness House was now a very active crime scene. Cops littered the lobby – maybe ten or twelve of them dressed up in full coveralls, armed with cameras and plastic bags. P

at could see a few items in fully transparent evidence bags sat on his desk as they walked through the foyer – including Johnny's penknife.

"So..." Joseph drawled as Pat wedged himself into a chair in the management office, "I heard there was an incident last night."

An "incident??"

"Yeah."

"Yeah?" Joseph swung his feet onto the desk. "That's all you've got to say? Yeah?"

Although he didn't expect anything more of Joseph, Pat was still flummoxed.

"What do you want me to say, Joe? I told it all to the cops last night. Yeah, Nadine had her throat cut on the fifth floor. Yeah, Nadine is dead. Yeah, somebody in the building probably did it."

Joseph's eyes narrowed.

"That brings me to my next point of conversation, Pat," he said, drumming his fingers on the desk. "How sure are we that nobody got in?"

There it was. The real reason for this meeting.

Time to find a scapegoat.

Pat huffed. "Security's watertight at night. I'm on the cameras all night, I do a sweep every few hours. There's no way someone got into the building."

"So what, someone in here did it?"

There it is.

"I guess," Pat shrugged.

Joseph grabbed a baseball off his junk-filled bookshelf and started tossing it hand to hand.

"That's a pretty big accusation, Patty."

"Pretty big body up on fifth floor, Joey."

Joseph's eyes turned to slits. He didn't like that. He didn't like that one bit. Pat didn't like saying it – he didn't like giving people attitude – but with Joseph he just couldn't help it. The guy was your quintessential asshole who'd gotten a six-figure job through connections his Daddy had made. Now he came in here, bossing people around about how things could be better around here while he did absolutely nothing at all.

"Get out, Pat. Don't let me see you around here until this evening."

*   *   *

Pat ducked out of the office as quick as he could. The cops were swarming the lobby. Some of them were taking photos, others swabbing surfaces. His desk looked like it had become a hotspot for bagged evidence and paperwork.

Lionel, Pat's day-shift equivalent, was sitting in a corner on the wheely-chair, staring vacantly over the scene.

"How's business, Lionel?"

"Aw, same old, Patty boy," he cawed.

Lionel was the type of man to genuinely not have a care in the world. He'd been in the business over forty years, and as a black man growing up in Queens in the 70s, he'd seen more than his share of dead bodies. For him, this was just another day.

"Any news on statements?" Pat asked.

Lionel looked at him, bemused. "How in the fuck would I know that?" he chuckled. "I ain't no cop!" He lolled back in his chair and closed his eyes, shaking his head at the absurdity of the question.

Worse than useless.

Pat's eyes drifted to a pile of paperwork on the desk.

Don't you even think about it.

But Pat did think about it. This was his job; his livelihood.

And if he was in here with a killer, he didn't just deserve to know.

He needed to know.

The cops weren't paying the two of them any attention, and Lionel was still staring into the abyss.

Just a few sheets down, there was a manila file. Witness testimonies. Handwritten copies. The real interviews were probably still ongoing, but this would give him some idea of where people were that night.

Marek's was on top, bullet-pointed. It was simple, with neat handwriting and sufficient detail that made Pat think he was cooperating.

He has to cooperate though, doesn't he?

Nadine was one of his employees – so his name was probably first on the chopping block if they came looking for a suspect.

Normal day. Drinks with Sal, Nadine & Franny – 5:30pm.

Franny was a longstanding trader at Mihok & Mihok. Young, pretty, funny.

Back to the office – 7:45pm, sans Franny. Toilet break – maybe 9:30pm. Drink with Pat – 11:15? Nadine acting unusual during the day, complaints of a headache and fatigue. Went upstairs, maybe 10:30? Didn't come back.

And that was it. Marek's experience of the day Nadine died, all summed up in a handful of short sentences. Reductive, at best. Lies, at worst.

Next up was Sal's, in the same handwriting. It was then that Pat realised it was probably a Detective, taking notes in an interview.

Probably Alvarez?

He looked up again, just checking to make sure she wasn't in the vicinity and kept reading. Sal's had nothing interesting in it – it was almost a carbon copy of Marek's day, bar no drink with Pat and a few cigarette breaks.

Pat knew Sal a touch better than some of the other people in the building, simply because they'd share cigarettes in the stairwells on nights when it was too cold to go outside. He was aloof; sometimes a little standoffish. But a murderer?

Hopefully not.

Monica's was next in the pile, followed by someone named 'Kathy Evans.' Pat didn't recognise the name, so it must've been her client; the one she'd offered to introduce to him.

The reports were almost identical – what seemed to be six hours of photoshoots and editing from about 5:30pm, with a break for a late dinner at 9. Pat remembered that; Chinese food had come through the lobby. It had smelt good; he had wondered where it was going.

The same neat, elegant handwriting was on the next few files as well; one for Mateo Brown, and one for Johnny Ray. Little notes on that one, just a single line.

Time alone in office after co-workers left. A few drinks.

Pat knew Johnny had been drinking, but the note made him realise something. He had seen Mateo and Catherine heading away from the office before he'd checked in on Johnny.

What had they gotten up to that evening?

Only one way to find out.

Pat rifled through the papers, until he finally came to one titled 'Mateo Brown'.

As he flicked through it, a voice boomed behind him.

"What the hell do you think you're doing?!"

Alvarez. Flustered, Pat dropped the folder as she grabbed him by the collar and hauled him away from the desk.

"What? You think just cause this used to be your desk, you can read everything that's on it?"

"I–I was just trying to help! I was seeing if anyone–"

"What!? You going to find a murderer for me?" she gasped, mockingly. "No shit, that makes twenty of us!"

Pat desperately tried to shuffle the papers back in order.

What if she locks me up? Fuck.

"I'm really sorry," he said. "It's just, I saw some people last night, and I was just trying to check if their stories lined up. I wasn't trying to cause any trouble, I promise." He caught sight of the management office behind her. Joseph's tiny feet were no longer on the desk.

Double fuck.

Pat desperately backed away from the door as Alvarez furiously waved a finger in his face.

"I'm telling you one time, and one time only, Mr. Dickson. If I so much as see your ass around my papers again, there'll be hell to pay."

Pat raised his hands defensively and backed out the door as Joseph emerged into the foyer, looking concerned. Pat couldn't hear what Alvarez was saying, but she was gesturing furiously in his direction, so he turned around and walked as briskly as his legs would carry him, right down to the car park.

It's fine. I'll get the full story tonight.

*   *   *

With cautious purpose in his step, Pat returned to Guinness House that evening after a day of enjoying himself in the daytime for a change. He was tired, no doubt about it, but it wasn't like he was going to go home and go back to bed. No sign of Alvarez, or Joseph, thankfully. He ducked inside and shook Lionel awake, before heading into the break-room to make them both a cup of coffee and grab a few packs of chips from the cupboard.

By the time he got back, Lionel had vanished, and Pat was all alone, so he set himself up with two cups for himself, squared his little bag under the desk and took a seat to consider his next move.

The management office door was open. The management office door – where Joseph would inevitably have taken his own set of statements from witnesses – was open.

Thanks, Joey.

Pat planned on conducting interviews of his own tonight, but that could wait. He checked that the coast was clear, and ducked inside.

The office was, in a word, gaudy. Joseph was a man who thought he was blessed with an incredible sense of style, but it was just a collection of eclectic junk. A big jukebox in the corner with flickering lights. A tacky lamp with bells hanging from the shade. Pat didn't know any better when it came to trends, or fashion…but at least he knew that he didn't know any better.

The drawers weren't locked – an absolute stroke of luck. As he rifled through the contents, Pat didn't have to try keeping things in the right place. Everything was haphazard and crumpled, and he doubted Joseph had enough brain cells to notice. He didn't have to look too far. A carbon copy of Alvarez's manila file was sitting right in the top drawer. Pat whipped over to the photocopier – after checking to make sure there were no late-night visitors again – made a copy of the file.

A breach of trust? Maybe.

A violation of confidential information? Definitely.

But it was worth the risk. He was trying to figure out if there was a murderer in the building!

What if they strike again? What if I'm next?

The ends justified the means. Pat placed the folder back where he found it and went on his way, making sure to close the door after him without locking it. Then, he took a seat at his desk, and started thumbing his way through the pages.

Marek's and Sal's were again, first up. Their own handwriting this time. Same content, different words. Pat skimmed past them to find one at the bottom of the pile.

I was drinking in my office. I did some work. I didn't leave the office all night. I saw nothing.

At least Johnny's story was consistent. One that was easy to get right, but Pat knew off the bat that it wasn't the whole truth. He'd heard Johnny's heavy footfalls around the building, maybe five minutes apart, a few times. He had definitely left his office.

Curious.

Pat put it aside for now. He rummaged through for Mateo's statement and matched it up with Catherine's. Surely enough, they were almost word perfect. They both detailed working until just before eleven, then eating dinner in their office breakroom, where they were joined by Johnny. Pat guessed that much was true; he hadn't let anyone in to deliver food to them, so they must have brought their own. Their statements also gave some credibility to Johnny – perhaps he was just light on details, and chose not to discuss his bathroom habits. Mateo and Catherine reported going for a walk just after eleven for "work discussion," and then Catherine described how she had left in her car, while Mateo had jumped onto another conference call.

Pat was sure that most of it was indeed true, but neither of them mentioned running into Pat just before 11.

If they were omitting that, what else were they omitting?

Little details mattered. Did Catherine maybe miss out on the fact that Mateo had a solo jaunt around nine, giving him just enough of a chance to commit the murder? Or was Pat looking at this wrong? Could it have been Catherine who ducked out "just to go to the toilet", whereas in fact she was up on the fifth floor and spilling blood? She was on edge when she was leaving. He'd chalked it up to late nights and cold weather.

Or was she ducking out quietly, trying to hide the evidence? And were they sure of Johnny's whereabouts the whole evening? He had a penknife in his pocket. Either way, he'd have to ask Catherine. She'd likely be upstairs, pulling another late night with Mateo. Frankly, he was surprised anyone had come in today, but all the usual cars were parked out front. Life goes on. Most of the other statements had nothing else of interest. Marek described their drink, and also noted that Nadine left "for unknown reasons" at around 9:30pm.

She was found on the fifth floor, so she must have gone up to see someone at Microceuticals. Had she ever shown up? Or was she dead before she got there?

What did Microceuticals have to say about it? Luka included Pat in a short statement, but there was nothing about Nadine.

Interrupted by security at both 8pm and 11pm. Pat chuckled; his first interruption was at seven, not eight.

Visionary? He doesn't even know what time it is.

Gopal's and Amy's stories were much the same.

Three people in lab all evening. Consistent work due to upcoming key projects. Short breaks, dinner eaten together. No significant interruptions.

The consistency of the statements meant they were probably clean.

Or they're all in on it together.

As Pat leafed through the rest of the files, there was one more file that piqued his curiosity.

Charlotte van De Berg's gorgeous handwriting detailed an incredibly thorough testimony of her whereabouts that evening, which seemed to be all confined to her office in PubStunt. She'd included a timestamped log of video conferences with clients in Beijing and London – a good excuse for being up that late. She detailed solo dinner plans, even including what she ate and how quickly; and followed it by admitting to some solitude in her office around 8pm.

Eric's note followed. His was essentially bare, even worse than Johnny's.

Late night, working solo. I was in my office.

No mention of any calls; or for that matter, of anyone who could provide him with an alibi. If he was in his office, would Charlotte – in all her thorough detail – not have included a little note with his whereabouts? On the other hand, if he had been out and about, perhaps arguing with Nadine…perhaps he didn't even know that Charlotte was there to attest to his whereabouts, given that she was quietly locked up on her own.

Malik's was possibly the most uninformative of them all. He was a doctor down on the second floor, and the only one in the clinic that night. *Admin work, research.*

Three words. Three words jotted down on the page, not even between the lines. No attempt to cover himself, no-one who could attest for his whereabouts. He was friends with Marek and Luka – did they ever get together? Did they that night?

All in all, none of the reports gave Pat any opportunity to point fingers. Hell, they hardly eliminated anyone as a suspect. Johnny and Eric were light on details and alibis, but was it obfuscation? Or just laziness? Charlotte's and Catherine's were heavy on detail, but was that a diversion? Why did Catherine leave the building if Mateo was still working?

So while there wasn't anything concrete, Pat definitely had some questions. He stowed the papers away in his bag and scanned over his cameras.

All was quiet. It was time to start doing his own interviews.

CHAPTER 9

Pat took the stairs, all the way up to the sixth floor. Karen would be proud. He'd call her later. For now, he wanted to talk to Monica. He needed some direction – some support – and she was the most likely place to get it.

He rapped on the door of Lafferty Inc. and waited patiently. The lights were on, so she was home. She had a few employees; lighting experts, editors, but none of them ever worked this late. He could only hope that the girl from the other night – Kathy? – was there too. If she had seen anything, surely she would say so. Monica appeared in the doorway. Her hair was slightly disheveled, her eyes wide.

Fear? Paranoia?

The other night, she looked positively radiant.

Tonight though, she seemed a lot more human.

"Pat?" He puffed out his chest.

"Can we talk?" he asked, tentatively. "Security's on double lock this evening. Nobody's getting in."

She looked concerned. "It's not like that every night?"

That threw him. "It…it is, but I made extra sure tonight–"

"Look, Pat, I really don't have time for this." She moved to shut the door, but Pat, in a rare moment of daring, did something he'd never done before.

He stuck his foot in the door.

It bounced off his shoe, and as he looked up at Monica, he saw something flare in her eyes.

Maybe that was a mistake.

"I have a theory," he stammered. "And – I just wanted, I just wanted to talk to someone about it." "Get your foot out of the door, Pat," she hissed. "This is my business, and you are not entitled to my time, or entry to the

45

premises."

Definitely a mistake.

Pat slid his foot back slowly, and she slammed the door so hard he was surprised the entire glass pane didn't explode on him. Instead, it bounced on its hinges as she flicked the lock shut from the inside, and her heels clacked away. He watched the light fade as she closed the door to the modelling studio.

Dejected, Pat turned towards the elevator. Thoughts raced through his head. Monica had never been like that with him before. She was normally unerringly patient, despite his social fumbles.

Has she got something to hide?

He'd have to talk to Kathy. If Monica was hiding something, Kathy would know. But that could wait. There was no way he was getting past her with anything less than a slap.

Pat pulled a notepad from his pocket and scrawled a few pointers down. *Monica. Possibly hiding something? Very angry. Need to speak to Kathy.*

He underlined the names a few times and circled 'Kathy'.

Back to the elevators. Time to speak to Johnny Ray.

*   *   *

Johnny was drunk again, but at least he let Pat through the doors of Collymore & Donovan without incident. The angsty young man beelined straight through the foyer and into the back room where he'd emerged from disheveled the previous night.

Pat followed him, warily.

Johnny still looked a mess. His hair was the same sweaty brown mop, his shirt was untucked, and Pat could smell the body odour and whiskey.

It's like he didn't shower last night.

The same bottle of booze as yesterday swung carelessly from his hand, but only dregs remained. He collapsed into one of many chairs, behind one of many desks.

"Take a seat."

Pat sat opposite him, never quite taking the weight off his feet, and took in the space. It was a chaotic mess of cables, screens and frames, linking computers up to three or four monitors that buzzed with numbers and charts that slowly ticked away. Filing cabinets crowded the floor space – Pat could see a stack of files that rose above head height on one of the desks. The floor to ceiling windows – just the same as every other office in the building – displaying the sparkling vista of midtown, finally starting to shut down for the evening. And again, no sign of Catherine or Mateo.

"Do you always work alone at night, Johnny?" Pat asked, gently. He shrugged, and swigged. "Sometimes."

Pat waited as Johnny set the bottle down and turned his attention to his computer. The screen flicked rapidly as he clicked furiously with his mouse before turning back to Pat, and the bottle.

"Sorry," he said. "They hire me to keep track of incoming billables."

"And do you?" Pat asked.

"Do I what?"

"Keep track."

Johnny laughed, and burped. "Yeah, I mean, I guess I do."

"You keep track of what goes on around here?" The smile faltered, and Johnny turned his back to Pat, clicking away on his computer again.

"Sometimes," he said, hesitantly.

"Did you see what happened last night?"

"Nope." "Were you drunk last night?"

"Yep."

"So, did you see anything?" asked Pat again, a little more forcefully.

Johnny whirled around and grabbed for his bottle, his untucked shirt flailing around him. "Look man, you're not a cop. I don't know what you're doing here, but I didn't see shit last night. I was here, I'd had a few drinks, I was just reading affidavits. I don't get paid to see who got stabbed in a corridor. That's your job, remember?"

Pat didn't have a counterpoint for that. Johnny's hands rapped relentlessly on the keyboard, his fingers moving so fast that Pat could hardly see them, pictures flicking around on the two monitors in front of him. As the windows flicked around, popping up and jumping from screen to screen, Pat caught sight of Johnny's PC background, with a much younger – and sober – version of Johnny on it, caught awkwardly in the embrace of an older lady.

"Who's that?" Pat asked.

Johnny looked perplexed for a moment, and then he caught on. "My Nana," he grunted.

"You guys close?" There was a pause, like Pat had hit a wrong note.

"Yeah. I love her, man. She's my Nana." He sniffed. "I love her so much."

Pat trod cautiously as he searched for an opening.

"I lost my Nana when I was twelve," he said softly.

Johnny mumbled, almost inaudibly. He'd had a warmth in his eyes for a moment, but it had soon vanished.

"That sucks," he said, not taking his eyes off the screen. "I'm sorry."

Pat let him tap away for another moment or so.

"You sure there's nothing you want to tell me about last night?" he asked.

The screens all vanished, flying into the taskbar at the bottom of the screen. Johnny stared straight ahead at his Nana, and groped for the whiskey bottle. Whether there was something else going on here, or it was just the alcohol, Pat was sure if he'd looked closer he would've spotted a tear.

"Johnny?"

Johnny set the bottle back down and shook his head. "Nah, man," he said. "I'm good. You can let yourself out."

No use wasting time.

The moonlight dripped through the clouds, illuminating the office in a bright white. A cold chill cut through the air as Pat ambled towards the exit, ready to leave Johnny all by himself, surrounded by a sea of chairs and computers.

"You wanna tell me where your co-workers went last night?" he called back.

Johnny flipped him off.

A bit unnecessary, no?

Pat let himself out of the back room and then out the front door. While Johnny hadn't given him anything useful, his 'interview' wasn't a total bust. He knew that some people drank because they had a problem, but some people drank to hide something.

With Johnny, it was entirely possibly that it was the latter. Pat pulled out his notepad and jotted down some notes. Spoke to Johnny. Nothing from him yet. Revisit this later. Catch him sober. He'd put a pin in this one for now. It was entirely possible he could get something more out of Johnny, but in the state that he was in…it was unlikely.

Maybe he needs some time. And he had to do his rounds.

*   *   *

For the first time in a long time, Pat did something he never hoped he'd have to do again.

He let himself into an office without permission.

The last time was after a report of thumping and screaming from a company in the old building, before the renovation. Pat had responded to the call, let himself in, and found a man having a seizure on the floor. His coworker was there too, and she'd almost lost her thumb, trying to stop him from choking on his own tongue.

Tonight, he was letting himself into PubStunt. He needed to speak to Eric Van De Berg, and wasn't going to let a locked door get in his way.

The lights were on in the back. Pat stumbled through the dark foyer, hands outstretched, groping for a wall to guide his way, all while struggling to figure the best questions to ask.

Where were you last night? What's your alibi? Was this really his prerogative?

It should be left up to the investigators, but he knew that time was of the essence in an investigation like this, and there was hardly anything in those reports. Pat knew these people, and if he could get any information out of them, he knew Alvarez would appreciate it.

The door at the back of the foyer – locked. It was one of those keyless deadbolts with a card reader attached. The red light blinked at him ominously. There was no way of getting through here without either knowing the code, or having a card in his hands.

He knocked, loudly. His plan was simple. Bombard Eric with questions and make him forget about the fact that he was essentially trespassing on private property.

Not his best plan, but still a good one.

The bolt clicked, the door swung open, and Eric's face shone in the darkness.

"What are you doing here?" he snapped. "Did you let yourself in?"

There goes that plan.

"I thought I heard a disturbance, sir," Pat bluffed. "One of the higher floors reported some screaming. Considering you're the only one on this floor, it's my job to look around. Make sure the premises are secure." He paused. "Particularly…particularly after the events of last night."

The anger faded, and Eric stepped aside to let him through into the back. Jackpot! Pat strode through, hands on his belt, chest puffed out. He made an overt show of peering into the room, as if to check for an intruder. He was actually checking for something else.

A knife on a desk? A razor blade, a pair of scissors? A homemade garrote-wire of some description?

None of that. All he saw was the back workings of PubStunt. It was a much smaller space than what he'd seen of Collymore & Donovan, and infinitely smaller than Microceuticals. There were no desks, no unruly cables joining together monitors; it was just a nice, cozy office with soft ambient lighting, courtesy of the high-standing lamps that towered high in the corners. Two sets of two black leather couches sat central in the space around old-fashioned coffee tables. There was a pool table in the corner, lit in the gentle glow of an overhanging lamp, and a retro Hi-Fi was tucked away in the corner, next to a small kitchenette. It looked more like an old-fashioned speakeasy than it did an office of one of the country's leading Public Relations companies.

The most dangerous thing in the room sat on the ornate desk in the corner; a letter opener, inverted in its sheath.

"Satisfied?" Eric asked.

Pat swung around and peered into the kitchenette, nodding slowly.

"All looks well, sir. I'll just let myself out, I guess." Pat paused, his hand on the handle. "Say, Mr. Van De Berg – you didn't happen to see anything suspicious last night, did you?"

The gentle approach, this time.

Eric sighed.

"I know you're typically in your office all night," Pat continued, "But I was just curious. Nadine was my friend, obviously, and it's terrible to lose her."

For a moment, Pat caught an unmistakable fleeting look of fear on Eric's face. Then, it was gone, and he floated over to the kitchenette and pulled a bottle out from under the counter.

"Sit with me, for a moment?" he asked, following the bottle with two small glasses.

Pat took a seat at the bar as Eric poured – a beautiful, golden bourbon, with a bright red chicken etched onto the bottle – and slid him a glass.

Eric sighed again, a deep, soulful breath.

"I have a confession to make," he said.

*   *   *

Eric always looked tired. Tonight, in the dim light of the kitchenette, he looked old.

Older than he should look, for a man in his mid-forties, worth millions. He pulled a plastic chair from under the bar and sat opposite Pat, grey hair shining in the darkness, bourbon dripping down his stubble. His suit was stunning – a textured, blue felt – but it was crinkled, like the lines around his eyes.

"I have a confession to make," he said again, his voice scarcely more than a whisper.

Pat waited, his heart in his mouth.

Was this it? Was he going to be the one to break the case?

"Nadine…is my wife," Eric said.

Pat did a double take.

"My ex-wife," Eric continued. He finished off the rest of the bourbon in one sip, and refilled the glass with a sniff. As he looked up at Pat, deep into his eyes, Pat could see tears starting to well up.

"What…what happened?" Pat asked.

A quarrel at home? A lover's tiff?

"I don't know," Eric said. "We were estranged."

Pat felt like his brain was aflame.

He did it! He killed his ex-wife!

"Estranged?" Pat prompted. He felt his heart racing inside his chest, and said a silent prayer to whatever God might be listening.

Keep talking, Eric.

"Separated, if you will," Eric replied. "We lived apart. She got the house, the car. I moved out, about 6 months ago. Don't get me wrong, it was a bit

50

ugly at times. And it was tough! Seeing her at work. Why do you think I shut myself in the office all the time? Why do you think I work nights?"

Pat was stunned. Now that he thought about it, Eric never used to be a shut-in. Up until about a year ago, he was a reasonably cheerful guy to see around the building. And then…Pat had started to see him less and less, but he'd never thought to ask about it.

"Why?"

If it were even possible, Eric's face fell a mile further.

"Nadine…Nadine had a bit of a crisis," he explained. "And, yeah, that's fine. I get it. People get to our age, and they start thinking that they've missed out."

Missing out on what?

Eric blinked back a tear.

"She kept saying she 'wanted to live while she was still alive.' And that's great, we all do, right? And yeah, Charlotte's all grown up now, but I still have to work. She hated that. Apparently holidays in Europe twice a year don't quite cut it as far as 'living' goes."

A draft trickled in from the door. Pat whipped around, cautious of the fact that he was all alone, and largely defenseless.

"So obviously, custody was never an issue," Eric continued, oblivious to Pat's concerns. "She doesn't live with us anymore. So that was that. Finances…separated. No divorce, or anything – her parents would kill her. And me." He chuckled wryly. "And then, she moved on. I never could."

"She was seeing someone?"

Eric chuckled. "Have you seen her?"

Pat nodded, and Eric smiled wistfully.

"She's still a knockout," he said. He paused for a moment, and the smile faded. "Was a knockout, I guess." He drained the drink again.

If he keeps going like this, he'll be the next one out of here in a body bag.

"So…she was seeing someone?" Pat asked.

Eric nodded, his mouth full of bourbon. "Dumped me for a younger model. You know, back in my day, I was in great shape. Had the big arms, the shoulders, veins popping out."

Pat could see it. Eric wasn't a small man by any means – just getting on a bit, and his glasses and the grey stubble made him look older. Pat was sure that beneath the wrinkled suit, he was still in good shape.

Eric reached to pour himself another glass, but Pat leaned forward and took his wrist, gently.

"It won't fix it," he said. Eric nodded. A tear dropped his cheek and splashed in the dregs of the glass.

"You don't have an alibi for last night, do you?" Pat asked.

Eric shook his head, his mouth tight with frustration. "I did what I do every night," he said. "Hole up in here, did a bit of work. I sent some emails, I read, I wrote for pleasure. Just couldn't stand going home to that damn empty apartment. It doesn't even feel like mine, you know?"

Pat nodded. "And what about Nadine?"

"Oh, well some nights she stays at her place, I guess. I don't know, I'm not there anymore. Other nights, I'm sure she's shacked up with that young fellow. That's why Charlotte stopped talking to her. Said that she found them going at it in the toilet, right here in the building."

Pat's blood ran cold.

Right here in the building.

"Who's she seeing, Eric?" "I don't know," he said. "But I know he works here. He works nights."

CHAPTER 10

As he puffed relentlessly on a much-needed cigarette in the concrete stairwell, Pat's head was spinning. That last conversation had unearthed a world of truths. But which ones were relevant?

Firstly, perhaps most importantly, Nadine was in a relationship. Pat was no cop, but he knew love was a strong motive for murder. What if her lover was unhinged? What if Nadine had tried to break it off with him, and he'd reacted badly? If it had happened after Catherine had gone home, maybe Nadine's death was the result of a midnight tryst gone awry.

Nadine's secret lover wasn't the only suspect, though. As her ex-husband, Eric's lack of alibi for the whole evening put him center-stage. Was it crocodile tears that Pat had seen from Eric that evening? Did he want vengeance on his wife? Was she a cheat? An adulterer?

Finally, Charlotte. If there was bad blood between family members, revenge was yet another motive. Was there an affair? Had it driven Nadine and Eric apart, and Charlotte blamed her mother for fracturing their family?

Unlikely, but still possible.

And then, there was Johnny. He was hiding something – but what? Was he a murderer? Was he a witness? Did Eric or Charlotte have something they were holding over his head? There were, of course, other possibilities, but Pat could hardly wrap his mind around these three options yet.

And so, in a fit of confusion, he called the one person he could really talk to about all this. He fumbled with his phone, his fat fingers hitting all the wrong buttons, but finally he got through.

"Karen," he whispered, peering up the concrete stairwell to make sure nobody was eavesdropping. "I've got updates."

His wife was cheerfully intrigued with all the distinct possibilities, exclaiming "Woah!" and "No way!" as he filled her in on the latest developments. He ran her through his conversations with Johnny and Eric as best he could, desperate for her insights.

"Well it's clear as mud isn't it?!" she whispered into the phone, her voice singing with enthusiasm. "Exciting, though! God, do you think you can crack this all by yourself? Are you safe?!"

"I'm as safe as houses, darling," he replied. "They can't touch me. I've got cameras everywhere."

"Well first I think you need to talk to the detectives," she advised. "Let them know what you found out."

"Surely they know that Nadine and Eric were married? They'd already have him down as a suspect! Wouldn't they?"

"But they wouldn't know about who she was sleeping with, would they?"

Her voice was full of glee. Pat shared the enthusiasm. But not because he wanted the bragging rights. He didn't care about being the hero in Nadine's story.

He just wanted justice.

Pat dragged relentlessly on the cigarette, and the butt burned at his lips as he got too close. A coughing fit ensued.

"Pat? Don't tell me you're smoking! I thought you gave up!"

"It's just one, my love. I mean, I'm going through a lot here!"

"Hmph," Karen grunted. "Well, get it sorted then. Figure out who did it. Go talk to the police!"

They said their goodbyes, and Pat wandered back to his desk. He would talk to the cops, he was sure of that – but not tonight. Alvarez wouldn't want to come back at this hour, and Pat didn't want to rustle any feathers.

With Netflix flickering in the background, Pat pondered his next move. He was going to break this case, come hell or high water. The question was – who to speak to?

The rest of his round was uneventful. He'd already been to PubStunt and the law firm, and Monica clearly didn't want anything to do with him, so he trekked up to MedHealth. As he stopped in front of the doors, he realised something.

He'd missed MedHealth on his last round yesterday. Just, forgotten it. *Fuck.*

There wasn't much he could really do about that now, just hope that the doctors hadn't said anything, otherwise Joseph would be on him like white on rice.

Malik opened the door before Pat even knocked, a cheek-splitting smile plastered over his face. He was a huge man, and in his loafers and pink linen shirt, he looked more like he'd stepped out of a GQ magazine than a surgery.

They weren't much for long chats, but Pat had read online that he was a first generation American, after his family had moved over from Egypt.

Despite his runway-style and dashing good looks, Pat noticed they had one thing in common – Malik's black, curly hair was quickly thinning out.

"Pat!" he exclaimed. "Good to see you! Are you going okay tonight?" Then his face quickly darkened, as though he had suddenly remembered the traumatic events of yesterday, and his voice softened. "How are you, though? Actually?"

Pat nodded grimly. "Getting by. It was a bit of a shock, really. My blood pressure won't ever be the same."

Malik puffed his cheeks out and sighed. "A tragedy. She was such a lovely woman." A lovely woman, eh? "You knew each other?"

Malik beckoned him inside. It was much the same as the other offices Pat had been in that night – a simple reception desk in the waiting room hiding the entrance to the offices out back.

Malik took a seat on one of the waiting room chairs.

"Yeah, I knew her well. Nadine, she did some admin work for the clinic from time to time. I'm sure you know – Marek, myself, Luka – we all went to college together, and we're working on a bit of a project, so Nadine and I..." he meshed his fingers together and interlocked them, "...interconnected. Friends of friends, and all that."

"Oh, I see." Pat had never been good at small talk. He'd always felt sort of awkward with the conversations he had on his rounds, except for with Monica. And now, as the burly Egyptian gazed down at him expectantly, Pat could think of only one thing to say.

"So, where were you last night?" he asked.

Malik looked a little perturbed. "I was here, Pat, just like every night. Days at the Manhattan General, night time here. Comes with the territory, owning the clinic and all. But you know that, don't you?"

Pat shuffled awkwardly from foot to foot. He almost felt bad for asking.

"I've just...I've heard that Nadine was involved with someone in the building. And you know, star-crossed lovers – always makes a good motive for murder, doesn't it? A crime of passion?"

Malik laughed heartily. "So what, just because we work in the same building, we're lovers? Hell, I'm not even here during the day. Come on, Pat. There must be half a dozen guys here who are here all night, every night. You gonna ask all of them the same thing?"

Pat's face must have given him away again. Malik rolled his eyes, smirking slightly.

"It's because I've got a reputation, isn't it? Tell me, Pat. What's my reputation around here?"

"You, uh..."

"I hook up with lots of women," Malik finished for him, nodding. He threw his hands up. "Sue me, Pat, I like a good lay. And I won't lie, Nadine's a good looking woman. But she wasn't interested. I shot my shot, maybe six months ago. She told me I was an asshole, and full of myself. 'Not her type'."

"I don't think you're an asshole," mumbled Pat. "You seem real nice."

'Real nice'. Yeah, good work, Pat. That'll get him on side.

Malik rolled his eyes. "Yeah, well...'real nice' or not, wasn't me. Like I said. No involvement with Nadine." He looked reasonably calm.

Pat watched his eyes, and they held his gaze firmly. Not even a bead of sweat.

"Have you asked the other guys here?" Malik asked, a tad more defensively. "You asked them if they're hooking up with Nadine?"

"Well—I haven't spoken to them yet," Pat said. "But I will! I'm going to get to the bottom of this!"

Malik chuckled. "You're here all night, but you really have no idea what goes on after dark, do you, Pat?"

"What do you mean?"

Malik chuckled. "Me, Marek, Luka...you know we all went to college together, right?"

Pat nodded. "I heard that, yeah."

"We're pioneers," Malik said. He pulled what looked to be a small tankard of water out from behind the reception desk and slugged it desperately. Pat waited, watching it drip down his chin, until he set it down by his feet.

"We're pioneers, Pat," Malik repeated. "We're working on...something new. It's in testing stages at the moment, but if it works....well..." He winked. "...let's just say I won't be spending my time with any women around here."

Pat smiled politely as Malik burst into bellyaching laughter at his own joke.

"But seriously, Pat," he said. "Seriously, I've hardly had time to sleep lately. The last thing I'm doing is getting involved with anyone romantically. Make sense?"

"Yeah. Yeah...I guess it does."

Malik stood, took Pat's hand in his huge vice and pulled him up to his feet.

"Look Pat...if you want to talk about this, I'm always around to lend an ear," he said. "But for now...I've got to get back to work." He stepped back into the office, but paused in the doorway. "You're a good guy, Pat. Let me know what you find out."

The door swung shut.

And with that, Pat was left in the chilly MedHealth lobby.

*   *   *

Pat needed time to think. He had paused his round and headed back downstairs, even going as far to turn off Netflix. A part of him was hoping the silence would suddenly impress upon him the answer to this whole mystery, but epiphanies evaded him, so he tried his best to think through the possibilities.

Malik was right; there were other single men in the building. Hell, Pat had let women into the building late at night to visit Luka. Pharmaceutical reps, mainly, but what sort of rep visits at midnight and doesn't leave until 3?

He could've slapped himself in the face as a bigger possibility dawned on him.

What about Marek?!

The single, good looking, charming Slovakian worked in the same office as Nadine! Surely, if she was estranged from her husband and on the prowl, he would be a likely candidate. And that wasn't the only thing. Jealousy was a surefire motive. What if someone else was involved with Nadine's secret lover, and this was a catfight gone wrong?

While Pat wasn't relying on Malik's statement – of course, who wouldn't deny a relationship with a dead woman? – and his revelation only meant that the pool of suspects had increased, Pat trotted towards the stairs with renewed vigour. He pottered up to the third floor to Mihok & Mihok, mentally preparing himself for what to say. Would he confront him? *J'accuse!* He could try and get him drunk, maybe he would spill the beans?

The floor was unusually gloomy. Normally around this hour he'd be hearing the whirring of printers and maybe some Middle Eastern folk music – Marek's go-to choice of tunes. But tonight, the normally dim lights of the sparkling office were turned off, and the only thing Pat could hear were the creak of his footsteps on the polished wood. As he neared the office, he could see the lights in the back office were on.

He doesn't even stop work when his assistant has been murdered.

Thoughts tumbling through his mind, Pat let himself in through the unlocked front door, and as the swathe of cold air conditioning whipped through his hair, he realised.

The front desk is empty.

Nobody knows I'm here.

He paused for a moment, taking in the scene. Dim light from the back office. No Nadine, obviously. No sign of Sal, Marek's second in command.

Was he the secret lover? What's your type, Nadine?

This was where his real investigation could begin. It wasn't the scene of the crime – the fifth floor windows had been cordoned off by police – but as her workplace, it wasn't a bad place to start.

What did police normally look for? Phone records? Bank statements?

In any event, the cabinet under the front reception counter seemed to be the place to start.

He tried the drawers – locked. Fumbling around the sides, his eyes still glued to the back door, Pat's chubby fingers stumbled upon the plastic butt of a small metal key. He turned it, tried the first drawer, and it slid open.

Pens, pencils, post-it notes. The next drawer; more of the same, plus a stapler and a magnificent stash of staples. The final drawer – a diffuser, and what looked to be bottles of essential oils; 'Soothing Lavender', 'Peaceful Rose-blossom'.

Pat stashed the bottles back in the cupboard as quietly as he could and locked the cupboard quietly. No luck. He wasn't expecting to find a file marked 'TOP SECRET', but something, anything that would tell him more about Nadine would be useful. Could he get into her emails? Only one way to find out.

He turned his attention to the laptop sat on the front desk. It was a sleek, silver model, one that he wasn't familiar with. Certainly nicer than his hunk of junk downstairs. But all he did with his was look at the cameras, so perhaps that was fair.

He flipped the lid open and was met with a bright login screen. Of course it did – everything was password authenticated nowadays. Pat wasn't stupid. This wasn't like the movies. It wasn't like he knew the name of her dog, or the name of the street she grew up in, so he had no chance of getting in there without someone letting him. He'd have to find something else.

Then, just around the corner, he heard the internal door to the back room open.

*   *   *

Marek strode out into the foyer, yawning. His footsteps slapped on the floor as they moved closer and closer to the front door.

Pat had miraculously managed to wedge himself under the desk after slamming the computer shut. Smells assaulted his senses; whiskey, a woody cologne, freshly laundered clothes. They grew stronger and stronger as Marek paused in the middle of the foyer.

What's he doing? What does he need?

Eventually, Pat heard the rush of cold air as the front door softly swung back and forth on its hinges. Then, the lock clicked.

Fuck.

Pat didn't have long.

Where was he going?

Could be a bathroom break. Could be to see Malik, or Luka. Could be to see anyone at Microceuticals, for that matter, or could be a late-night quickie.

He could be five minutes, he could be twenty. It was the ideal time to duck out.

But…Pat didn't have what he wanted yet. And while he didn't have much time…this was the best opportunity he was ever going to get.

Pat's brain screamed at him as his body beelined towards the back room. *What are you doing, you fool?! No, no, NO! He could be back any minute! And how are you even going to get out of here?*

But the rational thoughts were ignored. Pat practically ran through the doors, and time slowed as he used every inch of available brainpower to figure out exactly what he needed.

Big company. Lots of files. *Paper?* No, there was no paper. The space was the same size as Collymore & Donovan's, except about twice the number of TVs were pinned to the upper reaches of the walls.

But Pat wasn't interested in TVs.

A lounge area sat to the right, featuring robust leather couches and wooden coffee tables. Pat could see the same decanter he had been served from the night before sitting on the table with a single glass…

…and a laptop, brimming with light.

Pat hurried over.

It was Marek's laptop, no doubt about it. Silver and sleek, a carbon copy of the one on the front desk. He swiped the touchpad to reveal a picture of Marek in a T-shirt, grinning innocently. Behind him was a river, and a palatial building, complete with towers and decorative minarets. He'd seen it before on travel brochures for Russia.

No time for that. Just the usual icons on the desktop. Fingers sweating, Pat clicked on the file browser and a bright white screen flicked open, with a list of files sorted into browsers. 401K Archive Documents Users Microceuticals Pat clicked on the fourth link – 'Users.' A new window fired up, with even more subfolders listed. He only recognised three names out of the dozens listed – Marek Mihok, Sal Whiteman, and Nadine Matthews.

He opened Nadine's file.

Lots of documents. Many, many documents. Pat flicked through as fast as his fingers would allow. There were identity documents – a copy of her passport, her driving license, even her social security number!

This is her personal file.

Pat clicked furiously. He didn't even know where he was going, or what he was looking for.

But he'd know when he found it.

A bank statement flew up onto his screen. It was dated just over a week ago; a savings account with DeutscheBank. Page 1 of 12. He didn't have time to go through the numbers now; there were pages and pages of them! In a moment of clarity, he remembered the printer out in the front foyer. And all of a sudden, in this moment of intense pressure, Larry's attempts to teach him how to work a computer finally came back to him.

"The fastest way to print is to press Control-P," Larry said. "That'll bring up the printer menu."

Could he print from here? Did he have time?

Pat closed his eyes, said a silent prayer, and pressed the buttons. Miraculously, a menu popped up; Select your printer. There were three options, all just a sequence of jumbled letters and numbers. MHMH-001, MHMH-002, MHMH-003.

Did that mean three printers? Which one was the one in the lobby? He double clicked on the third one and pressed 'OK'.

Why? No idea, just seems like the right one.

With baited breath, he waited, like a call and response.

This is where it prints, right? Come on, dammit!

But the door to the foyer was shut. He wouldn't hear anything back here.

Pat dashed out to the front of the office, and sure enough, the grey monolith was booting up, whirring as a green light blinked furiously and the LCD flashed, furiously bright in the dim light of the foyer. In a matter of seconds, it spewed a catalogue of pages out into the output tray.

Okay, step one. Now, you've got to get out of here!

No. He needed more. He was a man on a mission, and one damn bank statement didn't prove anything!

Without even grabbing what was spewing out of the printer – thank God it was fast – Pat raced back into the back room and opened more documents, one after another. Thankfully they were all titled – he didn't even bother looking at the contents, just opened up half a dozen in a frenzy and pounded the keys that Larry had taught him.

Control-P, Control-P, Control-P.

He could hear the printer buzzing in the lobby. That's enough, idiot! After what seemed like a lifetime, Pat ceded control to the part of his brain preoccupied with his safety, and charged back out to the foyer, his footsteps echoing through the silence.

You didn't close the files!

Pat doubled back at record pace, sweat welling under his armpits, his breaths short and hitched. He'd never moved so fast in his life. He wished he was fitter.

For a second, he contemplated just taking the computer itself, but that would just cause bigger problems. Then there'd be another security issue to deal with!

He closed everything he'd opened as deliberately and carefully as his fingers would allow and backed away slowly, praying the laptop would return to its screensaver before Marek returned.

Back in the foyer, he snatched up a blank manila file from a stack on the reception desk and stuffed it with the documents from the printer, which were zipping out from the feeder at such a speed that some were drifting to the floor. Pat grabbed every single one, crumpling them into the folder, his heart pounding in his ears. Then, a higher power let him know that his time was almost up.

Through the pipes in the walls, Pat heard a toilet flush.

CHAPTER 11

Thankfully, the toilets were down the other end of the longer corridor. Providing Marek washed his hands, and depending on how fast he walked, Pat had at best a minute...

...and at worst, thirty seconds until he was caught red handed.

Pat knelt beside the desk, keeping the bank of wood between him and the door, his hands clasped in a silent prayer as the printer continued, spitting out pages upon pages of bank statements, credit reports, and whatever else he'd opened on the laptop.

Can I pull the plug out?

No, that would never work. He'd seen it on printers before – they had a memory. If you turned them off, it would just continue printing the next time someone booted it up, and then he would be back to the security issue again. He had to wait.

Pat peered out from behind the desk, the wood creaking under his knees. From here, he could see through the glass doors, down to where the bathrooms were, but the corridor faded into darkness. No movement, yet.

He looked back at the printer. It spewed the pages out relentlessly and consistently, no change in pace to account for the concerns of a mere human. He grabbed each page as it tumbled out, stuffing it into the folder, his eyes fixed on the door.

Come on...come on!

Wait.

The print queue!

He jumped to his feet and slapped a sweaty hand on the digital display. Queue: 1.

What did that mean? Was this one the last document? Or was there one more after that?

This document was another statement, so if each one was the same as the first that Pat had looked at, it was twelve pages long. Another twelve pages meant he had maybe twenty seconds to go before he was finished. But if there was another document...

He glanced back at the door, and to his horror, he saw a figure at the end of the hallway, definitively moving in his direction.

Pat dropped to his knees, behind the desk.

The printer continued to whirr. Another page, and another. Marek continued to approach as Pat cowered behind the desk, desperately snatching pages from the tray. As the banker passed beneath a light, Pat could see he was looking down at his phone, his fingers tapping away, the bright light beaming into his face.

The printer stopped.

Pat snatched up the last piece of paper and whipped his arm back to his chest, crawling hurriedly backwards and diving under the desk, just as a key jangled in the door.

*   *   *

Pat clasped his hand over his mouth, desperately trying to stifle his own breathing, and held the manila folder tight to his chest. The desk was too tight a hiding space – just large enough for Nadine's legs to comfortably swing around, but definitely not large enough for an overweight security guard to hide out for any prolonged period of time.

You know, if you just took the stairs like Karen told you to, maybe you wouldn't be in such a pickle.

Mercifully, the printer had turned itself off before Marek stepped into the office. Pat had held his breath and waited, listening intently to the slapping of steps on the wooden floors.

Marek swung past him, whistling merrily, tapping away on his phone, and squeezed past the printer to vanish into the back office without looking back. Had he so much as turned six inches, he would've seen the bright whites of Pat's uniform under the desk.

Now? Do I go now?

Pat hesitated for a split second, then scrambled out from under the desk. Blood pounding in his ears, he slipped on the wooden floor as he desperately made for the exit, practically throwing himself through the glass as he tumbled out into the hallway, not even caring about the amount of noise he was making.

Run! Run you fool!

The bathrooms were straight ahead, down the long stretch, and the entrance to the stairs on this floor was right next to them. The elevators were to the right.

Pat booked it to the right. Now was no time for self-aggrandizement; he just needed to get off this floor as quick as he possibly could, and hide the folder in his desk.

"Hey!" The voice boomed out from Mihok & Mihok as Pat reached the elevator, which benevolently creaked open for him as soon as his finger touched the button.

Pat's heart flew into his mouth as he stared, wide-eyed at the file in his hands.

No time.

He'll see me.

And so, as the elevator doors started to close, Pat did the only thing that seemed sensible.

He tossed the file forward and it landed with a satisfying slap on the floor of the elevator.

The doors closed, and Marek rounded the corner.

*   *   *

"Were you just in my office?" he snapped, irate. His eyes were alight, his expression sour. Normally, Pat had never seen a crease in his suit, but right now he looked genuinely perturbed.

"Oh, no!" Pat chuckled as he wrenched his eyes from the elevator's digital panel, which still read; '3'. "I'm really sorry. I slipped on the wood and, uh…bounced off your window. I'm sorry about that."

Good work, Pat.

But was it good enough?

Marek's eyes never left Pat as he swept over him from head to toe. Pat stood stock-still, like he was a suspect in a line-up. He felt beads of sweat forming on his forehead – partly from his scramble to get out of the office, partly out of fear.

"You fell into the door?"

"Yes, sir. Really, I'm very sorry. Won't happen again." Pat forced the most disingenuous smile he'd ever managed, but Marek remained stone-faced as he tried to determine if he was snooping around where he shouldn't have been.

Nothing in my hands, buddy. Am I home free?

The elevator rumbled.

Shit. Shit!

With a look of genuine disdain, Marek turned on his heel and swept back in the direction of his office. "Don't let it happen again!" he called out behind him as he disappeared through the glass doors around the corner.

Waiting until he was positive Marek was out of sight, Pat whipped around and hurriedly mashed both the elevator keys. It had gone up, but only as far as '4', thankfully, and the arrow indicated it was coming back down.

Finally, after an eternity of waiting, the doors slid open again…

…to reveal Catherine Kim.

Holding the file of financials.

Pat watched in horror as she moved to open the file, not looking up at him, her expression genuinely curious.

Without a moment of hesitation, he lunged forward and snatched it out of her grasp.

"Sorry!" he panted. "That's mine. Personal, uh – personal information, you know. Just dropped it before when I was getting out."

Catherine eyed him over. She glanced at him, at the folder in his hands, at the sweat on his forehead.

"Been exercising, have we?" she quipped.

"Uh, yeah," Pat grunted. "Been…uh, trying to take the stairs. Stay fit and everything."

Catherine's eyes narrowed. "But you dropped this in the elevator?"

Get your cover story straight!

Pat tried his best to laugh it off. "Ah, well…yeah. There was a disturbance I had to check on. Don't always have time to keep fit!" The elevator doors tried to shut, but Catherine slammed a hand into them.

"I pinged you to let you know I'm leaving. I still can't find my card. Can you let me out?"

Heading out early again, are we? Escaping, in the dead of night?

In his haste to run his own set of interviews, Pat had neglected his other duties by abandoning his computer.

"Yes, yes, of course!" Pat jumped in the elevator next to her, still clutching the file to his chest, and they headed downstairs to the lobby, where he swiped his card on the reader next to the door to open the gates for her.

"Can I walk you out?" he offered, stowing the file under his desk.

"I'd…I've got something to ask you about last night."

"Uh…no thanks. I'm good."

Catherine sauntered out of the front door and into the night, not looking back.

His heart still beating furiously, Pat collapsed in front of his computer and checked the cameras.

You did it.

You got out.

Nothing amiss. Nothing wrong. No Marek wandering around on the third floor. No outgoing calls on any of the building's internal phone lines, that he could see.

He'd made it.

With the benefit of hindsight, though, he had been nothing short of foolish. He could've – no, he would've – lost his job, and with an unsolved murder as a black mark on his CV, he wouldn't be getting another one shortly. It wasn't like he had any other marketable skills.

But still, the curious part of his brain – the part that was becoming increasingly obsessed with what had happened to Nadine – was ecstatic. He had his suspects, but now – for the first time – he had concrete information in his hands that the police didn't.

He was going to crack this case.

CHAPTER 12

"I don't know what you were thinking!" Karen shrieked at the top of her lungs, while Pat desperately tried to shush her.

He had gotten home about an hour ago, waving the file triumphantly, and Karen had gone ballistic, despite Larry being fast asleep across the hall. Pat's first mistake was waking her up so early – his second was admitting that he'd jeopardised his job to obtain information that he didn't even know he would be useful.

"I fully support you in finding out what happened, Pat!" she roared at him from the bathroom, as Pat sat up in bed like a wounded puppy. "I fully, fully support you! But you're breaking and entering, and stealing things! Don't get me wrong, I'm glad you got what you got, but you can't be jeopardising your job in the process!"

She stormed back into the bathroom, her hair in curlers, as Pat sat with his chin to his chest in bed, trying to hide under the covers.

There was no use interrupting her on a rant; it would just prolong the process. She re-appeared, whipping open the closet in a frenzy, and turfed out a selection of blouses to wear to work.

"Well?" she roared at him. "What's in the damn file, Pat!"

Pat picked it up off the bedside table, gingerly. "I haven't read it yet," he whispered.

"Okay! So all that, and you can't even be bothered to look at what you've got. You know what?" She flounced over to him and ripped it out of his hands. "I'm taking this. I'm going to read it. In the meantime, you can think about the fact that you jeopardised everything so hard you worked for. You know you could've lost your job? Your benefits? Our health insurance?!" She was positively wailing now as she stuffed herself into a pair of black pants and a tidy blouse.

"I was trying to help! The cops say they don't know who did it! I'm trying to help my friend!" Pat finally shouted back.

"Don't you shout at me! You'll wake Larry!" Karen hissed, before tucking the folder under one arm, grabbing her bag, and heading for the door. "Why did you even take it, Pat? What are you hoping to find?! I'm not happy, Pat! Not happy!"

She marched out the door, flinging it shut behind her, and Pat breathed a deep sigh of relief.

Much shorter than a normal fight. Perks of working nights.

The front door slammed. Pat rolled himself up in the bedsheets to hide out from the cold and forced his eyes. He needed to sleep, but the adrenaline was still pumping, and Karen's question echoing in his head.

Why had he taken the folder? What was he hoping to prove? It might take him some time to find something incriminating in the documents, but if he could at least tell Karen where his suspicions were headed, then it would give him something to go on.

So, who did he suspect?

There was Eric, the secret ex-husband…and maybe his daughter Charlotte.

There was Marek, the employer.

There was the possibly enraged lover – whoever that may be.

There was Johnny, the man who was drinking himself to an early grave.

And there was Catherine, forever ducking out early.

But so far, nobody had nobody was giving anything away.

Johnny wouldn't speak to him, Malik was tight-lipped, and Catherine – as nice as she was – seemed to be avoiding him, same as everyone else. Mateo had vanished into the annals of Collymore & Donovan, Microceuticals just shut the door in his face like always, and Monica was nowhere to be found.

So, what could he do…to rock the boat?

As the sun rose, Pat gave up on trying to sleep, and made a phone call to the one person who he thought might actually be curious about what he had to say.

*   *   *

Pat had only ever been in a police station once before, as a witness to a car accident. He paced awkwardly on the Midtown sidewalk for a minute, the huge concrete façade towering above him.

THE CITY OF NEW YORK POLICE DEPARTMENT – 26TH PRECINCT.

It had taken three buses to get here from home, but he sure wasn't going to try and drive his car into Midtown only to not find parking. But now, as he waited awkwardly in the cold, trying desperately to come up with what to say, he missed the warm comfort of his ride.

As if she was expecting him, Alvarez appeared at the front door and stuck her head out.

"Come inside," she said. "You'll freeze to death out there."

Thankful for the invitation, Pat ducked in and was met with the artificial warmth of space heaters running at full capacity.

It was a jam-packed office, with maybe twenty or thirty cops milling about in the small bullpen behind the front desk. A few more of them, uniformed and armed, were keeping watch over some people in the lobby; a woman and her child, a man missing some teeth. Pat spotted some people in suits, hiding in glass offices at the back.

Alvarez beckoned him through the foyer. Pat followed in her wake as she danced through the officers and into an interview room at the end of a corridor.

The room was stark and bare. Four chairs sat opposite each other against a table that had been shunted up to the wall to support an archaic tape recorder with dials and huge LEDs. The walls were largely concrete, but one of them housed a giant mirror. The floor was uncarpeted, unfinished, just dirty concrete under his feet.

Pat took a seat at the table, and Alvarez pulled out a notepad and pen before joining him. She smiled at him – a neon pink smile – and Pat couldn't help but feel that whole setting felt somewhat…intimate. He glanced up at the ceiling – cameras, two of them – and then at the mirror, which he presumed housed people listening in on the other side.

Not so intimate after all.

"There's nobody listening," Alvarez said as she caught him staring at the one-way mirror. She chuckled. "We're…understaffed, at the moment."

Pat forced a smile. His anxiety was peaking.

Is she trying to woo me? Get a confession out of me? Does she think I'm a suspect?

"I'll cut right to the chase, Detective," he said, trying his best to sound confident. "I think I have some information that you might find useful."

She flipped to a new page in the notepad, then looked up at him expectantly.

"Nadine," he explained. "In Guinness House."

She flashed her pearly whites. "Fortunately for the NYPD, Pat, there aren't so many murders that I don't remember you. And I must say, I was probably a little bit curt with you that night, so I'm sorry. Sometimes it's hard to remember who's batting for what team."

That made Pat feel good, like he'd done the right thing. Part of him wished that he'd brought the folder with the financials, but Karen's words about him committing a crime rang in his ears.

"I found something," he said quietly.

What if I'm hanging the wrong person out to dry? But won't they find out anyway? This is just speeding things along. I'm helping!

Alvarez waited patiently, pen poised.

"Eric Van De Berg…" he continued, "is Nadine's estranged husband."

Alvarez cocked an eyebrow. "And they work in the same building?"

Pat nodded. "Their daughter, too."

She hummed to herself, tapping her pen on the notepad. Her nails were pink, too.

"What else do you know?"

"He lives alone. They separated about six months ago. Charlotte, she works with him; she's their daughter."

Alvarez hummed again, scribbling away on her notepad. "So…that means he did it?"

"What?" Pat spluttered. "No, no! I mean – not necessarily, right?"

"So why come in?" Alvarez folded up the notepad and dropped it back on the desk. The beautiful smile was gone, replaced by an intense curiosity. She looked like a lion, eyeing Pat up like a wounded gazelle.

"If you don't think he did it, why are you here? Don't you work nights? Shouldn't you be sleeping?"

Suddenly, Pat was regretting his visit. "I don't know that he did it, but he could've!" he spluttered. "I mean, I'm just trying to help!"

Alvarez shrugged. "Yeah, okay. We're pretty confident it was an intruder, anyway."

That made Pat's blood boil. "It was not an intruder. I keep that building locked down, safe and sound. Nobody gets in and out without my permission!"

"Oh yeah, watching the cameras all night were we?" Alvarez's tone was dismissive, and she'd even put the pen down, like she'd already concluded he wasn't going to say anything else of value. "Even when out for cigarettes in the stairwell? I've met your friend, the other guy. What was his name? Lionel, I think. Has he got an opinion, too?"

Pat couldn't handle it anymore. He flew to his feet, knocking the chair backwards, his ham hands balled up into fists. He saw a flicker of fear in Alvarez's eyes – she was, after all, a lone woman in a closed room with a much larger man – but then it vanished.

To be replaced by fury.

"Get out."

Her voice was little more than a whisper, but it told Pat that he was inches away from being arrested. He didn't care – he had come here to help, not be insulted.

He whipped around the desk, back down the hallway and into the waiting area, and then into the cold of the street.

If they're not going to listen, I'll solve this myself.

*   *   *

He slept for about five hours that morning, Alvarez's comments tormenting him.

Who does she think she is? I'll show her. I'll show her what I can do.

Eventually, just after three in the afternoon, he rolled out of bed and put on pants. This was an 'early morning' for him; normally, Karen would wake him when she got home around five, if he was lucky enough to sleep through Larry getting home from school.

He made himself a light 'breakfast' – eggs on toast – and called her, but she didn't answer. Just as he settled in front of the TV with a cup of coffee, the phone rang.

Unknown number.

Hesitantly, he answered.

"Hello?"

"It's Lionel, Pat," came the drawl from the other end of the line. Most unusual. In all the years they'd worked together, he'd had exactly one phone call from Lionel, and that was to tell him a joke about a goat walking into the bar. Frankly, he was surprised that the guy knew how to use a phone, let alone that he still had his number.

Pat waited expectantly, but Lionel left him hanging.

"Yes, Lionel?"

"Cops…cops are here," Lionel yawned. "They've got the old guy in, down here in the lobby. One of the girls said you're really invested in all this, so…thought I'd give you a bell."

"Lionel, you're fantastic. I'll see you soon."

"Ciao, friend."

Pat hung up and raced upstairs, jumping as quick as he could into his work clothes, which were still dirty – owing to the fact that he'd hardly been out of them in the last twelve hours.

They had Eric in custody? Was that because of what he'd told Alvarez?

Stinking of body odour and with Doritos stains all over the front of his shirt, he texted Karen to let her know he'd be gone when he got home and dashed back downstairs. He found Larry sitting in the kitchen, eyes glued to his phone.

Was Pat like that in his youth? Of course not. But he found no reason to get on Larry for it – he had good grades, an active social life, he was fit and healthy. What more could a parent want, even if his eyes were going square?

"Morning," Pat grunted as he rushed to make his coffee.

"It's almost four," Larry laughed, eyes never leaving his phone.

Pat filled up his coffee, wrestled his tie into a suitable knot and was out the door, giving Larry a quick kiss as he departed. Leaving this early meant he likely wouldn't see Karen until the early hours. Probably for the best, given her furore that morning.

Like ships, passing in the night.

Light traffic had him at work in record time. He slammed his car into the parking lot and bolted quickly up the front steps, breathless and determined.

Lionel awaited him.

"Where is he?" Pat panted.

There were no cops in the lobby, no more yellow tape; no sign that anything untoward had happened at all. Lionel waved indifferently towards the back of the building, past Joseph's office.

Pat started towards the conference rooms, determined.

If anyone deserves to know what's being said here, it's me.

Joseph's beady eyes were watching through the crack in the blinds as Pat stamped past his office. Joseph wouldn't come out for the cops. He felt himself too important. But he was also a nosy little weasel, so Pat had a little satisfaction that he – "just a lowly security guard" – knew more than the boss.

This is my chance to shine. Hell, I know as much as the lead Detective!

Heading through the double doors that led to the rarely used back of the building, a threatening sight loomed up ahead of Pat. Two cops – burly white men with poor excuses for moustaches – flanked the conference room doors. Sunglasses, tattoos, guns on their waistbands. They didn't move as Pat hustled in their direction.

Detective Alvarez and Eric Van De Berg were visible through the glass walls of the conference room. He was seated at the large wooden table, and she was pacing, a resolute glint in her eye as she looked to be peppering him with questions. His body language was nervous – shuffling, fidgeting, and Pat could see from here that his face was covered in sweat.

A confession? Or an interrogation?

Pat had routinely surprised himself since the murder took place. And in that moment, this new trend continued as he beelined directly towards one of the two cops standing in front of the door.

"You can't go in there, sir," one of them said, sticking a hand out, but Pat marched forward and let the man's arm slap off his chest as he wrenched down the handle and strode into the room.

Alvarez looked up – shocked – and then her expression turned sour.

"This isn't a walk-in show, Mr. Dickson," she said icily. "You're going to have to leave."

Pat felt the blood roaring in his ears. One of the cops clapped him on the shoulder, and he shrugged him off without breaking eye contact.

"This is my building," he said firmly. "I need to be kept in the loop.

Especially if you're accusing me of not doing my job."

Eric looked somewhat relieved at his arrival. Pat nodded at him.

I've got your back.

He got a nervous smile in return.

Alvarez blew air out of her nose, dissatisfied, then glanced at Eric.

"I'd like him to stay," Eric said quietly. "He already knows this."

"Fine." Alvarez whirled around to the other side of the table. "But I'm not repeating myself. And I don't think I need to. You have no alibi from nine thirty-five through to…eleven thirty? When everyone convened in the lobby?"

Eric shook his head, and Pat took a seat next to him. Alvarez continued to pace.

"Mr. Dickson," Alvarez continued. "You actually may be able to help us with this. Can you confirm Mr. Van De Berg's whereabouts at all?"

Pat bit his lip. He couldn't. As per Eric's own admission, he spent most of his time inside the building holed up in his office.

He shook his head. Eric looked dismayed.

"You didn't check on him?" Alvarez asked. "As part of your round?"

Pat shook his head again. "I tried, but…"

"But what, Mr. Dickson?"

"But the office was locked."

She pursed her lips, nodding. "It was locked?"

"If it's just Charlotte and I, it's not unusual for us to lock the doors," Eric offered. Alvarez waved him silent.

"Were the lights on?"

"They…they were off," admitted Pat, now feeling like he was on the back foot.

"But he still could've been in there."

"So, the lights were off, but you think he was inside?"

"Excuse me! Is this a court of inquiry?" Eric snapped.

"No!" Alvarez hissed. "But Mr. Dickson practically forced his way into this little confessional, so I think we should make him useful while he's here, shouldn't we?"

Eric retreated into silence as Alvarez rounded on Pat again. He was regretting pushing her buttons.

"I'm sorry, Mr. Dickson," Alvarez said, that same glint in her eye. "But do you believe Mr. Van De Berg committed this murder, or not? Because yesterday, you showed up at the station to offer incriminating evidence, did you not?"

Pat flushed white hot, and Eric's mouth dropped open.

"You did what?!" he roared, but Alvarez flapped a hand at him again.

"Quiet! Or I'll actually arrest you!"

Pat felt his blood simmering as Alvarez paced around to his side of the table, her lips inches from his ear. Her perfume smelled sweet and light, and he caught a hint of rosewater.

"So, he's got no alibi," she purred. "Motive – she's his estranged wife. We had a good chat before you got here – seems they weren't on the best of terms! Charlotte confirms that as well. Means – that's quite easily covered. Plenty of sharp objects in this building. And well...we know from your statement that he had the opportunity. So, I think we know what's next, don't we?"

She clapped Pat on the shoulder and beckoned the officers over from the door before slamming her hands on the table, her nose inches from Eric's.

"Eric Van De Berg, I am arresting you for the murder of Nadine Matthews. You do not have to say anything, but anything you do say may be used against you in a court of law. You have a right to an attorney. If you do not have one, one will be appointed to you by the State of New York."

The cops marched in and dragged Eric to his feet. His face – getting progressively more weathered and grey by the minute – had that forty-thousand yard stare that Pat had seen in the movies.

As the cops slapped the cuffs onto their prisoner and Alvarez cast him a smug smile, Pat's heart sank.

Had he cost an innocent man the rest of his freedom?

CHAPTER 13

Alvarez ushered Pat out of the room as she consulted with the cops.

What have you done, Pat? You've thrown him in it!

Pat slumped down at his desk, his eyes glazing over the security cameras as guilt pinched his chest. Lionel had vanished, presumably abandoning his duties the moment Pat had shown up.

Alvarez chatted with the two cops in the doorway. Eric was standing in the middle of the three of them. The rage was gone; he just looked shrunken, defeated. He was just a simple, lonely man who was wallowing in the aftermath of a failing marriage.

There was love lost, but there was no hatred.

Only sadness.

Conversely, Alvarez was practically beaming. Pat wanted to say he didn't understand her, but he did. She was all about closing the case.

He'd seen in cop shows on TV that they had targets. Homicide rates, solved crimes and so on.

Was this how she hit her quotas? By not caring? Or did she know something that Pat didn't?

For half a moment, Pat was tempted to head back in there and start shouting about Nadine's secret lover. Or perhaps there was something in the manila folder that would acquit Eric?

But he couldn't tell them about that. Bringing any attention to the fact that he'd stolen documents would cost him. And as he watched Alvarez with that triumphant smile on her face, he wasn't even sure that showing her his takings would bear any fruit.

No, he'd have to wait. Wait for something concrete. Karen still had the files, so he just had to hope she'd find something in them. Some sort of motive, tucked away in emails and bank statements.

Alvarez broke away from the cops and marched over to Pat, smug with satisfaction.

"I'd like a report from you detailing what's happened here tonight," she instructed. "If you remember how to write one, that is."

Pat practically snarled at her as she pranced back down the wall, a spring in her step.

Oh, I'll give you a report.

Onlookers had started to gather. In the late afternoon, there were many more people present on the night shift, but he still spotted the usual suspects.

The three amigos – Marek, Malik and Luka – watched from afar, their expressions unwavering. Amy Morales – the young girl from Micrcoceuticals – was standing next to them. She was a gorgeous young woman – no doubt that was why she was still around, what with their abysmal staff turnover – but her normal sharp cheekbones and sparkling eyes were sullied with abject terror. Monica was lurking by herself in the corner, eyes glazed over. Whether that was to do with the fact that she worked in a building with a murderer, or at the whole drama surrounding it, Pat didn't know. She briefly met his gaze – with disapproval? – then turned on her heel and vanished into the elevator.

Pat had disappointed her. He could feel it. He'd made this whole situation worse than it had to be.

You have to fix this.

Alvarez broke away from the conference room, and the two cops dragged Eric in her wake. Handcuffs were clipped tight around his wrists. Pat couldn't make eye contact.

Who was Nadine's secret lover?

Someone burst through the throng of onlookers. His shirt was wrinkled, but no bottle swung from his hand.

Johnny Ray.

"He has an alibi!" Johnny roared. "I'm his alibi!"

Alvarez stopped dead in her tracks, Eric and the cops pulling to a halt behind her. The murmuring crowd fell silent, collectively holding their breaths.

"We're lovers!"

As if it was a scene from a film, the crowd gasped in horror.

"Yes!" Johnny continued, moving forward towards Eric. The cops stepped to block him, but Johnny darted around them and grabbed at Eric's hands. Alvarez, looking perplexed, tried to shoo him away, but he just pushed past her, clearly intent on making a very public statement.

"I am his lover!" he shouted again. "We were in my office, on Tuesday night. We've been together for months now. He's ashamed to say it! He's so ashamed that he'd rather be imprisoned than accept himself for who he really is!"

Pat looked for Charlotte Van De Berg, and spotted her off to the side by the staircase. She was slack-jawed, paler than ever, a hand covering her mouth in shock. Johnny's colleagues – Catherine and Mateo among them – were exchanging hurried whispers. Marek looked furious. He mumbled something to Luka, and the three of them hurried up the stairs with Amy, Gopal and Sal lagging behind them.

"It's true!" Eric bellowed, shaking free of the officers. "It's true, all of it! I swear to it!"

Alvarez couldn't keep it together. Pat watched her flounder, whipping from left to right as Johnny literally shoved through the officers who were trying to keep him apart from Eric and planted a huge kiss on his lips. It seemed almost forceful, as though he was trying to prove a point. Eric's hands gingerly wrapped around Johnny's waist until Johnny let him go with a triumphant exhalation.

"Enough, enough!" Alvarez roared as the officers. "You, and you!" she yelled, pointing at Johnny and Eric, "with me, in there, right now!" She stormed towards the conference room, heels cracking like gunshots on the marble floor.

Pat was stuck to his seat with shock, utterly flabbergasted. He watched the pair link arms and Johnny whisper something in Eric's ear. This wasn't lovers talk; his expression was grave as he spoke hurriedly, so quickly that Pat couldn't read his lips.

Eric nodded twice, and they disappeared into the room behind Alvarez. As the door to the conference room slammed shut, the spell was lifted from the crowd. A hushed, excited whispering broke out as they dispersed in groups, up the staircases and into the elevators.

Pat watched them go, but his mind was on something else.

That look of fury that he'd seen in Marek's eye before he'd vanished up the stairs.

*   *   *

Pat's brain ran slowly through the rest of the afternoon, like he was driving through a fog. He'd tried to call Lionel to see if he planned on returning for his shift, but his phone went straight to voicemail. Leaving the building unattended would only add to his list of troubles, so he called Karen.

"I'm going to have to work a double shift," he said, tentatively. They hadn't spoken since the fight that last night.

"Oh well!" she chirped. "More money on the table, right? Do you want me to bring you some food after I finish?"

He thought on it. What with Monica not speaking to him, it would be nice to have some company in the building.

I can't put her out like that, though. She works hard enough.

"It's fine, honey. Get some rest and I'll see you in the morning."

"I'll get you some dinner on one of those App things," she sang. "I know what you like. Love ya, hon."

And that was the rest of Pat's social contact for the day. Eric and Johnny were in the conference room with the police for about another hour or so before Alvarez – her face like thunder – finally departed, with a snap of her fingers to get Pat to open the doors. Eric and Johnny trudged out after her – Eric looking relieved – and then they went back upstairs.

Separately.

Pat didn't bother doing Lionel's rounds – they definitely weren't his responsibility – so he just spent the rest of the afternoon hiding behind his desk, attempting to look busy while also avoiding Joseph's eyeline. The little man stared up at him from his office through the gap in the blinds. Pat had no doubt that the cogs behind those beady eyes were whirring furiously, trying to find an excuse to fire him.

Thankfully, he left as the sun was setting, with the rest of the office fodder. As the last of the day shift departed, the winter cold whipped through the front doors, and Pat was left alone at his desk.

Along with all the people who were in Guinness House on the night of Nadine's murder.

But when Pat started on his 7pm round, he wasn't thinking about office safety.

He was thinking about Eric's alibi.

Was it true? Were he and Johnny 'hooking up?'

Pat had no more information on the financials – he'd texted Karen to ask if she'd found anything but she'd responded with a single, 'nope'. Obviously still not happy with his extracurricular work activities, even if she was offering to bring him dinner.

He wandered up to Mihok & Mihok. Part of him was hoping there'd be another glass of scotch on offer. Yet again, Marek was seated at the front counter.

In Nadine's seat.

He glanced up as Pat entered.

And he didn't look happy.

"Not knocking anymore, are we?"

"Uh," Pat stammered. "I just…just came by to see how you were doing?"

Marek slammed his laptop lid shut. "Doing great, thank you." His face remained sour as he packed up and headed into the back office. "Shut the door on your way out."

The door to the back swung shut and the lights flicked on, leaving Pat by his lonesome in the foyer.

Pat ducked out, and a message came through on his app.

Catherine: Hey, can you let me out?

Pat took the stairs down to the lobby again – Karen would be proud – and found Catherine waiting, looking slightly flushed, in front of his desk. He could see the chilblains on her skin – the heaters were on the fritz, and the weather outside was merciless.

"Everything alright?" he asked. She nodded meekly, looking at the floor. *What does she know?*

He punched his code in under the desk and she started towards the door, before turning back towards him.

He could see the hesitation in her eyes.

"Walk me out?" she asked.

It was freezing outside. Pat had grabbed his jacket as he followed Catherine out, and now he zipped it up to his chin, trying to protect himself from the icy wind. They strolled down to the gate, side by side.

She said nothing. Pat unlocked the gate, the rusty chain clanging against the steel bars, and snow started to fall. Soft white petals covered her shoulders as she looked up at him for the first time that evening.

"I…uh, found my key-card," she said softly. She pulled it out of her jacket and dangled it in front of him. Pat was perplexed – and frankly, a bit annoyed at having to hurry downstairs for no good reason.

"So…?"

"—there's something you ought to know," she said. She toyed with her hair nervously, as though she was afraid of saying too much, but then took a deep breath and nodded resolutely.

"I know…" she said, "…I know who was sleeping with Nadine."

Pat's breath caught in his throat. Catherine sighed again, and pushed past Pat to through the gate, fumbling in her bag to get her card keys. Her headlights across the parking lot flickered briefly in the dark.

"I didn't want to say anything, because…well, I was so sure that Eric did it. But…now he's got an alibi, what with Johnny…"

Pat was hanging on every word, but he didn't want to force a name out of her too quickly.

"Did you know?" he asked. "About Johnny and Eric?"

Catherine shook her head. "I mean, I've never met Eric. And Johnny….well, he's kind of gone off the rails since Nadine died, so it makes sense, doesn't it? He's sleeping with her ex-husband, he's a prime suspect, he starts freaking out. He really hasn't been himself the last couple of days. All adds up, doesn't it?"

Pat nodded. Their relationship sure explained Johnny's weird behaviour over the last few days. He'd always been a heavy drinker, a partier, but he was becoming completely unhinged.

Public declarations of love? So very high-school.

"And what about Nadine? Who was she with?"

Catherine sighed again. She was a pretty girl, but she looked tired. Like what she knew was taking a toll on her.

"We had some time apart, the night of the murder," she said. "So technically, I lied on my witness statement." Her face narrowed. "If you tell anyone I told you that, I'll deny it. But I didn't mean to do it. I didn't mean to cover for him."

Pat felt the wind stinging his eyes, but he couldn't take them off Catherine.

"Who was it, Catherine?"

"Mateo," she said. "She's been sleeping with Mateo."

CHAPTER 14

Catherine left in a hurry, desperate to get out of the cold. Pat let her go, his mind whirring.

But he still had a job to do, so as soon as Catherine pulled away he immediately beelined around the perimeter of the building to check the gardens. A small doubt lingered in the back of his mind.

What if I did miss an intruder?

But all was clear, and quiet. No teenagers hiding behind fences with their skateboards.

And no murderers with knives trying to sneak in by the fire exits.

And so, after an agonizingly long detour, Pat headed back inside to immediately call Karen.

"Mateo!" he hissed into the phone. "That's who Nadine was sleeping with!"

"Ooooh!" she purred. "The hotshot lawyer? He didn't have an alibi?"

"Well, I guess not! And he had condoms in his pockets!"

"Dead to rights!!" Karen shouted into the phone. "Slam dunk!"

Pat ran her through the entire conversation with Catherine, his teeth chattering. He paced frantically in the lobby, trying to keep the cold from his bones.

It's like I'm a detective!

"It could be either of them," he whispered. "Eric, or Mateo. I mean, I never knew about Eric and Johnny, but it does make sense. If they were uh…."

"…fucking?" Karen finished for him.

"Yeah, I mean, if they were…uh, 'fucking', then that explains why Eric was so secretive about his whereabouts on that night. But Johnny was in his office the whole night, I think? And I didn't know Eric was gay!"

"Well he might be, what – bisexual? Isn't that what the kids call it these days? Swinging both ways?" Karen was chuckling on the end of the phone.

"Karen! This serious!" Pat hissed. "And yeah, I guess he could be. But I'm not entirely convinced. Johnny normally brings…younger men, to the office. And Eric is well…older."

"Silver fox?" queried Karen. "Maybe he's got a massive wang."

So crude. Pat loved Karen, but she really did have a mouth on her sometimes. Nevertheless, in this situation, she was really the only person he could talk to.

Eventually, after much prodding, they came up with a plan.

"So I talk to Mateo?" Pat asked. "And say I've got a nice lady to set him up with?"

"Yes, yes," said Karen. "You say, 'Hey Mateo, I've got a lovely young thing who's looking to date a hot lawyer.' Tell him she's an accountant or something, you know, career driven."

"And then what? He'll turn around and say, 'Sorry Pat, my girlfriend just died?'"

Karen scoffed. "Don't be silly! Get a read of him, see what he says. Or what he doesn't say. Sometimes people say more when they don't say anything at all."

She was a lot smarter than Pat, that was for sure. It was a good plan.

"Did you find anything in here documents?" he asked in a hushed whisper.

"Oh, Patty, I had a look for you today," she whined. "But it's all so foreign to me! Just money in, money out. School fees, I think. Coffee, coffee, coffee. There are some bigger transactions though…but it just doesn't mean anything to me. I think maybe we can look at them together when you get home?"

"Sounds great, my love."

The conversation was drawing to its natural end, and Pat felt the nerves creeping in.

"Should I really just go talk to Mateo?"

"Well, someone's got to! I still think you should report this to the police though. If that lady's not going to tell them herself. Can't you do it anonymously?"

Again, Karen was right. The sensible thing to do was report it – for two reasons. First off, despite Pat's reservations about Alvarez, Pat generally knew the best course of action was to give this information to people who had far more resources than he did. And second, if Mateo *was* dangerous, then it would be best that they knew Pat had been grilling him.

But Pat wasn't going to call them now. He had a bone to pick, and he wasn't going to give Alvarez the satisfaction of swooping in just yet. What if she made another premature arrest? What if she twisted his words again, just like with Eric?

"I'll do it, I'll do it. But I just want to talk to him first."

"But it's past 8? Didn't you see him on your first round?"

Shit.

Pat checked the time. He'd been on the phone with Karen for over an hour now, and he hadn't even bothered finishing his first round after he'd let Catherine out. He'd only been to Mihok & Mihok and that was it!

"Gotta run, my love. I'll call you with updates."

Pat hustled his butt up to six, taking the elevators for expediency, to find the doors of Lafferty Inc closed and no view of any lights from inside. He knocked and waited, only briefly, and then headed towards the stairs. Disappointing, but probably for the best considering he was catching up on work he should've done an hour ago.

He just really wanted to speak to Monica. She'd been his best friend in the building up until that point – a horrendously flirty one, at that – and he couldn't stand not talking to her regularly. While at that second, his heart was set on avenging Nadine, he knew he'd have to make amends with her at some point. The nights were already far too isolating.

As Pat trudged towards the stairs, he thought about Karen.

What a godsend she is.

Pat's mind could get muddled at the best of times, so it really helped having her in his corner to keep him organised…even if they did disagree. And he was sure of his next steps now; finish his round, then talk to Mateo. He didn't know if Eric was in the clear from the cops, but given the fact that he hadn't actually walked out of the building in handcuffs, there was a possibility he was at home, safe and sound.

So that was the plan. Talk to Mateo, get to the bottom of all of this, and drop his notes in Alvarez's lap. Hell, if he solved it all by himself, maybe she'd even offer him a job on the force! The pay would surely be better, the benefits, and he wouldn't have to work these damn twelve hour shifts anymore.

I'll do this myself. Show them what I'm made of.

He rounded onto the fifth floor, his eyes gravitating to where he'd found Nadine's body.

The police tape was now gone, the floor was clean, courtesy of the cleaning crew. Not a spatter of blood in sight. No evidence that this was the spot she took her last breath.

As Pat turned the corner, his heart plummeted. Ahead of him, the lights of Microceuticals glimmered a pale white at the end of the landing. The large industrial lock, guarding one of the most protected offices in the building, had been smashed into pieces.

The door was wide open.

*　*　*

"Fuck, fuck, fuck!" Anxiety flooded Pat's chest as he barreled down the corridor.

The company's doors were reinforced glass – you'd break them off their hinges before cracking them – which meant ironically, the locks were the weak point. They were replaced on an annual basis as the metal housing started to slip freely around on the glass panel. If they were weak, one good wrench would set them free…and allow access.

And it was Pat's job to check if they were loose.

He pulled his walkie-talkie out of his belt and stepped into the office, broken glass from where the handle had fallen crunching under his feet. The walkie was useless in its official capacity – there was a matching one in the front desk, and in his whole time here, Pat had only ever used it once to communicate with Lionel, courtesy of their separate shifts.

But if there was an intruder, then at least Pat had something better than his fists to defend himself.

"Hello?" he called out. "Anyone here?"

The lights in the back room were on, so Luka and his little gang were probably still in the lab. The reception area itself looked as normal as it could be – but Pat had hardly been allowed in here, so he couldn't know for certain.

It was a reasonably run-of-the-mill front office space. A classic marble-topped desk, bright-white tiles on the floor, a set of double doors that presumably led through to the 'official' research facility, a few lamps, and closet that said 'storage'. No turfed tables, no wires hanging out of the wall, nothing looked askew.

So what did they take…?

…or have they not left yet?

"Hello?" Pat called out again, his voice shaking. "If there's anyone in here, I'm armed!"

He peered over the reception desk. The fancy all-in-one computer was still there, alongside a lone stack of post-it notes.

They didn't take the computer…

Luka burst out of the lab, covered head to toe in a hazmat suit. He pulled off the helmet with a gasp, his eyes burning with fury.

"What the fuck are you doing here!?" he bellowed, sweat pouring off his face, his hair slick to his forehead. His eyes met the broken handle of the door.

"DID YOU BREAK IN?!"

And with all the tension of the last few days, and forgetful of the fact that he was an hour late for his sweep, Pat's blood boiled over.

"HOW DARE YOU!" he roared back, rising to his full height. "How dare you! I am here for my rounds, as I am every night of the damn week!

Seven days a week, fifty weeks a year, like I have been here for years! If you ever speak to me like that again, Nadine won't be the only person leaving in a body bag!"

It felt amazing. The blood pounded through Pat's ears as he shouted down at Luka, who was shrinking under his wrath for the first time in history. Gopal and Amy burst out of the room, pausing in the doorway to rip off their masks, curious to see what the commotion was about. Pat took a breath, panting with fury.

Luka squared up to him, nose to nose. Instinctively, Pat felt his hand tighten around the walkie-talkie.

Go ahead, make a move. I dare you.

"How the fuck did you let someone break in here?" Luka snarled at him, his upper lip curling with rage. "Isn't this your whole job? I have no idea? You have no idea – no idea! – what we're doing back in there, but we pay your rent!" He jabbed Pat in the chest with his little fingers, and Pat mustered every once of available self-control to stop himself from grabbing the man's hand and ripping the digits clean off.

He exhaled a full, controlled breath, and cleared his throat.

"Luka," he hissed, "Unfortunately I am unable to be in all places at once. Evidently, someone has broken in here, so I need you to make sure that nothing has been taken."

Luka scoffed. "What, you want a full inventory? We don't leave anything out here! We aren't idiots!" His tone was mocking and cruel, as he cast his eyes over Pat.

"Personal effects, small items. Anything specific."

Gopal was patting his pockets, but it was Amy who looked the most panicked. She dived forward for the reception desk, tearing through the drawers furiously, her little hands groping for the dark corners. After a moment, she turned to Luka and Gopal.

"They've taken my phone." Gopal's face went white, and Luka's lips curled even further. Pat, however, was more curious about something else.

"They? Who's they?"

"Nobody!" Luka spat, waving a hand to silence his co-workers.

Pat glanced at Amy.

"I misspoke," she admitted. "I guess – I guess I just assumed it was…I assumed there was more than one person."

Nope. Nope, nope, nope.

"A murder, and now a robbery in the building," Luka breathed. "You're not doing very well here, are you, Mr. Dickson?"

Pat whipped his phone out of his pocket. "I'm calling the cops," he announced, but Luka snatched the phone out of his hands. For a second, Pat thought he spotted….fear?

"You'll do no such thing!" he shouted. "We will report this to the building manager ourselves. Police cannot be involved – our reputation is too important. If people know that trade secrets may have left these premises, well...." His eyes locked into Pats, "...let's just say I'll be coming after you. Personally."

Pat stared him down as Luka offered his own phone back to him. The room was tense. Amy and Gopal were lingering next to the double doors to the lab, evidently desperate to make their escape.

How could anyone work for a man like this?

Pat took his phone and shoved it back into his pocket, before turning on his heel. He stopped to look at the door. The locking contraption had fallen into two pieces, a handle on each side of the door, suspended by a thin wire straining over the hole in the glass.

Pat reached out and grabbed the internal handle.

"I'm taking this," he said. "Evidence."

The cable snapped as he yanked on the handle, and its other half fell to the floor of the office with a clang. It was cold in his hand as he wandered away from the office, leaving Luka, Gopal and Amy in his wake.

What now?

Pat didn't know. But it wasn't unlikely that this wasn't connected to Nadine, somehow. And now, with the door handle in his grasp, he had evidence.

*   *   *

Pat took the broken door handle into the men's toilet on the ground floor. He could still feel his pulse echoing in his head, his blood roaring through his ears. He needed space, he needed time, he needed quiet, and he wasn't going to get that in the foyer at his desk.

And so he took a seat on the toilet, locked the door, closed his eyes and sucked in a huge breath, as Karen had taught him. But he could still see Luka's face in his mind's eye, burning with anger, and he felt that same fury welling in his chest.

He inspected the handle. It was cold steel; expensive, heavy. The same as any of the others in the building, just ripped clean of its housing. He ran his finger softly over the residual glass that was hanging off the metal plate in splinters, and some of it tinkled to the floor under the touch of his fingers. The cable was loose where it had snapped, snaking delicately across his thigh.

But what really interested Pat were the heavy scratches right down the front of the plate.

After enough deep breaths, Pat left the toilet and took the elevator up to the sixth floor, praying it wouldn't stop on five. He knew Monica would be locked in her back studio, and – what with the way she'd looked at him earlier – she probably wasn't in the mood for a conversation. Which was good, because Pat was in no mood for conversation. He stopped in front of Lafferty Inc. and inspected the door handles.

Then, he called Karen.

"Someone broke into Microceuticals tonight," he said quietly.

"Not like you to skip a hello!" she chortled. "Who was it?"

"I don't know," Pat said. "And Luka – the boss, the owner – he's really pissed. I mean, what was I supposed to do about it?!"

"Did you check the cameras?" Pat could've slapped himself. The cameras! "No! Oh my God, Karen! I need you here with me. Like a little version of you in my pocket!"

"You can always call, my love," she chirped. "Anyway, what happened?! I want details!"

Pat was inspecting the door handles as he cradled the phone to his ear. No heavy scratches on Lafferty Inc's door. They were the same make, the same model, but the one he held in his hand was much more roughed up.

It confirmed his suspicion – this wasn't done by hand. While Microceuticals' door handles were used hundreds – if not thousands – of times a week, they were still sturdy.

"I don't know," he said. "But they took a girl's phone. And they didn't do it without a tool. Like a crowbar, or a tire iron or something."

"Where would they have gotten that?" mused Karen.

The supply closet.

He said a quick goodbye to Karen and booked it back to the elevator, heading for the maintenance room that was hiding out just behind the toilets. While Pat had been in the lobby for most of the evening, he'd spent a little time outside with Catherine, then checking the gardens. If executed carefully – no, expertly – that was surely enough time to break into Microceuticals…and get away with the goods.

But as Pat rummaged through the brooms and mops, he realised something. Nothing was disturbed. Indeed, he'd practically knocked open a bucket full of dirty mop water that the cleaners would've put back, and everything was in place – terribly disorganised – but all on shelves.

If someone had dug through to grab a crowbar, wouldn't they have tossed things on the floor? Wouldn't they have kicked the bucket over? Hell, did they even keep a crowbar in here?

Pat didn't think they did.

Which meant somebody brought their own crowbar.

Pat rolled up to his desk and pushed aside his Netflix windows to find the camera feed.

There were about thirty or forty cameras in all, covering most angles of the building, but some of them were worse than useless. He could see all the elevator access points from three different angles, but the quality wasn't good enough to make out identifying details, and some of the exits of the stairwells weren't covered. In the stairwells themselves, there were no cameras at all! He'd pointed that out to Joseph.

Lionel never had any complaints, so why do you?

It's probably just your eyesight.

If you do your job properly and make sure the gate is locked, we shouldn't have any intruders, so there shouldn't be any problems.

He was right in a way; Pat's eyesight was getting worse. He whizzed the cameras back about half an hour, and caught himself talking to Catherine in the lobby. There they were, as she asked him to walk her out.

Wait a minute.

Wait a damn minute.

She was asking him to walk her out. She never did that – well, he always did it voluntarily as it was a good chance to check on the front gate and check the grounds as she always seemed to leave during his first round – but she asked him tonight!

But she told me about Mateo.

Pat mulled it over as he watched the pixelated versions of the two of them walking out of the lobby. If she was baiting him to go outside, then she must be covering for someone, but she spent all her time with Mateo, and she did seem genuinely worried.

Also, if she was trying to distract Pat so that Mateo could break into Microceuticals, then why on earth would she be telling tales on him for sleeping with Nadine? He scrolled the clocks backwards a few moments, and enlarged the recordings that showed the fifth floor.

And sure enough, he found the intruder.

CHAPTER 15

Unfortunately for Pat, there was absolutely no way of telling who the burglar was. Aside from the backpack slung over his shoulder and the hooded sweatshirt obscuring his face, the thief didn't have any sort of identifying features. He didn't have a hunchback, or walk with a limp. The camera quality was too spotty to make out any details, but Pat would've put him at an average height, average build. Maybe a bit too small to be one of the bigger men in the office – he wasn't as broad shouldered as Malik.

But it was definitely a he. Pat tracked his target as best he could, jumping from camera to camera, scrubbing the recordings back and forth. He found him on the second floor to start with, emerging from the darkness of the east stairwell. Then, he'd moved right across the building and – strangely – taken the elevator up to the fifth floor.

That's when he knew I'd left. He knew Catherine was distracting me, so he swept the building first to make sure it was quiet.

The intruder drew something from his sweatshirt when he appeared on the fifth floor.

The weapon.

And then, he disappeared off camera. Was this Mateo? Was there some evidence in Microceuticals that he was trying to get rid of? The hooded figure appeared again a few minutes later, bar still clutched in his hands, moving with purpose along the fifth floor. His backpack looked about the same.

Did he only take one phone?

And then, he disappeared down the staircase on the fifth floor.

Pat clicked furiously, rewinding and fast forwarding as he backflipped between trying to get a better look at the man's face...and trying to find out where he'd gone.

Blind spots. He knows the blind spots.

He had disappeared, into the darkness. Whoever this man was, he was experienced. It could be Eric, it could be Mateo, it could be Marek or Johnny or any of the other men that worked in the building. Pat had always taken Sal Whiteman – Marek's second in command – to be something of a slippery snake.

But what would any of them want from Microceuticals? What did they want with Amy's phone?

He tried Karen, but no answer. For a second, his mind jumped to the worst. *What if Mateo has gotten to her?* He shut down the intrusive thoughts. She'd be at home, of course. Maybe having a nice bath or chatting with Larry.

There were two things he had to do tonight. The first was to keep his job – he'd never hear the end of it from Joseph if he didn't report this right away, so he opened his emails and started punching away at the keyboard.

Dear Joseph,

Unfortunately, there was a break-in into the Microceuticals Office tonight. I was out checking the grounds and ensuring a staff member got to her car safely when it happened. I can see the perpetrator on the security cameras but I am unable to determine their identity. They appear to have stolen a personal item from Amy Morales – her cell phone. I will be doing my usual full sweeps of the building until Lionel reports in tomorrow morning. I'll call you at the first sign of trouble.

Regards, Pat

He read and re-read the email a few times, his cursor hovering over the 'send' button. He knew it had to be done, but no doubt that the fallout of this would put him firmly in the crosshairs as someone who wasn't doing their job properly. Unless he could put someone else there first.

He hit send.

Now it's time to talk to Mateo.

*   *   *

Another cigarette first, though.

In the quiet of the east stairwell, he bumped one out of the packet and – with a cursory glance up the stairs – fired it up. The smoke filled his lungs like it was always meant to be there, filling his veins with glorious nicotine. He checked his phone.

Missed Call: Larry

"Dad?" Larry picked up straight away.

Not surprising; he's always glued to that thing.

"Hey buddy, sorry – I must've missed you earlier. Everything okay?"

Larry sounded a little stressed. "It's fine, Dad. Just…just wanted to check in on how you're doing."

Pat couldn't help but smile.

What sort of universe am I living in, where my son is always the first to ask me how I am?

"I'm fine, buddy. Everything's going okay over here. Just a double-shift, is all."

"Well…" Larry sounded uncertain. "It's just…with the murderer. Did they find who did it?"

Pat puffed hard on the cigarette and blew an exuberant exhale, smoke pluming up the stairwell. "They didn't, bud. They didn't. They think they did, but…they didn't."

Silence on the other end of the line. Then—

"—You'll figure it out though, right, Dad?"

Pat's heart melted. That was why Pat didn't mind working so hard. He wasn't a lazy man by any stretch of the imagination, but he would've been happy working less and living more. They could afford to, as well. But the twelve-hour shifts, the solitude at home, the missed barbecues and work parties; he did it all with one thing in mind.

Larry's college fund.

He wanted Larry to have better opportunities than he ever did. Growing up, his family wasn't impoverished, but they were certainly lower-class. Pat had gone to a third-rate college and then had to drop out to support Karen after they got together. He didn't have that financial support of being able to ask his parents for money, and he'd envied all his friends who could.

So every spare penny went in the fund.

"Dad?"

Pat came back to reality. "You think I can figure this out?"

Larry chuckled. "Dad, you're the smartest guy I know." He dropped his voice to a whisper. "Smarter than Mom. Just don't tell her that."

Pat laughed, dragging on his cigarette again, and then heard footsteps from the stairwell above him. "Gotta go, bud. Sorry. I'll call you later."

As he clicked off, a pair of feet descended the stairs next to him.

Sal Whiteman ambled into view cigarette already in his mouth, and Pat breathed a sigh of relief. He only knew Sal on a surface level – favourite beer, sports teams – but at least he wasn't going to rat him out to Joseph. They'd always smoke here through the winters, when it was too cold to go outside, and even though there were two stairwells in the building, they always seemed to meet in the same one. Pat took that to mean that Sal enjoyed his company - at least on some level.

"Big night?" Pat asked. Sal took a seat on the concrete stairs, fired up his smoke, and dragged.

"Always is, isn't it?"

Pat nodded glumly as he struggled to find words.

Time for an unofficial interview, perhaps?

"You hear about Nadine?" he asked, immediately regretting the question. *Of course he knows about Nadine, he works with her! Idiot.*

Sal rolled his eyes. "Yeah, well, it's over and done with now, isn't it?" He took another extended drag and blew the smoke up the stairwell. "People just gotta let sleeping dogs lie."

Pat was bemused. "Over and done with?"

Sal chuckled. "Well, everybody knows that someone broke in, man. Cops'll find them eventually. Life goes on."

Pat felt his eye twitch. "Nobody broke in here. I was watching the cameras. All night."

Sal shrugged. "If that's what you want to believe, man."

"It's the truth."

Sal puffed relentlessly on his cigarette like it was a lifeline. The look in his eye said that he didn't actually care what Pat was saying; that he wasn't going to be convinced. Like he didn't want to be convinced. There was no use trying to convince him…

…but Pat just couldn't help himself.

"Nobody broke in," he repeated. "And I do sweeps every few hours. Someone in here did it. I know it."

Sal's expression turned dark. "Big accusation, Pat," he whispered. "Big accusation."

"You know it, I know it."

"Well…" Sal finished off his cigarette and flicked the butt forward, right between Pat's shoes. "…like I said, if you want to believe that, you believe it. But if you start accusing people in this building of murder…" He stood, and dusted off his pants, "…you'd better be sure you know what you're talking about."

And then he was gone, back up the stairs, whistling merrily, leaving Pat alone…

…and feeling ever surer that he needed to watch his own back.

*   *   *

Pat walked up to the fourth floor, headed straight for the law offices of Collymore & Donovan. The wood floorboards creaked under his feet. Questions raced through his head.

Could it really be Mateo? Was Catherine in on this with him?

…was this even really about Nadine?

Pat was still totally unsure as to how the break-in and the murder related, but he did know a few things. Firstly, between the accusations from Catherine, and the condoms in his pocket when everyone first met in the lobby, Mateo would be firmly in the crosshairs next time Pat spoke to

Alvarez. Whether or not Catherine was involved to some extent was possible...but Pat didn't see how he could figure that out without a confession.

Pat also knew that everyone was holding their cards close to their chest. Luka was furious about the missing cell phone, and there must've been a reason to steal it in the first place. Pat hadn't seen a security breaches for years, and then two in the same week! This wasn't a coincidence.

And naturally, Nadine was a link between Marek and Luka. They all worked together, some sort of collaboration. He'd even seen them on the news doing interviews just the week before.

"For the first time, Jamie – the first time ever! – we're seeing some developments on a drug designed to treat Huntington's Disease."

"What's that, Frank?" "Well, we've got Marek Mihok here to explain it to us. With his business partner and long-time friend, Luka Vasilj, they're working on a neurological treatment for condition with an incredibly high mortality rate..."

Business partners, friends, working in the same building. Nadine, dead. Luka, defensive.

And Marek...looking a bit too angry about Johnny jumping to Eric's defense.

The whole Eric and Johnny relationship didn't quite make sense to Pat, so he was set on investigating that a little bit further. He could ask around. Had anyone seen them together? Did they have any sort of public history? A little tongue action at the Christmas Party, perhaps?

Pat had much to work on, but it had to be done in secret. No-one could be definitively trusted. The night shift at Guinness House was an incestuous little community, and he definitely couldn't afford any more close calls like almost getting caught under the desk at Mihok & Mihok. From hereon out, he would make sure that he trod carefully.

And he did so, right down the down the paneled wood of the fourth floor corridor to where the lights of Collymore & Donovan were beckoning.

Beckoning him towards his reckoning with Mateo.

His heart flipped as he reached the front door.

What if he's not there? What if he is, but he's armed?

Yet again, Pat felt for the walkie-talkie on his belt, his only defensive tool aside from his fists. But Mateo was a strong man, and he was younger than Pat. In any sort of physical confrontation, Pat wouldn't put himself as the front runner.

Particularly if there's a crowbar in the mix.

He knocked, twice, the glass shimmering slightly beneath his knuckles, and waited with baited breath. A figure appeared from the back room a few moments later. Pat couldn't tell who it was in the darkness, just a silhouette of a man ambling towards the door, slightly lopsided.

Johnny Ray.

He opened the door, and as he did, Pat recoiled. His breath– no, his whole body! – stank of alcohol. He was in a suit, but it was the same one as last night…and he looked even more rough around the edges. The buttons were done up wrong, his eyes were only half open, and uneven stubble was sprouting on his chin.

"What?" he burped. "Whaddya want?"

I'll deal with you and your fake affair later!

"Is Mateo here?" Pat asked, hand still on his walkie-talkie. Johnny said nothing, but stepped aside and waved him towards the back. A bright white light shone through the small window, and a soft orange luminescence glowed from the conference room as Pat strode past it. Johnny didn't follow him – he ducked into the conference room off to the right and slammed the door behind him, then pulled the shutters down, leaving Pat alone in the darkness. For a second, he felt a spot of relief at the fact that Johnny was still in the office.

Better than being alone with a murderer.

Pat braced himself…and walked through the door to the back room. He was met with the same bullpen he'd been in the other night, and yet again there was only one person present.

Mateo, at a desk facing the door.

He glanced up as Pat walked in, and did a double take.

Fear? Or just stress?

He looked tired. No, he looked exhausted. His suit was crumpled, blue woolen fibres unthreading at his shoulders. His large round glasses were mucky and stained, and his eyes were bloodshot. Not the normal, picture-perfect gorgeous man he was used to seeing around the building.

"Can I help you?" he asked softly. Pat didn't wait for an invitation, just strode around the desk and squeezed himself into the closest available wheely-chair, before scooting himself as close as he could without coming across as inappropriate. Mateo looked at him expectantly, his eyes borne with sorrow.

"We've met before," Pat said. "I'm security. I do the nights."

Mateo chuckled half-heartedly. "Pat, it's been a rough few days, but I haven't forgotten who you are."

"Right," Pat said. He was buying time. At this point, it was probably obvious, but he just had to work up the courage to say what he needed to say.

He sized up his combatant. Smart, handsome. The glasses were filthy, but expensive. As was the watch on his wrist – a beautiful, gold-clasped Rolex. Pat's father had collected vintage watches all through his life – only ones he could get cheap, of course – so Pat knew a little about them. It was a classic model, with tiny diamonds set into the numbers.

Even for a hotshot lawyer, that's an expensive piece of kit.

Mateo caught him staring. "You like it?" he asked.

Pat nodded. "My Dad collected watches."

Mateo sighed, unclasped it, and threw it on the desk. "I hate it," he mumbled. "Blood money. Just reminds me that the only thing that matters in life is time." He paused a second. "You can keep it if you want."

Pat's eyes went wide. Was this a diversion? A distraction, with gold bling? He prised his eyes away from the gorgeous timepiece and set his sights back on Mateo.

"Where were you?" he asked. "The night Nadine died?" He saw it in Mateo's eyes. The question hit him like a truck, his breath leaving his body. His mouth opened, but then he choked on dry words. Pat waited as he composed himself.

Patience.

"I— I was here," Mateo stammered, "with Catherine. We...we had a conference, with London."

Pat nodded. "But Catherine told me that you guys weren't together the whole night." He paused. " And I saw her leave."

Mateo nodded. Pat could see the cogs whirring, as though he was trying to come up with another lie to cover his tracks.

Busted.

Pat glanced around the room, cautious of anything that could be used as a weapon. But unless Mateo planned on strangling him with an HDMI cord, he couldn't see anything in the immediate vicinity that looked to be a threat.

"I...I was in here," he finally said. "We finished up our meeting. Used one of the conference rooms on the floor."

"Don't you guys have a conference room?"

"Yeah, but...Johnny, he was in there."

"No, Mateo. He wasn't."

Mateo swallowed. Pat leaned forward. He had a feeling burning in his gut. Whether it was a desire to get to the truth, or just the fury of being lied to, he didn't know.

"I'll ask you one more time, Mateo. Where were you the night that Nadine was murdered?"

*　*　*

For a second, Pat could've sworn a tear crept into Mateo's left eye, but then he coughed and wiped the sweat from his row.

"I was here," he repeated. "I remember now. We've been having some issues with connectivity in the conference room, so it wasn't stable enough to use for the meeting. That's why we used one of the other ones." He paused for a second. "What does that matter, anyway?"

Truth be told, it didn't matter at all. Pat wasn't concerned about Mateo's meeting; Catherine had already told Pat that he was present for it. What Pat really wanted to know was where he ended up afterwards.

"It doesn't, really," Pat shrugged. "Where'd you go after that?"

"Uh….I, uh, I came back here."

"Immediately?"

Mateo gulped. "Yeah. Yeah, right afterwards."

Liar!

Pat stood up and took in the view of the room. He often wondered how much these guys were getting paid; how much their jobs were worth to them; how much they'd keep from their employers.

"You know, Eric Van De Berg was arrested the other day?"

"I saw. I was in the lobby."

"You think he did it?"

Mateo went white as a sheet. "Uh…did what?"

Pat couldn't help but scoff. "Do you think he killed her?"

Mateo paused, and Pat could practically see his inner demons wrestling. "I don't know."

An interesting response. On the one hand, Pat thought that someone trying to cover up a murder would be jumping at the prospect of another suspect.

But maybe Mateo never meant for it to go that far. If he was consumed with guilt, did he have enough of a conscience to let another man take the fall for what he did?

Although, it's not like you can half-cut someone's throat.

"Were you sleeping with Nadine, Mateo?" Mateo's mouth dropped open, and his eyes flashed with fear.

He knows I know. The next few moments seemed to happen in slow motion. Pat's brain was whirring as he watched Mateo glance around the room.

Is he looking for a weapon?

His hand tightened on the walkie-talkie, and he instinctively edged his chair back towards the door.

But finally, Mateo dropped his head into his hands and let out a heart-wrenching wail.

"I was!" he sobbed. "We…we were together!" He stood up, wringing his hands, tears now flowing freely from his cheeks. "I'd never hurt her, Pat, I swear to it. But…" The tears were flowing freely, blessing his blue suit with darker stains as they streamed from his chin. "I was looking for her, Pat. When you found her, I was looking for her! That's what we do! We have a little rendezvous every now and then, night times, after Cathy goes home. She wanted to keep it…keep it quiet, keep it from her husband. From Eric!"

Pat stayed quiet.

Let him say what he needs to say.

Mateo's sobs finally subsided, and he wiped the tears from his eyes with a loud sniff.

"So yeah, we…we were seeing each other. If that answers your question."

"So you didn't see her that night? Before?"

Pat's voice was catching in his throat. He was the one doing the questioning, but he still felt the gravity of the situation.

On the plus side, he was reasonably sure that the blubbering man sat opposite him wasn't about to attack him.

But did he attack her?

And if he didn't, who did?

"I didn't. I texted her, but she didn't answer. So I went looking. She wasn't in her office, but I knew that…I know that Mihok & Mihok is doing some stuff with Microceuticals, and I went looking for her again! And I couldn't find her, until—until I went upstairs!" He burst into full blown hysteria again, wailing like a wounded animal.

An act? If so, it's a good one.

"Have you got the texts?" Pat asked. His heart was still thumping, but his breathing had steadied. He felt focused, and in control. A litany of questions were whirring through his head, but he knew he had to do this one step at a time.

Mateo shook his head. "I figured how it would look. Woman and her ex-husband, the jilted lover always stuck in the middle. I erased everything."

"Is that why you broke into Microceuticals? Was there evidence on Amy's phone?"

For the first time that night, Mateo looked puzzled. "Break in? What? Why? Why would I break in there?"

Pat shrugged. "Evidence?"

"When?"

"Maybe an hour ago?"

Mateo grimaced and shook his head. "Pat, my man, I've been in my office crying all night. Do I really look like I'm fit to be stealing And Amy Morales? I've spoken to her maybe – I don't know – twice?"

He had a point. But Pat wasn't ready to write him off as the culprit. He'd been in the building both nights.

Maybe Amy had caught them together. Maybe Amy had taken photos, implicating him.

Whatever convoluted motive Mateo had for the robbery; Pat was sure of one thing. The whole time they'd been talking, Pat been sweeping the room with his eyes. He'd come up with naught, until his eyes finally fell to the floor.

The floor under Mateo's desk.

A crowbar, on the floor under Mateo's desk.

CHAPTER 16

Pat flew out of the room as fast as his legs would carry him. The instant he'd spotted the crowbar, his brain had gone into overdrive, his feet reaching speeds he didn't think were possible. He tripped and staggered across the slippery wood, a blanket of terror covering him as he tried desperately to keep at least one eye on Mateo.

Mateo, who remained in his chair, looking totally bewildered.

Pat made it to the door of the bullpen and wrenched it open, stumbling into the foyer, and then out of the office and onto the fourth floor landing, gasping for air over the glass balcony, his head spinning from fear and adrenaline. Like a viper, he spun, to see if Mateo was chasing him—

— but he wasn't. The only movement was the glass door of Collymore & Donovan, still swinging slightly from where he'd thrown himself through it.

Pat caught his breath as he moved apprehensively towards the elevator, his eyes still locked on the door of the law offices. He mashed the button, scarcely daring to move more than he had to, shaking with terror.

The doors hummed open. Pat jumped inside.

He's not chasing me.

The doors slid shut, locking him in a box of wood and metal.

He was safe. He hit the button for the lobby, and as it slowly descended, Pat desperately tried to piece together the evidence.

Motive to kill Nadine? *Love. Lust.*

Motive to break in? *Removing evidence. Evidence on Amy's phone.*

Opportunity? *Here, both nights.*

Means? *A crowbar, in his office.*

A crowbar, under his desk.

It seemed so obvious. Pat could've kicked himself. He'd had the gut instinct from the start; Nadine, the victim of her secret lover in a midnight tryst gone wrong. It all made sense.

Except the break-in. But surely Alvarez could get to the bottom of that. He'd called the watch blood money. What did he mean?

Maybe someone had paid him to do the deed. Hell, maybe it was one of Eric's old watches. Maybe he'd stolen it.

Yeah, Alvarez would have to figure out the rest. As much as her sickly pink smile made his guts turn the wrong way, Pat had to tell her. She had to know. Perhaps they'd get on better after this. Perhaps she'd have a bit more respect for him.

Could she recommend me to join the force? A better job? I'd make a great detective, that's for sure!

Pat's heart was still racing as he exited the elevator and strode across the lobby. The clock had ticked past nine, so it was late, but she'd left her number behind. He rummaged through the top drawer of his desk – a mess of highlighters, rubber bands, pens that were never used, and a few filthy notepads – before extracting the crumpled business card. He dialed, and she picked up almost immediately.

"Hello?" She sounded alert. Likely not asleep yet, not like Karen.

Karen! He'd have to call her after this.

"Detective Alvarez! It's Pat, from Guinness House."

"Pat? What's going on?" Her voice tensed up. "Has there been another incident? Is everything okay? Remember, if something's happened, you need to call 9–"

"No, it's fine", Pat interrupted. "Well, it's not fine. But there was a break-in, and I was investigating–"

"–a break in? Did you report it?"

"Well, not yet ma'am, it only happened about an hour–"

"Mr. Dickson! You are a security guard! You are working in a building where there has just been a murder! If there is anything, anything out of the ordinary, you are to do your job and report it, to the appropriate authorities!"

Pat took a breath. He could hear her furious panting down the phone.

"I found the murderer," he said, quietly. "I think you should–" –and at that very moment, a finger slammed down on the switch hook of Pat's desk phone.

The line went dead.

*   *   *

Joseph was staring down at him, his pinprick eyes enraged in their deep sockets. He was so close that Pat could smell the gel coating his thick black hair as he leaned over the desk, his face inches from Pat as he cowered next to the phone.

"My office," he hissed. "Now." Pat trailed behind him, meekly maneuvering his bulk through the door frame, squeezing himself into one of the chairs as Joseph sat opposite him. He looked furious; most likely because he'd never been in the office this late during his whole tenure. Under the office's soft lighting, Pat could see the stress-wrinkles. It looked like he'd come in just for this conversation.

"Tell me what happened tonight," he snapped.

You know what happened; I emailed you about it! Why can't you just cut to the chase? You can never cut to the chase, can you?

"Oh, just the usual." Pat held his gaze, firmly. "Did my rounds. I had a really interesting conversation with Mateo Brown, down on−"

"Cut the crap, Pat!" Joseph's patience had run out. His eyes tried to burn a whole in Pat's forehead as he stared him down across the desk.

Pat folded his arms. "There was a break-in at Microceuticals," he said. "It happened while I was walking Catherine to her car. She asked me to, by the way. But you already know this, don't you? I emailed you about it."

Then, a minute too late, Pat caught on.

"Luka called you, didn't he?"

Joseph said nothing, but his face told the truth. He pulled out a pen and paper and dated it.

"I need a detailed account of everything that happened tonight," he muttered. "Everything. Don't skimp on details."

So Pat told him everything.

…well, nearly everything. He included painstaking details of toilet breaks and took Joseph through every step of his rounds, all while his boss grew more and more irate. Eventually, the only sound that came from the other side of the desk was the scratching of pen on paper.

But all in all, Pat made no mention of Mateo's affair.

Would it have been wise to share?

Probably.

But Pat already planned on doing that with someone who would make use of the information. Not with someone who could take credit for it.

Finally, Pat recounted being walked into Joseph's office, and the words he expected came quickly.

"You're fired."

Pat shrugged. "And?"

Joseph looked a little stunned. Evidently, he was expecting some sort of muster and bluster. Shouting, perhaps. Maybe a fist-fight.

God, a fist fight would be good.

"What did you say?"

"You said I'm fired. Anything else?"

The beady eyes narrowed. "What are you playing at?" Pat locked his gaze with Joseph's, his tone mocking. "Oh, sorry. Is there anything else, sir?"

"Get out."

"Fine by me."

And so, Pat stood, unclipped his keys from his belt and pelted them at his boss' chest. He slammed the walkie-talkie on the desk and strode out of the office, leaving his boss in his wake.

We aren't done here.

He'd be back. But first, he had to report his findings.

*   *   *

"You're dreaming, Pat!" squawked Karen from the bathroom as she wiped off her makeup for the day. It was an unusual break in their routine, but Pat's dismissal from work meant they'd actually be going to bed together.

Except, much to Karen's dismay, Pat was far too excited to roll over and sleep.

"Hear me out!" he insisted from under the flowery quilt. "If I go to the cops now, Mateo gets arrested, then I get my job back. I'll be a hero! Plus, Alvarez already knows half the story. I called her. She knows I know who did it, so if I don't go to her, she'll come to me."

Karen stuck her head out of the bathroom. She looked cynical. "How sure are you that he actually did it?"

"Positive." He wrapped himself as tight as he could in the blanket, desperately trying to stave off the cold. "He had the crowbar in his office, he has a motive because he was sleeping with her, and he has opportunity because Catherine wasn't actually his alibi! He did it! It all makes sense!"

Pat was quite proud of his performance. Because, as much as he hated to admit it, he was trying to convince himself as much as convince Karen.

The facts added up, but something was gnawing at him.

Like he knew something, but couldn't remember it.

Focus, Pat. Look at the facts. That's what detectives do.

Karen rolled her eyes and stripped off for bed. "You're forgetting one thing, big man", she cooed as she snuggled up to him, and poked a finger in his chest. "Mateo, he said he loved this woman, yeah?"

"Yeah?"

"And you believe him?"

"Well…I think so? Yes?"

"And I love you!" she purred. "You're my big teddy bear. How could I ever kill a man I love?" She peppered Pat with kisses as doubt tumbled around his head.

She smells like apples.

"But…he did it, didn't he?" Pat whispered. "He must have!" That same gnawing feeling.

Karen rolled over and flicked the lights off, perturbed that her attempts at affection weren't getting her anywhere. "You said it yourself, Pat. There's about a dozen people in that building, and all of them sound pretty shifty one way or another. And one of them is a murderer!"

"So?"

"I know it' s been fun, but…might it just be better – might it be safer – to let the whole thing go?"

"Karen—"

"—Pat, listen to me." Karen looked frustrated now, which was worrying. She never got frustrated. She dug through the blankets and took his big, meaty hands in hers. "You just lost your job. Now I don't doubt that you'll get another one, but I need your focus to be on that. That, alone."

The lights went off for a second and final time, and somehow – like there was a switch in her head – Karen was fast asleep.

But Pat was not. A thought crept into his head. You're unemployed. Anxiety ricocheted up his chest and emerged on his face as a hot flush. Pat felt his breathing quicken, and suddenly the warm covers were so very hot on his stomach.

You've never been unemployed before! What are you doing?! What have you done?! What about Larry, and his college fund?

Pat sat up, sweating, taking deep gulps of air through his mouth. It's okay. You just…need a plan. A plan. That's all.

And a plan came to him quickly.

Maybe it was the anxiety, but there was only one way forward. Pat wasn't a terribly employable person. Yeah, he could probably pick up a shift at some grocery store or a gym, but good hours were hard to come by.

Particularly without a reference.

At Guinness House he could work twelve-hour shifts, but that was only because night work was quiet. And he got paid overtime for half of them!

Go to the cops. Be a hero. Get the job back.

His breathing slowed. His heart, punching in his chest, slowed slightly.

You can do this, Pat. You can solve this.

Do it for Larry.

And as the goal echoed in Pat's head as he rolled over and tried to sleep, the gnawing sensation of having missed something finally faded. He tossed and turned, desperate for tomorrow to come, but there wasn't a chance in hell of that happening this early after so many years of the night shift.

But Pat forced his eyes shut, letting the dark envelop him.

And eventually, his body gave in.

* * *

The phone blared its way through Pat's subconscious the next morning.

It was early – too early. Plus, now that he was unemployed, who the hell was calling him this early?

Alvarez.

"I need you down at the station, pronto," she barked down the line.

Not even a hello?

"What for?" Pat grunted, his eyes still only half-open. "I've got Eric Van De Berg here," she said. "Still insisting on his innocence. And considering that little phone call you made late last night, I'm hoping you've got some evidence for me."

Pat's jaw hit the floor. He rolled over – Karen was already at work. Her scent lingered on the pillow.

The sole breadwinner, now. Pat forced himself up in bed.

"Mr. Dickson?"

"Uh—yeah, sorry. Come down to the station?"

"Post. Haste." Her voice was like thunder.

But Pat's voice churned at the thought of having to see Eric's face again.

He lost his wife, and I dropped him in it.

"Uh…can we do somewhere else, Detective?" Pat groaned. "I…it's hard for me to make it down to the station on such short notice."

"I spoke to your building manager this morning," she said. "He fired you yesterday."

"Uh…yeah?" Pat didn't see the relevance.

"Then you have no other commitments. Get down here, and maybe I can put in a good word for you to get your job back. But either way, you're coming down here, or I'm coming up and dragging you in myself. And if I have to do that, I'll throw in a citation for wasting police time with that phone call last night. Within the hour, Mr. Dickson."

Click.

Pat pulled on a pair of jeans and headed downstairs. Karen – still hoping for him to reprioritize – had left the paper out for him, opened to the classifieds. Pat paused for a minute, staring at the offerings. She'd circled some offerings with a red pen.

'Part time security – 12 hours a week'. 'Campus Safety Officer – golf cart provided'. 'Customer Service Agent – no experience required.'

This is it. If I don't get my job back, this is where I'll end up.

He could see it in his mind's eye – a headset pinching at his ears as he fielded calls to people who were trying to eat their dinner. Or rolling across the golf course in a beat-up cart, yelling at kids to get off the lawns. He couldn't let his life go down that path. He'd worked at Guinness House for years, and he was good at it, this last week notwithstanding. He wasn't going to let one smarmy, weasel-eyed bastard get one over on him, particularly when that bastard was Joseph.

Setting his trepidation aside, Pat grabbed his coat and took off out the door.

CHAPTER 17

Pat barged through the front doors of the police station less than a half an hour later. He was ready, he was prepped. He knew what he was going to say, and he didn't let anyone stop him. Alvarez emerged from one of the back doors, looking surprised to see him.

"That was fast."

"I parked out front, in one of the patrol spots," Pat said. "Is that going to be a problem?"

Alvarez looked him in the eye cautiously, like she was about to fight him on it, then shook her head. "I guess not," she said. "Come on."

She waved him through to the same interrogation room where he'd been a few days prior. They took seats on opposite sides of the desk and she flicked the tape recorder on, just like last time. But it was different this time.

Because this time, Pat was in control.

Because he knew who did it.

"Mateo Brown killed Nadine Matthews," he stated flatly before she'd even pulled out her pen and paper.

Alvarez stared him down. "That's quite an accusation, Pat."

"It's not an accusation. It's a fact." Pat shrugged. "I went to speak to him last night. There was a break in at Microceuticals, and there was a crowbar under his desk. He confessed to me."

"That he killed her?" Alvarez was on tenterhooks, not breaking eye contact as her pen raced across the paper.

"No, not quite," Pat admitted. "But he did admit that they were having an extra-marital relationship. Plus – his alibi that night, it doesn't add up. You need to check it."

"He wasn't with his co-worker?"

"She left about an hour before," Pat said. "You would've known that if you'd read what I wrote down about my movements that night."

She didn't like that, but didn't say anything. Just more scribbles.

"No-one can account for his whereabouts," Pat continued. "A jaded lover, that's his motive. He had the opportunity. I don't know where the murder weapon is, and I don't know what he wanted from Microceuticals, but other than that it's open and shut."

That last comment was the straw that broke the camel's back. Alvarez slammed her pen on the table.

"I don't think I have to remind you of this, Mr. Dickson, but you are not a detective. There's only one person who decides if a case is open and shut around here, and it's me."

She flipped to a fresh page in her notepad.

"Other than that, you made yourself painfully present for Eric Van De Berg's initial questioning, so I'm sure you're aware that we're still questioning him. He says, despite your earlier comments, that you can account for his whereabouts that night. Is that correct?"

Pat paused a beat. He knew he had to be careful what he said here – or she'd be throwing it back in his face again. "He was in his office. Just like always."

"He says he was with a Johnny Ray, a lawyer on the fourth floor. Can you corroborate that?"

Pat hesitated a second, Karen's words about motive echoing in his head. Feasibly, it still could've been Eric who committed the murder.

But then, why was Mateo breaking and entering if he had nothing to hide?

Pat chose the easy way out and said nothing.

Alvarez studied him, like a vulture.

"We…will pursue this line of inquiry," she said, breaking the silence. "Other than this – surprising – accusation, is there anything else you'd like to share?"

Pat thought for a second. He still wasn't comfortable admitting to stealing the files from Mihok & Mihok, which was looking to be more and more of a mistake if he couldn't do anything with them. He wasn't absolutely sure of Mateo, but at the least, but the crowbar was pretty damning evidence.

"That's it," he said. "That's all I know." The clock ticked past ten. Alvarez nodded and led him out. They dodged through the crowd of cops and she let him out the front door, back into the cold, before slamming the door shut behind him without a word. As the December chill nipped at Pat's collar there on the sidewalk, he finally felt some satisfaction. He'd shared enough to have done his duty, but not too much to be getting people into trouble unnecessarily. Now he just hoped she would keep his word. Because he had one more stop to make.

*   *   *

Pat practically danced back into work that evening. He'd called Karen to give her the good news, right after he'd gotten out of an impromptu meeting with Joseph following his visit to the police station.

"I got my job back!" he sang. "I'm back honey!" It was something he never thought he'd be ecstatic about, but the immediate stress of the mortgage and Larry's private school fees had been feeding his anxiety through the day. He'd felt weak at the knees as he realised it was his final pay check would be awaiting him that Friday.

So, after his visit to the police station, he'd headed over to Guinness House. Pat had walked up through the open front gate and right into the building. Right past Lionel, whose eyes were almost closed as he lolled back in Pat's favourite chair, creaking it at the hinges. Bemused, Joseph had let him into his office, and then a fire had flickered in his eyes as he'd realised that – yet again – Lionel was almost asleep on the job.

"We do one thing," Pat had said. He didn't plead or beg, but he was firm. "One thing. We go through the cameras. If anyone entered or exited the building without my knowledge, I'll leave. You can even keep my severance pay, and I'll let you rely on Sleeping Beauty in the lobby out there."

Thanks Lionel.

Weary and already out of options, Joseph had agreed. No doubt he would've been exhausted from sticking around to cover the rest of the night shift.

Pat had been counting on that.

Together the two of them combed through hours of security footage of the outside of the building. It was only the outside that was necessary, as that alone would prove that there was no intruders on either the night of the murder or the night of the robbery.

It took almost two hours, but finally, after re-winding the most recent recordings for the fifth time, Joseph had cracked.

"So what now?"

"I get my job back," Pat said. "I already figured out who broke into Microceuticals. I reported it to the police an hour ago, in my own time. You need me here on this job, or else you're stuck with him." Before he'd even jerked his thumb back at the sleeping Lionel, he could see the resignation in Joseph's eyes. With a sigh of relief, he'd handed back Pat's walkie-talkie and dug his keys out of the desk.

"Usual time tonight?" he asked. It was perhaps the most genuine Pat had ever seen him. For good reason, though; he was desperate. There was no way he could employ someone experienced enough to cover a night shift that quickly. He'd have to end up doing it himself again.

He's got his own Joseph, somewhere.

Pat agreed. He took his leave, but not before taking a moment to roll up Lionel's newspaper and slap him across the forehead with it as he departed.

From there, he took the day to himself. The anxieties of unemployment vanished more immediately than he would have ever expected. He took a walk through midtown, called Karen and Larry to check in, and even closed his eyes under the roof of a lovely warm greenhouse in the late afternoon.

He took some time to ponder the mystery that had fallen into his hands, and he took some more to think of Nadine. She wouldn't want to be remembered as a body on the fifth floor, someone dead after dark. He thought of her baked treats and warm smile, her sassy jokes and headstrong attitude.

And he'd be damned if he was going to let someone get away with taking all that away.

Finally, Pat headed home for dinner. Karen had done Mac 'n' Cheese. They ate as a family, celebrated his return to work with a few beers, and then Pat suited up and took himself and two pots of coffee back to work. He loved being out during the day, but his eyes were already heavy.

As Pat's headlights lit up Guinness House an hour later, he felt a twinge of excitement. Frankly, he was excited to see how the night played out.

Would Eric be back? What about Mateo? Have they arrested him yet?

And knowing that Luka had put in the call – and doubtlessly pushed for Pat to be made redundant – he couldn't wait to run into him on his rounds. He'd be livid!

After dropping his food in the fridge and fixing the chair that Lionel had abused, Pat doubled back outside to check the parking lot.

Mateo's car was still there. Maybe he'd been taken away into a cop car? More likely Alvarez hadn't made the arrest yet. Probably checking his alibi.

That might take some time.

He settled in for the night, turning on Netflix and throwing his feet up on the desk. There were so many people he wanted to talk to, but for tonight, he was just thankful to be employed again. While it was only a short break, it had really made him realise how much to be thankful for.

At least it's all over now.

Right?

And then, a familiar face appeared at the top of one of the staircases that led down to the lobby.

A face that didn't look happy.

Marek descended the stairs, a smile on his face, but his eyes lifeless. He glided over to Pat's station and planted his hands on the desk.

Pat daren't move.

"A busy few days for you, eh, Patrick?" Marek chuckled. "First you're gone, now you're back! What's it to be, hmm?" He was grinning, like a cat who'd found the cream.

Pat shrugged. "Just a misunderstanding."

Marek nodded knowingly. "A break-in? Microceuticals?"

Pat nodded cautiously. "I can't really say much," he said. "I think there'll be an investigation. Don't want to be getting myself stuck in the middle of anything." "

Ah, but Mr. Dickson!" Marek rounded the desk and clapped him on the shoulder. "That seems to be your modus operandi, no? I mean, first you're the one to find poor Nadine, and then you're the first at the scene of the crime with the break in…?"

Pat didn't appreciate the implications.

"It's my job, of course," he said. "Just an unlucky week!"

Marek nodded again and rotated Pat in the chair so he couldn't see his face, but he could feel the banker's hot breath in his hair and on the back of his neck.

"Man to man…" Marek whispered, "…wouldn't it be best if you kept out of trouble for a while?"

Pat whirled around, but Marek's hand somehow stayed put on his shoulder. It was like a vice, clamping into the base of his neck.

"What exactly are you implying, Marek?"

"Pat, I'm just saying that I think it's best if you just do your job."

That felt a lot less like a suggestion, and more like a threat.

"I know you've been doing a little more than your rounds in the building. You've been…asking many questions."

His eyes narrowed, and Pat could see a glint of something, hiding under that plastic smile.

Something frightful.

"We all think it's best if you let sleeping dogs lie."

Were you involved in this?

Marek let his hand go and wandered slowly back towards the stairs. Pat, frozen in his chair, watched him slink away. Halfway up the stairs, he turned.

"I think we all know that someone in this building is capable of murder, Pat. We wouldn't want you putting yourself in the line of fire, would we?"

*   *   *

Pat laid low for the rest of the night. He'd wanted to keep an eye out for Mateo, but Marek's words had chilled him so much that he daren't even complete his rounds. It was like what Sal had said to him in the stairwell, but coming from Marek, was much more frightening. He snacked on his Doritos with the quietest of crunches. He opened his lemonade and it sounded like a gunshot. Even sitting in his chair in the wide-open expanse of the front lobby, with locked doors behind him and security cameras all around, Pat found himself constantly looking over his shoulder.

As he was slurping up the remnants of his dinner, an email dinged on his computer.

ATTN: ALL STAFF

A break-in occurred last night. Personal items were stolen from the office of Microceuticals. There will be a staff meeting tomorrow afternoon at 2pm where this will be discussed. We will be looking to determine if anybody else has had items taken from their office. If the guilty party could please return the items, there is an empty cardboard box outside the offices of Mihok & Mihok, to save you a trip upstairs. If you give back what you stole, you will not be prosecuted. Please confirm your attendance at the meeting.
Regards, Marek Mihok
Mihok & Mihok Investments

Pat's brain whirred.

If the phone was stolen from Microceuticals, why was Marek the one sending this email? Shouldn't it be Luka, or Gopal? Or even Amy herself?

He could smell the desperation. There was something on that phone.

This isn't over.

Pat had always known Microceuticals to be secretive to the point of absurdity, but was their new drug the only thing they were hiding? The seconds ticked by. Then the minutes. And as the hour passed, Pat realised...

...the gnawing feeling was back.

He had to talk to someone about this. And then he heard the clack of her footsteps, five floors above him.

Monica. She'd always been his friend, always listened to him in times of uncertainty, and he needed someone who he could confide in. Marek's words felt like a shadow around him, and he needed someone in his corner.

Like a buddy system, right? Looking out for each other?

Pat grabbed his lemonade and beelined for the elevators. The sixth floor was quiet, as usual. From up here, as he glanced over the balcony, he saw a few of the familiar night-time faces floating around downstairs. Catherine, Johnny.... ...and Mateo. They were moving like a pack. Catherine and Mateo led the way at the front, while Johnny lagged behind. Even from up here, he still looked a little unsteady on his feet. Still getting over Eric, perhaps?

Pat knocked on the door of Lafferty Inc, and waited. Monica answered a few moments later, lips pursed.

"What? What now?" Her tone was sour like milk, and Pat's frustration almost took over for a second, but he caught himself just in time.

"Are you alright?" he asked, his tone coming out a touch brusquer than he would have liked. She looked taken aback. "It's just, we used to talk all the time," he continued. "You used to be so friendly to me, but...now it's like you just don't have the time. What's going on?"

Her eyes narrowed, and she folded her arms across her chest. "You mean, how come I'm defensive since a woman was murdered in the building? Is that what you mean, Pat?"

Okay, 1-0, Monica.

"Well, look..." Pat fumbled for his words, "...I just need some help. I'm trying to figure out who did this. You were always someone I could bounce ideas off, someone I could talk to!"

"Pat, this isn't about new ideas for a podcast, or me joking about setting you up with one of my latest honeys," she snapped. "A woman was murdered, and the police are looking into it. I'm just trying to stay out of the way while convincing every poor woman who comes in here for a shoot that they're not going to have their throat slashed walking back to the lobby!"

Pat breathed a heavy sigh. He was starting to see her point. "I just, need some help," he repeated, his voice reeking of desperation. "Just someone to talk to. Just...for a few minutes."

She paused for a moment, weighing up the options. And after the longest five seconds of Pat's life, she finally swung the door open, and beckoned him inside. Pat stepped through.

The room was a huge space, cosy with warm lighting and soft rugs, camera equipment and a luxurious wooden desk. A week ago, Pat would've been more than cautious about coming in here. He always felt like Monica was ready to snap him up – or snap off her dress – but tonight he was relieved. He needed to talk to someone he knew he could trust – he needed to talk to her.

Monica leaned back on her desk, crossed her arms, and shot him a steely glare.

"So?" she asked. "You want help? Talk."

Pat dropped into the couch. "I don't know who murdered Nadine," he began.

"Nobody does," she quipped. "That's why we let the detectives do their work." Her tone was icy. She'd invited him in, but everything about her was telling him that he needed to get out.

"Right..." Pat replied, "but I know a bit more than other people." She sighed wearily and took a seat behind her desk. Her hand fell below the table for a second and reappeared clutching a seltzer. She didn't offer him one.

"Can I speak to Kathy?" he asked gently. "The girl who was with you that night? I...I just need to know if she saw anything."

Monica scoffed. "Nope. No way. I'm not having you dragging that poor girl into your….mess."

"It's not my mess, Monica."

"Doesn't matter. Just because she was unlucky enough to be here doesn't mean she has be party to your deluded whims."

The words stung. Pat wasn't going to get her help; that much was obvious. But if he couldn't talk to Kathy, then at least he could use Monica as a sounding board.

"Eric was Nadine's ex-husband," Pat said. "They split up. Recently." Monica shrugged. "We've all heard that by this stage."

"Right. Well, obviously…everyone thought he was the…the murderer. But apparently he's shacking up with Johnny?" She said nothing. "Did you know about that?"

She shrugged. "Unlike some people here, I try to stay out of people's business." *Ouch. 2-0.*

Pat carried on. At least this was a good place for getting his thoughts out in the open. "So then, including Eric, everyone else has an alibi. But…I walked Catherine out to her car the other night, and she told me something." He had Monica on the hook now. He saw it in her eyes, in the way she leaned forward ever so slightly.

"She told me that Nadine was sleeping with Mateo. Outside of her marriage." He paused. "And… that he was alone during the time of the murder." Monica stayed quiet, watching him closely.

"So I went to talk to him, and he told me they were sleeping together," Pat continued. "And then there was the break-in at Microceuticals, and there was a crowbar in his office. Under his desk."

She shrugged, seeming awfully nonchalant considering she was listening to Pat detail possible motives and means for burglary and murder. "Seems pretty obvious then, doesn't it?"

"But I found him crying in the bathroom, the night she died." And that was it. That was the gnawing feeling that had been plaguing him about Mateo. Pat had seen those tears in the bathroom, just hours after they'd found her. He'd seen them again, when he'd interrogated the man in his office, but he'd been so focused on the fact that he might have cracked the case that he'd just dismissed it.

And what made that gnawing feeling so much worse was the fact that now both Sal and Marek seemed to want to keep Pat far, far away from this, despite seemingly having nothing to do with it.

Am I wrong about Mateo?

Monica shrugged again, and wiggled the mouse at her computer, bathing her face in a bright white light. Whatever interest she had in the conversation seemed to have dissipated.

"I don't know, Pat," she sighed. "People who do things like that…they have no sense of empathy. Crocodile tears." She scoffed again. "Not that you'd know what that means."

And at that moment, with yet more snark in her tone, something inside Pat snapped. "Is something wrong?" he snapped. "Have I done something? Upset you in some way?" For a second, the front that she had been putting up over the last couple of days fell. It was as though a barrier in front of her face swung away. Just for a moment, she looked kind and innocent again. Like his old friend. But in the fastest of turnarounds, the barrier returned.

"What did you say to me?"

"Yeah, I get it. Somebody died in this building. Someone we knew. But I didn't murder anyone! So why are you taking this out on me?"

She paused for a second, her lip curling as she chose her words carefully. "You know, Pat, I'm not obliged to talk to you about anything. I do it because I like to maintain good relationships with people. Particularly the one person who's whole job is supposed to be about protecting my welfare."

She stalked back to the entrance, swinging the door open for him in a firm invitation to leave.

"There's been two security incidents in one week, while you've been on the clock," she said. "Nothing when it's Lionel downstairs. Personally, I thought you were better than that."

Pat stared her down for a second, but her expression was stone cold.

And so, he heaved himself up from the chair, and walked out, away from the warmth.

She double locked the door behind him.

CHAPTER 18

Pat fumed silently as he strode over to the elevators.

Fuck it. Nobody wants me here, apparently I'm crap at my job. Maybe I'll just sit on my ass all night, see how they like it then. See how she likes it when I don't check the security cameras, or the parking lot. See how she likes it when she's walking to her car at night knowing I haven't checked if there's a murderer in the gardens.

But, as much as he hated to admit it, Monica's words rung true. Pat had hardly had any incidents in his whole tenure as a security guard, and now he'd had two – two big ones –in a matter of days. Plus, there was no killer outside in the gardens, or the parking lot.

Nope. They're inside the building.

Pat didn't bother doing his usual rounds. He texted Karen to see if she'd managed to figure anything out from Nadine's financials, but she didn't reply. She had been a little bit iffy with him when he'd told her he'd gotten his job back – not as enthusiastic as he would've liked. But Pat knew that he had to come back. He had no choice.

As dusk fell, and the night swallowed him, Pat felt that anxiety in his chest again. And it wasn't anxiety about not having money, or about Larry's college fund. It wasn't the lack of confidence that he wasn't skilled enough to find another job – though that didn't help.

It was because his friend had died. And Pat needed to find out why. And he was never going to figure it out without free reign of the building after hours.

And so, he worked. No, he didn't head up over to Collymore & Donovan, because as much as he'd love to shake Johnny by the collar and figure out why he'd become a binge drinker overnight, he wanted to avoid Mateo at all costs. Knowing Alvarez, she'd find some way to throw the book at him if they were even caught exchanging hellos. He also didn't visit PubStunt, for similar reasons of keeping distance from Eric Van De Berg, having seen the fire in his eyes when Alvarez was making her initial arrest. And he daren't travel by Mihok & Mihok for fear of running into Marek after what seemed like a threat on his life.

He did however, visit one very important place that night.

Microceuticals was by far and away the most mysterious of all the offices in the building. In any normal week, Pat wouldn't even think of letting himself into their offices.

But he'd already let himself in once this week...

...and this was far from any normal week.

In for a penny, in for a pound?

At about half past ten, Pat shuffled his way to the elevators and took them up to five. The stark white light of the office beamed brilliantly on his left as the elevator doors dipped open, but Pat opted to turn right, making his way around the long way, down the squeaky wooden landing and in front of the floor to ceiling windows.

When he reached the spot where he'd found Nadine's body, he paused.

The floor was polished again – the cleaners came in most nights. Not a trace was left of the woman who'd worked here. And yes, it easy enough to write it off as a jealous husband or a frenzied lover, but what was really going on? He touched the hardwood floor where he'd found her laying, the soft squeak of bleach and peroxide under his fingers.

Who were you?

What did he really know about Nadine? She had always given him the impression that she was single, but he now knew that wasn't the case.

She had a kid! Older than Larry!

Nadine hadn't been herself for the last couple of weeks. Pat had noticed. She looked more tired than usual. Normally, she had a full face of makeup – tasteful makeup – but particularly over the last week, Pat had noted an absence of it. He remembered seeing the crow's feet by her eyes.

Was it Mateo? Were you fighting?

Pat left the cursed space in front of the windows and looped around to the front of Microceuticals. His heart tightened in his chest, those familiar knots of anxiety squeezing his stomach as grasped the door handle.

You're the only one who can figure out what's going on here.

Pat pushed on the door and stepped off the parquet flooring onto the bright white tiles, his body suddenly feeling warm under the soft lighting of the reception area. Then he made eye contact with the person behind the reception desk.

Amy Morales.

He'd seen her in passing a few times. Most of those times she was attached to Gopal at the hip, just another one of the many young twenty-somethings hired to do his dirty work in the lab. While Luka was the visionary, Gopal was the brains and the experience, and so he had a string of potential proteges dogging his heels at every turn. Amy was the latest. White, young, and gorgeously presented, she was wearing a short cut blazer with the sleeves rolled up over a white blouse. Piercing blue eyes hit Pat full on as he stepped through the door.

"Uh– hello!" Pat stammered.

She should be in the lab! Why is she here?

"Hi!" she squeaked back. She looked surprised, but not freaked out. A good turn to a bad start. Pat obviously wasn't meant to be coming in unannounced, but given she was reasonably new to the role, whether she knew that was the next thing to figure out.

Okay Pat, building rapport. The most important part.

"Not in the lab today?" he asked, jerking his thumb towards the double white doors.

She chuckled wryly, then looked away – embarrassed. "I've been banned for now," she said. "You know, what with everything that went on."

"They banned you because your phone was stolen?" Pat asked, incredulous. "That's...not very fair, is it?"

Amy chuckled nervously, her eyes sparkling in the dim light of the foyer. "Yeah, life's not fair, hey? 'You shouldn't have left it in the reception, Amy!' 'If you're fucking that up, what are you going to fuck up in here, Amy!'" She laughed again, more heartily. "You know what they're like. But, it's my own fault I guess. I'm just trying to get back on his good side." Her eyes had a slight twinkle. "I...I need to be on his good side."

Pat was stunned. "Who, Gopal?"

"Luka," she sighed. That made sense. Pat had been in the same role for years now, but he knew as well as everyone else how important a good recommendation was for anyone interested in furthering their career. But Pat wasn't interested in Amy's career aspirations. He leaned across the desk, getting his pudgy cheeks as close to hers as he could without coming off as creepy.

"So where were you?" he asked. He kept his voice low, aware that his presence wouldn't be appreciated by Luka. "The night it all happened?"

Amy's dreamy smile faded, and her face dipped down towards the desk, solemn.

"I was here," she said flatly. "We were working all night. Just, in the lab. We didn't even know anything had happened until the cops showed up."

"Just the three of you?"

She shrugged noncommittally. "Always the three of us. You know how it is. Work's the most important. Work comes first. Work, work, work. I tried to get them to come out for a drink with me once, but you know..." she giggled, "...you can take a horse to water, but you can't make it drink!"

Pat glanced at the back room. No movement back there. "You get your phone back?" he asked, keeping his voice hushed.

She shook her head. "Nothing, yet. I'm praying it turns up. I've been checking the box like – five times a day. But nothing."

"Who's got it?" he asked. Something shone in Amy's eyes, like she knew – and then vanished. She shrugged. "Don't know. Probably some perv, looking for naked pictures." Her eyes met his.

Trying to distract me?

Pat desperately tried to focus as Amy giggled gleefully then resumed tapping away on the laptop in front of her with perfectly manicured nails.

The white door of the lab was behind her. He needed to get in there! He probably could've played it off if she wasn't here, but doubtlessly she'd tell him to stop if he went for that door.

Amy paused for a beat, then glanced up at him. "Was there anything else I could help you with?" she asked, batting her eyelashes.

Pat shook his head, knowing she couldn't – or wouldn't – be able to answer his question.

What are you hiding in there? With one last look at the door, he departed.

*　　*　　*

Pat managed to creep out by the end of the night with any major incidents. Marek had stalked through the lobby just after two, so Pat glued his eyes to the desk and avoided looking at him as best he could. Earlier, Eric's daughter Charlotte had literally courted her father out of the door – she came down personally to ensure that the front gate was unlocked, and then hurried the bedraggled man out of the lobby and into the carpark, with nothing except an icy glare for Pat. Pat was grateful that neither of them had said anything further; he'd had enough confrontation over the past few days to last him a lifetime.

After Lionel rolled through in the early hours of the morning to take over for his shift, and Pat's time in the chair came to a close, he got home quickly and his eyes were closed before he hit the pillow.

He felt Karen kiss him goodbye through his light slumber under the morning sun, and then, there was peace.

Unfortunately, the peace didn't last long. He'd had maybe five hours sleep at most, and then the phone rang.

It was Lionel.

"Get down here, fast," he grunted. "Cops just called. They're planning on making an arrest. I just opened up the building for them. They said they'll be in within the hour."

While Lionel enjoyed the occasional nap on the job, he was no snooze.

Pat changed his underwear, skipped showering and threw on his work uniform as quickly as he could, before hurrying downstairs and tearing off towards Manhattan.

Pat hurried up the front steps, puffing, to where Lionel awaited him.

"You've beaten the cops here," he mumbled. "Ten minutes, my guess."

They ducked inside and Lionel filled him in. He didn't have much; just a notice that the front gates had to be opened up for squad cars, and a warning from Alvarez that firearms would be present. That was standard procedure, Pat knew. Nadine's murder was what they called a violent homicide, and from the TV shows he'd seen he was pretty sure that meant a whole load of armed officers, and handcuffs.

"Does anybody else know about this?" Pat asked.

Lionel said nothing, but jerked his head up towards the higher floors. Onlookers were gathering. Pat could see dozens of people hiding by the lobby staircase as they muttered anxiously amongst themselves. He spotted Malik, with his big head of bushy curls, peering out from near the elevators, flanked by two equally debonair colleagues. Marek and Sal were loitering near the doorway, their faces blank slates.

There was no sign of anyone from Collymore & Donovan. No sign of Catherine, or Johnny. No sign of Mateo either. News travelled fast in this building, but only ever in appropriate circles.

He doesn't know the cops are coming for him.

Pat waited patiently with Lionel, his hands white-hot with anticipation.

Did I do the right thing? Did he do it?

Finally, Alvarez flung open the front doors, three police officers hot on her heels, weapons drawn. A squad car outside had the blue and red lights pulsing, lighting up the front of the building, and a larger van slid in behind it as Alvarez strode towards the centre of the lobby.

She paused underneath the watchful eye of the crowd, drinking in the attention. Pat could tell she liked to make a grand entrance.

"Everybody!" she called out to her audience, "There is no need to be alarmed! Please return to your offices. There is no cause for concern!" The onlookers didn't move.

Alvarez waved her offices forward to the elevator. As the doors closed, she caught Pat's eye and held it, determination etched across her face. Pat felt the blood return to his fingers as the elevator hummed its way upstairs. Lionel had hardly batted an eyelid. The crowd dissipated slightly, but for the most part, they chatted amongst themselves from above. Pat hadn't let his suspicions slip to anyone, and the only conversation he'd had about the break in was with Monica, but he couldn't see her flaming mop of red hair up on the sixth floor.

Did she tell people? Or does nobody know what's about to happen? Then, triumphantly, Alvarez emerged from the elevator with her security detail.

Sandwiched between the four of them was Mateo. He looked haggard and beaten down. His eyes were puffy, like he'd been crying again, and the cops had him underneath the arms and were practically dragging him towards the doors as he stumbled to keep up. One of the officers were clutching a plastic evidence bag. It was opaque, but even from the front desk, Pat could see what was inside.

The crowbar.

Gasps rang out from the gallery as Alvarez escorted Mateo in the direction of the front doors, right past the security desk. Her eyes met Pat's again, and she gave him the slightest of nods.

Good work.

Pat cast his eyes up towards the audience and caught the briefest glimpse of Eric Van De Berg. The man's face was steeled, giving nothing away, and as the front doors swung shut behind Mateo and Alvarez, he turned away from the balcony, vanishing back into the depths of his office.

And then they were gone.

Guinness House was abuzz for hours after the arrest. Pat's shift hadn't started, but he stuck around, sleep deprived and short of food, for a reason that he would never dare to admit to Karen.

He was getting attention. Everyone had obviously heard of his role in this whole crisis – finding the body, discovering the break-in – and it was like they viewed him as some sort of hero. The daytime employees – normally quiet, somber folk who were just looking to get through their day – now saw him, properly, as a person. It was thrilling! They milled through the office with poorly subdued excitement, chattering nonstop about the events of the morning. Pat caught whispers of their conversation as he meandered aimlessly around the floors.

"I knew he did it!" they were saying. 'Well, we all suspected him, didn't we?!'

When they saw Pat, they smiled and waved, or gave him a thumbs up. One of the lawyers from Collymore & Donovan even stopped to thank him, clapping a hand on his back.

"You did great work, Patrick," he had said. "We all know you keep us safe. Fancy switching to the day shift?"

And the attitudes of the night workers – or at least, all those that Pat had come across – made Pat seriously consider that as an option. Catherine was practically in tears as she tore up the staircase after lunch, and Johnny Ray made sure to maintain eye contact as he aggressively slammed the door to the bullpen. Pat didn't see either Eric or Charlotte, but he could feel the fury emanating from their office as he traipsed around the fourth floor.

Meanwhile, Marek's words from the other night echoed in his ears.

I think we all know that somebody in this building is capable of murder, Pat.

He didn't see Marek until a few hours later, when an email popped up on Lionel's computer to remind everyone to gather in the lobby for the security meeting. Pat shoved the sleeping Lionel aside and read it.

Lobby in five minutes, everyone.

Pat found it rude, but evidently everyone else was heavily invested in the security of the building, as they all did as instructed, gathering under the great skylight that illuminated the lobby a few minutes later.

There were maybe forty or fifty people, total. Pat could see Monica lurking in the back, her eyes down. She had the look of someone who was there to be ticked off the attendance list. Gopal Tendulkar – Luka's lead lab tech – stood off to the side, surrounded by a throng of young kids who couldn't have been more than a year out of college. He was watching the staircase, unblinking. But it was the person next to Gopal who caught Pat's attention.

Amy Morales' gaze was locked on Pat. He held it. She didn't waver. She wasn't even blinking. Pat turned away for a second, hoping – praying – that he was mistaken and she was looking at someone else, but when he turned back to catch her eye again—

—she was still looking at him.

I need to tell you something.

That's what she was saying. Nothing like the unbroken stare she had the other night, a sparkle of joy with a hint of lust. Tonight, she was a portrait of fear and apprehension…

…and there was something else there as well.

Marek, Luka and Malik arrived last, trotting down the stairs to the awaiting crowd. Luka's lip was curled up in its usual snarl, and Malik looked a touch nervous, but Marek…

…Marek looked furious.

Why are you so caught up on this phone?

They paused in the middle of the atrium and turned to face the crowd.

"It has been a day!" Marek boomed, clapping his hands. Pat scooted his chair to the side so he could see their faces. Lionel remained motionless, eyes still half closed.

"After the events of the other morning, I just wanted to check in with everyone and make sure that no other valuables have been stolen from offices," Marek continued. Pat baulked slightly.

That's my job!

"Obviously," Marek continued, "our security has been a little overworked, which makes for the evident lapses in our safety." He turned with a sickly grin and gestured towards Pat – looking like a deer caught in the headlights – and Lionel – still asleep – behind the desk. Pat elbowed Lionel perhaps a little too vigorously and he jolted awake, his cap falling from his head.

Luka stepped forward. "We'll be reviewing some internal security protocols at Microceuticals and would suggest that you all do the same," he said. His tone was sharp and brusque, like he was reading from a pre-prepared statement. "Evidently it's time to remember that a two-bit security operation cannot keep us safe at all times. Our thoughts go out to Nadine and her family."

Two-bit security operation?

Pat's lip curled, but he stayed quiet.

Best to let this blow over. Can't be making enemies at work.

Eric Van De Berg was watching him from the crowd.

Well, can't be making any more enemies.

Then, it was Malik's turn. He read from a piece of paper.

"Um…just wanted to let everybody know – obviously, you come to us for, uh, appointments! But no patient data has been compromised. No security breaches from us. Sorry. Thanks."

He ducked back into line, and Pat could see the heads of his fellow doctors and a few nurses bobbing in agreement as they chattered amongst themselves.

Amy Morales was still staring at him.

"Unfortunately, the personal items that were stolen from Microceuticals have not been returned," said Marek. "I'll be retiring the box from outside my office. No need to cause any unsightliness around the place if people aren't willing to step forward and do the right thing."

"Didn't he take the phone?" someone called out from the crowd. Pat had no doubt which "he" they were talking about it.

"Yeah!" someone else shouted. "Check his office!" Marek held up a hand to silence the masses. "Collymore & Donovan have been incredibly helpful in letting us go through their office to determine if Mateo had stolen the phone," he explained. "Unfortunately, he's either hidden it at home…or he wasn't the one who took it. It has not been recovered."

Murmurs from the crowd. Pat was a little surprised – if Mateo was foolish enough to leave the crowbar in his office, then surely he wasn't too great at covering his tracks.

But if he didn't take the phone, who did?

"Suffice it to say," Marek continued, "that we have accepted the items won't be returned, but we're happy to leave it here at this stage." He turned and stared right at Pat, as though addressing him directly. "I also think it's safe to say that there is no need for any further investigation."

Pat held his gaze as best he could, a hot flush running up his face.

"Dismissed!" Luka shouted, then abruptly turned on his heel and stormed off up the stairs. Marek stared down Pat for just a few moments longer, and then followed, Malik at his side. The crowd slowly dispersed, but one person hung around a little longer than the others.

Amy Morales.

Pat could see the hesitation in her face as Gopal and his gang of young women meandered towards the elevator. She started towards Pat.

"Amy!" Gopal snapped. Quick as a whip, Amy turned on her heel and hurried over to the elevators, and they all disappeared back up to the fifth floor. And then all was quiet again….

…except in Pat's head.

Something wasn't adding up. Amy was trying to tell him something – there was something on that phone. Something Mateo – or someone else? – broke into Microceuticals to find….and now, they were feeling threatened.

They don't want me near this investigation. They know I'm onto something.

"Move over!" Pat hissed at Lionel, shunting his chair sideways and knocking his counterpart out of the way. He pulled up the security camera archives in a hurry, flicking through for the night in question, trying to confirm that it was Mateo on those cameras. He saw the figure armed with the crowbar, flitting up and down the stairs. It could have been Mateo – it could've been anyone else. Sal, or Johnny, or hell; even Marek or Luka. Pat watched as the man emerged from the stairwell on the second floor, and reappeared on the first. He skimmed the recordings forward as Lionel watched over his shoulder, perplexed as the man appeared on the second-floor staircase, and then took the elevator up to the fifth before disappearing again, just like he had last time.

Where is he going? What's his game?

At that point, Pat realised what was happening.

This man wasn't trying to stay hidden. He knew the blind spots. He knew them so well that Pat had no idea where he'd come from. But he'd walked across the landings in full view of the security cameras, crowbar in hand, no less than a dozen times. He was almost in clear view as he emerged from the staircase and beelined right for Microceuticals.

If he knew the blind spots, why didn't he use them?

Because this man, whoever he was, was trying to tell his viewer something. Because he was trying to draw attention to himself, as subtly as he could.

He was trying to show the world that Microceuticals was compromised.

CHAPTER 19

Pat could've kicked himself. He mulled his thoughts over in quiet despite Lionel – for the first time ever – pestering him repeatedly until he finally packed up his bags and traipsed out into the dusk.

As night fell, and the day shift went home one by one, Pat grabbed some leftovers he kept in the fridge for emergencies as he tried to wrap his head around what was happening.

Eventually, he called Karen.

"Here's what I'm thinking," he said. "The break-in at Microceuticals wasn't a break-in. I think they broke into their own office, and planted the crowbar on Mateo."

Karen spluttered laughter into the phone. "Patty, my dear, you really do live in a dreamland some times. This has been hard on you! But seriously, you need to let it go. Isn't that what the man said earlier?"

"Marek?! Of course he said that!" Pat's eyes flicked up to the higher floors, cautious of anyone listening in. "Why else is he so desperate to find Amy's phone?! She doesn't work for him, Karen! He doesn't even care that his receptionist had her throat cut!"

"Okay, hold up hon. Calm down a second, and you tell me what you think is going on, here."

Pat composed himself, and tried to lay out his thoughts as best he could. "I think Marek is a murderer. Either him, or him and Luka – Nadine was found on the fifth floor after all. Then, I think they staged the break-in to get the heat off them. Make themselves look like another victim. They make a big deal out of Amy's phone being stolen, it makes them look innocent. That's why they're making a big show out of the phone. You know, I bet you it isn't even missing. It's probably in a trash can somewhere."

Karen scoffed. "That's ridiculous!"

"No!" Pat hissed. "What's ridiculous is that Mateo – who is apparently smart enough to get away with murder – is also stupid enough to keep a crowbar under his desk after he used it to break into an office. And I saw the guy on the tape! He's running all around the joint! I'm telling you, Karen. If it was Mateo, he'd be smarter than that. Everyone here is smarter than that. This guy was trying to get spotted!"

"Pat, my love, you need to calm down," Karen cooed. "The doc said stress isn't good for your heart, remember? Look, just take it slow. I'm a bit bored, so I'm combing through that lady's financials now. It's quite interesting!"

Pat could've kissed the earth beneath her feet. He wasn't smart enough to figure out if there was anything interesting in there, but Karen was.

"Okay, okay, get to it!" he said. "Let me know as soon as you find anything. I have to go talk to someone."

"Who?"

"Marek. And Eric."

"The one who told you to leave it alone? And the one who you accused of murder?"

"I didn't accuse him of murder!"

"Pat!" Karen sounded impatient. "I'm telling you, you need to be careful with this! You can't go around all willy-nilly just shouting at people. Write it down! Practice what you're going to say. And be safe! My God!"

Eventually, with enough assurances that he wasn't going to get himself into any sort of physical danger, Karen let him hang up. He fired up Netflix and ate his dinner – a beautiful bolognese – but his mind wasn't on the television. Finally, he threw down the food and headed up to the third floor.

He was ready for a talk. A man-to-man, 'lets-get-to-the-bottom-of-this', talk. Pat swung through the glass doors of Mihok & Mihok without knocking, and at that point he realised that it wasn't going to be man-to-man at all.

Marek was sitting at the front desk in Nadine's seat, his fingers flickering over the laptop. Behind him, brow furrowed, lip curled, was Luka. The latter stared daggers at Pat, who had paused in the doorway, unprepared for two of them.

Marek slapped the laptop shut and sprang to his feet.

"Yes?" he spat. "What?"

Pat's hands curled into fists by his side.

"Why are you so against finding out who did this?"

Marek took a long, deep breath and gestured to a chair in front of the desk. He glanced at Luka, with a look that said more than Pat could possibly know. Luka slunk back into the shadows.

Out of sight, out of mind.

Marek rested his arms on the table and spread his hands. He was wearing a suit today, a crisp black with thin grey pinstripes descending its length, and a textured sky-blue shirt with an open collar. His expression was soft as he gazed into Pat's eyes.

"I gather you think there's a problem here, Patrick?" he asked solemnly.

"You're pushing me out," Pat said, sternly. "I'm trying to figure out who did this. Trying to figure out who killed Nadine."

Marek sighed gloomily. "I think that has already been established, no? They arrested Mateo this afternoon."

"Bullshit."

"There's no need for foul language, please."

Pat could've punched him. "What is it?" he probed. "What do you know? Why are you so desperate to get some admin assistant's phone back? What's on there?"

Luka started forward as if to say something, but Marek's finger shot up, silencing him.

He thinks he can handle me.

Marek leaned back in his chair and steepled his fingers.

"Patrick, I'm going to give you the benefit of the doubt for a moment as I know you have had a difficult week." His tone was icy. "But rest assured, I do not take accusations like this lightly. Are you implying that I had something to do with my employee's murder? Or that I know something about it?"

Pat said nothing.

"Good," continued Marek. "Glad we could clear that up."

He motioned at Luka. "The reason my colleague is here tonight, and the reason I am so intent on finding Ms. Morales' phone is because our companies are working together on some very valuable research, and there are evidently some significant security concerns in this building right now. Wouldn't you agree?"

Pat nodded, slowly. He could hardly disagree, but he also felt like this was a terrible self-indictment.

"What happened was obviously a terrible tragedy," Marek said, "and whether or not it was Mateo who did this, I guess we will find out soon enough. That is a job for the police. Not for you, not for me. For the police. The reason that I am suggesting you stay out of it is because you have already made an accusation towards Nadine's ex-husband, am I correct?"

Pat nodded slowly, not daring to say anything. Marek shrugged. "So...what we have established so far is that you have potentially distracted – or shall we say, impeded? – the police during their investigations, while also being lax in your duties, correct?"

"I am not lax in my duties!"

Marek shrugged again. "I beg to differ. But Patrick, I like you. You seem

126

like a nice fellow, and I'd hate for you to lose your job. I am simply suggesting that if you stay away from the police investigation, then we may be able to minimize subsequent events like this. Is that fair to say?"

Pat remained silent. He hated him. He hated how he could twist words to make it sound as though Pat was incompetent, or not doing his job right. And those words – both Marek's in the lobby, and Sal's in the stairwell – were far from being mere 'suggestions.' They were threats.

Marek stood and gestured towards the door.

"Sal will walk you down to the lobby," he said. "I think it's best if you keep to your duties there for the next few nights. Let the police do the interviews."

Sal Whiteman emerged from the shadows. How long he'd been lingering there in the darkness, Pat didn't know.

The other attack dog.

He didn't wait for Sal, but strode out of the doorway, leaving Marek and Luka in his wake, and headed down the stairs. Sal tailed him down to the first floor and then waited at the top of the stairs, watching him.

"Be safe!" Sal called out. "Don't need anyone else around here getting hurt."

Pat didn't respond. He sure as shit wasn't going to let a lapdog – or his boss, for that matter – tell him what to do. So he waited, pausing at the foot of the stairs on the second floor, until Sal disappeared back into the darkness.

Then he turned on his heel and beelined to the west side of the building, heading straight towards PubStunt.

* * *

Pat was seeing red as he strode down the corridor. He wasn't afraid anymore, he was furious. He was tired. Tired of being stepped on, of being treated like a lower-class citizen in this building.

Tired of feeling like a pawn in some greater game. Tired of the way that they were treating him like a criminal, when he seemed to be the only one fighting for justice.

His heart beating dangerously fast inside his chest, Pat strode through the front doors of PubStunt and marched right up to the door to the backroom. He punched the keypad a few times with no success, the red light blinking at him and an insistent beeping alerting him to the fact that he wasn't allowed any further without permission. He knocked – three loud bangs – and stepped back to wait. Eric's curious face appeared in the window as he peered out to see who was making an appearance. He saw Pat, then his expression narrowed and he flung the door open.

"Are you sleeping with Johnny Ray?" Pat asked sternly, interrupting Eric before he could even get a word out.

Eric paused.

"Yes?" he offered defensively, sounding remarkably unsure of himself.

"Were you sleeping with him on the night that Nadine was murdered?"

"Y-yes," Eric nodded. "Yes, I was." Pat saw red.

More lies.

"Were you – a previously married man – sleeping with a young boy and using it to cover the fact that you don't have an alibi for the night of your estranged wife's murder?"

Eric almost stopped breathing. His eyes widened, then narrowed defensively. "Just because I was married doesn't mean I can't be gay. Or bisexual, for that matter."

Pat didn't care for semantics. "Were you fucking Johnny or not?"

Eric couldn't keep it up any longer. He deflated with a long, drawn-out sigh, and swung around into the back room, kicking the door open with his foot.

Pat followed him in and lingered awkwardly next to the pristine couches as Eric made for the kitchen.

"Sit," he grunted, before pulling out the same bottle of bourbon that he had been abusing the other night. He set two generous glasses on the coffee table and dumped himself into a seat opposite Pat.

Neither of them spoke for a moment. Eric drained the glass. He still looked tired – exhausted. The silver stubble was longer now.

But it would be, wouldn't it? If your wife had just died?

"Funeral will be about a month from now," he said softly. "You coming?"

Pat nodded. "She was my friend."

Eric sighed. "St Paul's, 10am." He paused a beat, reminiscing. "She'd have wanted you there. She mentioned you, from time to time. Said she liked it when you stopped by. Said you made her feel safe."

The words were like a knife in Pat's heart. It had been such a chaotic few days that he'd hardly had time to process the fact that he wouldn't ever see his friend again. His cheeks quivered, ever so slightly.

But he wasn't here to reminisce. He was here for answers.

"So you weren't sleeping with Johnny?"

Eric shook his head. "I wasn't." He chuckled wryly. "I mean, it'd be good if I was. Hell of an alibi. But no, I'm as straight as an arrow. Unfortunately."

"So why'd he say you were?" Eric puffed a big sigh. "Honestly, I don't know." He ran his finger around the rim of the glass. "He just...offered me a way out. And now he won't talk to me. He won't talk to anyone, by the sounds of it. Michelle from downstairs – I know her quite well. He won't talk to her. He's definitely not talking to Mateo, the fucking sick—"

Pat cleared his throat. Eric glanced up at him apologetically.

"Sorry," he said. "With all due respect, Mr. Van De Berg," Pat said, trying to keep the mood focused, "it's been a really confusing few days. I'm just trying to get some answers here, and quick enough before someone gets on my back for coming and talking to you." Eric laughed. "Mihok? Yeah, I've heard." He finished his glass and refilled it straight away before taking another swig, then glanced at Pat and saw the uneasiness in his eyes.

"Sorry," he said. "But… this is a long conversation. Hard to do it sober. Let me catch up a second."

Down went the whole glass in one go, followed by a solid burp. Pat took a sip of his, trying to put the poor man at ease. It was warm and sweet on his tongue, and hot in his chest. His phone buzzed in his pocket.

Not the time.

"I don't know why Johnny said what he said," Eric continued. "Honestly, I don't. But I had no solid alibi. I was sitting in here watching bullshit newfangled content and surfing the web. Charlotte was in the next room, but she was on a conference all night, and she's too straightlaced to even try and lie to the police…so I never asked her to."

"And you just went along with it?"

Eric smirked. "What is it they say? Don't look a gift horse in the mouth, right?" He paused. "I mean, don't get me wrong, I want the police to get to the bottom of this. But – I like murder shows, podcasts, true crime, y'know? It's always the husband, or a family member. Like that guy in Colorado, a few years back. Shot his wife and his daughters, buried them in oil drums. He was a plumber, I think. Then went on living his life. Sent a few fake texts to make it look like she'd run away."

Pat hadn't heard of that story.

One murder's enough for my lifetime.

"So no alibi, a love of true crime, and an estranged wife who's just been found having an affair…" Eric ticked the list off on his fingers, "…I'm sure I'm a lovely suspect. And I can't afford to be tied up in anything like that right now. Even if I got off, my business would go under. It'd wreck my reputation, my clients would leave, naturally. They're high profile – they can't be associated with someone who's looked at as a murderer." Pat strummed his thigh.

It's official – he has no alibi.

Eric seemed like a total wreck, completely distraught, but could these be crocodile tears? Was he being manipulated? Was he being played?

Sometimes, your strongest tool is your gut, his father used to say.

"So who did it then?"

"Well, the answer's pretty obvious, isn't it?" Eric scratched at his stubble thoughtfully. Pat's phone buzzed again. "I mean, you've got a man just downstairs who was sleeping with her! And he had a crowbar in his office!"

But Pat didn't quite buy that either.

"Do you think he actually did it?"

Eric cocked his head to the side, his eyes filled with a morose curiosity. "I don't know, Pat. But I think at this stage, you need to let the cops do their job. Just…leave it alone."

*　　*　　*

Leave it alone.

Eric's words echoed in Pat's head as he scurried from the PubStunt office and made his way back down to the lobby. A message he'd heard before. A message from Marek Mihok.

He'd planned on visiting Johnny Ray, but he didn't have the energy tonight to corral a drunkard. He crashed into his chair behind the desk and called Karen, ready to have her help him wrap his mind around what he knew.

"Pat! Pat! Oh my God, I've been trying to reach you!"

He checked his phone. Four missed calls in a row, just under ten minutes ago.

"I was talking to Eric! Did you find something?"

"Pat, listen up, and listen carefully," Karen said. Her tone was deadly serious. "We've got something going on here. I combed through all the financial records. Microceuticals, who runs that company?"

"That's the one on the fifth floor. That's…." Nadine's face flashed into his mind's eye, and Pat choked on his words, "…that's where I found the body."

"They've got an IPO in three weeks. Do you know what that means?" Pat had no idea.

"What?"

"I've been doing some research, I Googled it. It's called an 'Initial Public Offering'. So apparently companies can be either privately or publicly owned. If they…if they're private, then they use an IPO to 'go public', - I think, I'm not totally sure of the details. That's when investors give them money for shares. It's a big moment. Real big."

It was a little too late for a crash course in financial consulting. Pat tried to hold onto the words as best he could.

"What does it mean?"

"Well, first of all, the paperwork you gave me — was that Nadine's private information?"

"I mean…I think so? It's got her name on it, right?"

Karen blew a huge sigh down the phone.

"Okay, we can be pretty sure it's attributable to her, then," she said. "So, some of the documents are detailing a new drug being worked on. They're doing trials of it now."

"Trials, what – with real people?"

"Yep, that's it. I Googled that as well," Karen fired back. "Now here's the interesting bit. In the financial records, I can see that she's being paid by them. She's had four lump sum payments of just over $12,000, all in the past three months."

She was being paid by them.

But Karen wasn't done. Pat held his breath.

"So they're doing human trials, and they're paying her off. And that's big money, Pat. She just earned half your salary in three months. Three months, Patty."

Pat swallowed. "Could she be working for them?"

"What, working for Microceuticals?"

"It must add up somehow, right? What else could they be paying her for?"

Karen's voice was practically a whisper. "That's the thing, Pat...I found a patient chart."

She was a patient?

"They were giving her the drug, Pat. Weekly injections. And...I think they were paying her to take it."

A cold wind blew through the gap between the doors as a hot flush ebbed over Pat's body. He struggled out of his chair, his mind whirring so fast that his vision went pink for just a second. He could hear his heart beating in his chest, and he spun around in his chair to make sure nobody was listening in.

"It goes out of her account the next day," Karen continued. "To two different accounts. Personal ones, apparently. I don't know whose they are, it doesn't say. And it gets worse."

Pat was on a knife edge as Karen rustled through the papers.

What has she found?

She read a headline to him, fumbling to get the words correct.

"Microceuticals IPO will be expected to go public early in the New Year, with Chief Executive Luka Vasilj working in tandem with two of his longstanding friends in a joint venture."

Her words felt like a gunshot. Pat tried to breathe. Karen kept reading.

"The drug – Hydroxycephaline – is marketed as a neurotransmitter stabiliser which can potentially slow the progress of Huntington's Disease, a rare degenerative disorder that results in mobility and cognitive disorders."

Did Nadine have Huntington's Disease?

"A full course of Hydroxycephaline treatments is expected to cost up to $480,000, and rebate systems will see professionals flourish if they are licensed to prescribe. The clinical trials are conducted at Guinness House and include almost a thousand patients. Following their completion, there will be two physicians in the nation who will be able to prescribe Hydroxycephaline, which affects approximately 30,000 people in the U.S. alone."

She paused for a second. Pat saw the gut punch before it arrived.

"Those physicians are James Joseph of the Mayo Clinic in Minnesota…and Malik Wahba, of MedHealth, in New York City."

CHAPTER 20

Pat's head spun. He hardly said goodbye to Karen, just spat out a few gurgled words and hung up the phone, as he desperately tried to process the information.

Nadine was being paid by Microceuticals as a test subject for their drug. That's why she had been looking so sickly these last few weeks. Eric had mentioned Nadine having a crisis.

And a life-threatening disease was good enough reason for a crisis.

But then, a potential cure. Luka was developing it. Marek was bankrolling it. And Malik would be the one distributing it. For almost half a million dollars for every patient they treated. Those three men were able to not only create a lifesaving drug, but also make a fortune from doing so.

But why Nadine? What did she know? And then, why would they kill her?

Pat paced frantically in the lobby. His hands were sweating, even in the winter chill.

What if they were paying all their test subjects that? That would be…millions of dollars. Tens of millions. Was that legal? Who could he even talk to about this? He needed someone on the inside, someone he could trust. Gopal?

Not likely. He was so deep in Luka's pocket that he was practically falling down his pant leg. Sal Whiteman?

Not a chance. Pat had seen him with Marek, in conversations with clients in the lobby. A viper, waiting to strike.

Amy?

The only choice; and then, Pat realised – the obvious choice. He'd seen her face earlier that night. A quiet desperation of someone aching to share their secrets. She was only young; too young to be burdened with a woman's death. And she worked in the lab with them. While he had no doubt that it was Marek, Luka and Malik masterminding the entire operation, he would put money on someone in their proximity knowing at least enough to blow the whole case wide open. He'd talk to Malik, as well.

The weakest link.

But Amy first. And not in the office. That wouldn't work.

Luka would have ears everywhere.

He'd have to be more subtle.

And so, as the clock ticked past eleven, and the graveyard shift continued their work at this ungodly hour, Pat devised the most subtle plan he could think of. It may not have been the most delicate maneuver, but Pat knew there was one place Amy always went where Luka, Marek, Malik – or anyone else in their incestuous little party couldn't follow – and that would therefore be the best place to have their conversation.

So, Pat hurried up to the stairwell, sights firmly set on the women's bathroom on the fifth floor. On his way up, he took the time to peek in on the second floor.

Just part of my regular check-up, he'd say if anyone questioned. *Doing a few extra rounds tonight, just to make sure that everything is safe. You caught the criminal? Of course, but that doesn't mean we shouldn't be on high alert.*

Malik's silhouette was moving swiftly around inside MedHealth. He had good reason to think things were going well. A clinical drug that could cure one of the deadliest diseases known to humans. A death sentence for anyone who had it, and being one of only two men who could distribute the treatment.

He'd be a God amongst men.

Pat slipped back into the stairwell and continued upwards, his legs cramping under the sheer weight of his immense bulk. He'd taken the stairs more in this past week than he had in the whole year. *Let's hope Karen notices!*

The eerie lights of Microceuticals seemed almost threatening tonight. He slipped out of the fifth floor stairwell, looped around on the balcony with the glass window and came face to face with the door to the women's bathroom. Nobody else would be using it tonight, not on this floor. All of Gopal's youngsters had gone home. Plus, if the stalls were anything like the ones in the men's bathroom, he could peek through to the sinks and see if it was her.

Now or never, Pat.

For Nadine.

He checked if the coast was clear one last time, and then ducked inside.

*   *   *

Pat heard her shoes on the bathroom tiles first. They didn't clack like some of the other women's. He was reasonably sure it was her, but an inkling of doubt picked away at him as he remembered that some women

134

liked to go to the bathroom with their friends.

Was he doing the right thing? Was it right, to be crouched on top of a toilet in a woman's restroom so as his shoes wouldn't be seen, just so he could jump someone with questions about whether or not their employer may have been complicit in a murder?

Probably not.

But right now, that wasn't his biggest problem.

How in the hell do I show myself without coming across as threatening?

He could hear her shuffling around at the sink, and thanked God she hadn't gone into the cubicle next to him, which would've been horrendously awkward.

Now or never, Pat.

He slapped his size 10 feet back onto the tile floor and prepped himself, then opened the door. She was in front of the sink, applying a vibrant pink lipstick that matched her dress.

In immediate hindsight, he realised how terrifying it must've been for her.

Alone, in the bathroom, with a murderer on the loose, and all of a sudden a massive security guard pounces on you in the women's toilet.

Amy screamed.

Pat was on her in two steps, clamping his hand over her mouth. "Stop, stop! I just need to talk to you!" he hissed.

She wrenched herself free, panting, backing away furiously towards the entryway to the bathroom.

"What the fuck are you doing in here?!" she screeched, as Pat desperately put a finger to his lips. He felt himself bending over slightly, as though coming down to her height would make him less threatening. Her eyes were locked on her phone, which she'd left on the countertop.

New phone?

"I'm just here to talk!" Pat whispered. "I swear. I just needed a minute of your time. Just one minute!"

She was still panting, eyes wide, like a deer in the headlights.

"This was the only place I knew you'd be alone!"

"And there's a damn good reason for that!" she hissed. "This is the women's bathroom!"

Pat hurried over to the sink and grabbed her phone, then passed it to her.

She backed up, her hand fumbling for the door handle as he passed it to her. A peace offering. She snatched it off him.

There's something going on here!" Pat said. "Nadine's murder. It wasn't just random chance. And I think your boss is hiding something."

Amy was frozen solid.

"What do you know?" Pat pressed. "Whoever broke in – they took your phone. And you were looking at me earlier – why? To tell me something?

What do you know?" He took one more step towards her as she stood, mutedly at the door way, her eyes locked with his. "Did Luka do this?" he asked softly. "Is that why they took your phone? Is there evidence?"

She shook her head, ever so slightly.

"Did Nadine have Huntington's disease?" he asked. "Why was she being paid so much?"

Pat was so focused he didn't see her hand go into her handbag, and he certainly didn't expect what came next.

Amy's hand struck him hard across the face, scraping something hard and metallic across his cheek. He felt it gouge a chunk out of his left cheek as he recoiled, head spinning, Amy whipping out of the door in a flash of vibrant pink.

Dazed, Pat tripped towards the door, in hot pursuit, falling out into the corridor—

—but she was gone.

*　*　*

The cut was still stinging a few minutes later as Pat nursed it with an ice pack at his desk. It must've been a key of some sort. Thankfully something that wasn't intended to be a weapon, but still packed a punch when it was used as one.

Even though it hadn't panned out the way he'd expected, Pat was far from disappointed.

"I'm so close!" he hissed to Karen down the phone. "But I can't figure out why they killed her!"

"Well..." Karen mused. "Wouldn't it be a good step to figure out why they're paying her?"

She was right. *Again.*

Pat's brain was like fireworks. He hustled her off the phone as she nagged at him to be careful, and heading up to the second floor. His legs were cramping from all the stairs; he'd never moved so much in his life.

Worth it, if I crack the case.

MedHealth was largely deserted, as usual.

But Malik Wahba was still present. He bobbed his big curly head up with a cheeky smile as Pat entered the room, sour-faced.

And ready for a fight.

"A peaceful evening so far, Pat?"

Pat threw himself into the seat opposite the gorgeous oak desk and stared down the man.

This is it. This is the guy who's due to make millions off this deal.

Pat didn't choose his words carefully.

"Why were you paying Nadine Matthews thousands of dollars?"

Malik's jaw dropped. His pen clattered to the desk, and he immediately fumbled for it. "What are you talking about?"

"I know you were paying her. I've seen her bank statements."

The doctor hesitated. "Why do you have her bank statements?"

"Not important. Why were you paying her?" Pat drummed his fingers on the table. A lame effort to look even remotely intimidating.

Malik paused, then his expression darkened. "It's not a good look to go through dead people's things, Mr. Dickson."

"Yeah, but it's not a good look to be paying off someone who ends up with her throat cut either, Dr. Wahba."

They sat for a moment. Lions, sizing each other up. There were secrets at bay here; million-dollar secrets for Malik, felony secrets for Pat. It was just a question of willpower.

He'll break first.

And he did. With a blustery exhale, Malik pulled a huge water jug out from under his desk and chugged from it. Pat watched and waited as it dripped down his beard and onto his shirt.

Slowly and deliberately, Malik closed the jug back up, stowed it away, and leaned back in his chair.

"It's very hard," he started, "to tell you what I need to tell you." Pat shrugged.

"At the moment, all I think is that you and your buddies up and murdered someone, so you can't exactly go downhill any further."

"Touché."

"So?"

Malik breathed a long, drawn-out sigh. "Nadine has Huntington's Disease," he offered.

"Yeah, I knew that," Pat said. "But why were you paying her?"

Malik bit his lip, as though he was unsure how much he should say.

"As I'm sure you know, in clinical trials, we need to see a certain number of patients." Pat nodded.

"Nadine...well, she's a member of a few support groups, so..." Malik waited as Pat tried to piece together the information, but his patience ran out.

"So Nadine referred people to us," he explained. "It...it's not exactly a kosher process. She...she told people that Hydroxycephaline – uh, that's the drug that we've made, up at Microceuticals – she told people that it was great. It was making her feel great. And...that's how we got people in for trials." He swallowed. "And then we compensated her."

Pat paused.

Something doesn't add up.

"If the drug's so good," he said. "Wouldn't that get people in by itself?"

Malik smiled sadly. "Unfortunately, Nadine wasn't on Hydroxy. We needed her connections, her influence. But randomised control trials mean that we can't pick and choose who gets the treatment. Everyone else gets a placebo. It's the only fair way of doing it. The...bonuses we gave her...it's not exactly kosher, but considering all she was doing for us, I had to give her something."

"But...I saw her in the building," Pat said. "She's been – she's been sick! Really sick!"

Malik shrugged. "Do you know anything about Huntington's disease?"

Pat shook his head.

"That can happen. Whenever, wherever. You...just start getting sicker."

"That doesn't sound right to me."

"That's because you aren't a pathologist."

Fair enough.

"Who runs the trials?" Pat quizzed.

"I do. They design the drug upstairs, but I handle patient care. All of it. Only me." He chuckled softly. "That's why I'm always working so late. And that's why I'm up there."

Pat mulled it over. They had Nadine, firmly in their financial clutches, bringing them people who were vital to the success of their product. He'd heard about random trials; certain drugs getting through, others not. They were a crucial part of the process, and she was their connection.

So why kill her?

"Was she blackmailing you?"

Malik rolled her eyes. "For what? She was getting a good deal. Send her friends our way, she gets cash in her pockets, some of her friends get treatment. It's a win-win for everyone."

"Except she ends up dead."

Malik stood up, frustrated. "Pat. Nadine was crucial to the success of our trial. She died. It's horrible. She's been referring people to us now for what – eighteen months? Two years? And we've been entirely supportive business partners the entire way." He sighed. "And now...now we've lost someone that we considered a friend, a confidant, a colleague. She was butchered, horribly. But if I can promise you one thing – anything – it's that none of us had anything to do with it."

Pat wasn't sold. Some questions remained unsolved, and if there was some motive for the group of grown-up college frat boys to be killing Nadine, then maybe everything would tie itself up in a neat little bow.

But he just couldn't see it.

Malik slumped back into his chair. "What can I do to convince you?" he asked, tossing his phone onto the desk. "You want to see my correspondence? I hardly talk to those guys. We were friends in college, now this is a business opportunity. I'm a doctor. I took an oath. And yeah, maybe I shouldn't have been giving Nadine a referral fee, but you know what? I don't regret it. This drug could make history, and she gave us the contacts that we needed to get past the trial stage."

"And it could make you millions."

That upset him. Pat saw it in his eyes.

"You think that's what I care about?" Malik asked, incredulous. "You think I'm in this for the money?"

"I don't know."

"Well I'm not. And I think it's time for you to leave."

*   *   *

The first floor seemed colder than usual. The breeze was still licking in under the front doors, and rain had started to patter down on the windows.

Pat felt lost. He thought he had been onto something with looking at Microceuticals, and he had indeed discovered a whole web of interconnectedness, but still nobody with a clear motive, and more than a handful of people with the opportunity.

There were too many unanswered questions. Was Mateo really the guilty party here? Why had Johnny covered for Eric? What did Amy want to say? Why so much desperation over a single lost cell phone?

His first question was about to be answered. A buzzing in his pocket jolted him from his thoughts. He didn't recognise the number, but it started with '212' – an original NYC line.

It could only be one person.

"Pat, it's Alvarez. Are you busy tonight?" Pat groaned internally.

Nope, but I don't want to be.

"Not really, why?"

"Bit of a courtesy call for you. We don't have enough evidence to hold Mateo Brown, and he mentioned offhand that he was planning on heading by the building to pick up some things. I was just curious if Eric Van De Berg was still in the building. I know there's some unresolved tension there, and I'd rather avoid any more drama."

Pat hurried up the stairs to PubStunt, phone swinging at his side as he puffed his way to the front door. The office was dark, but that didn't mean anything, what with Eric's propensity for sleeping inside his office.

But if he's asleep, it should be fine?

"I don't think he's here. Lights are off."

"Great. Then no need to send any backup. Thanks, Pat."

She clicked off. Her demeanour eased Pat a little. She spoke to him like he was a friend. It was nice, especially on these lonely nights.

But he still missed being able to chat to Monica.

The night ticked on with nothing eventuating. Nobody arrived in the parking lot until Pat mulled over closing the front gates, and then the bright beams of a taxi shone through the front glass windows.

Mateo came through the lobby a few moments later. He didn't look great. The rain had matted his hear to his forehead. His skin – normally smooth and shiny – was greasy and pockmarked, and he had dark circles under his eyes. Grimacing, he nodded at Pat as he made his way towards the elevators.

Pat glanced upstairs as the elevator doors shut. He could just see PubStunt's front windows from down here, and the lights were still off.

Everything was quiet. Mateo re-emerged from the elevators a few minutes later, clutching at a box of personal belongings, Catherine Kim at his side. His eyes glazed over as she chattered anxiously. Then she spotted Pat, and froze.

What now? What on earth have I done now?

Catherine held his gaze for a second and then darted back into the elevator as the doors closed.

Mateo, on the other hand, didn't have similar inhibitions. He dumped a box onto Pat's desk. It was piled high with papers, a few files, some cables, a headset.

Everything a man needs to work from home.

"Mind if I sit?" he asked quietly. "My brother's coming to pick me up."

Pat shook his head. "Go ahead."

Mateo sank into Lionel's rickety chair and propped his feet up on the desk as his fingers danced over his phone. Pat tried to read his face. He looked like a man who had run out of steam. Distraught. Tired.

They sat there in silence as Pat fought for something to say.

Conversations with a murderer?

"How long were you in there?" he finally mumbled.

However long it was, you basically put him there.

Mateo glanced up. "Too long," he muttered. "Too damn long."

The fingers danced relentlessly over the phone.

"I don't blame you," Mateo said. "For reporting me to the cops. I guess it didn't look good, huh?"

It didn't. A crowbar in the office, condoms in his pockets, no alibi.

"No," Pat admitted. Mateo sighed. "Well Pat, you seem like a nice guy. And I hope you're not like most of America, and you know that it's innocent until proven guilty."

"I guess."

"In that case…" Mateo offered a hand, "…can we have a fresh start?"

Pat froze.

Is this what murderers do? He took Mateo's hand and shook it tentatively. It was a refreshing moment. There was a frankness and openness to it that Pat hadn't felt with anyone at Guinness House recently.

Then a voice came from the top of the stairs, fracturing the peace.

"You killed my wife, you motherfucker."

*   *   *

Eric descended the stairs slowly, looking ever more the part of a vengeful ex-husband. Pat and Mateo scrambled to their feet as he sloped towards them, his grey hair shimmering under the dim lights.

As he got closer, Pat could see – worryingly – that both of his hands were full. In his left, a bottle of bourbon. This time the chicken on the bottle was green…but just like last time, the bottle was half empty.

A new bottle.

And in his right hand…

…he was clutching a letter opener.

Pat groped for his walkie-talkie as Eric approached. The blade – the razor sharp blade – glinted menacingly in the moonlight.

The rain started to pour.

Mateo was holding his hands up in the air defensively as Eric approached. He slid backwards towards the front door, Pat following his lead.

"I didn't do anything to your wife, man," Mateo insisted. "We had a thing. But I didn't hurt her. No way. No way at all."

Eric shook his head just a fraction. Pat realised too late that he should have hit the emergency call button underneath his desk.

The desk that was now on the other side of Eric.

"Eric," Pat said, daring to inch forward, "I think we all need to calm down a little. Why don't you and I step outside? We can take a walk, talk about this."

The rain hammered defiantly against the glass windows.

Eric jabbed the letter opener in his direction. It twinkled furiously under the soft lighting.

Could that be the murder weapon?

"Sit down, Pat. Now."

Eric rounded on Mateo, sending him skittering away from the doors and towards the east staircase. He took a huge swig from the open bottle, and then it slipped from his hand and exploded on the tiles, whisky and glass bounding in every direction.

"Eric, man!" Mateo pleaded. "I didn't do anything! I didn't hurt her!"

"Liar!" Mateo tripped backwards onto the staircase and Eric lurched forward. Suddenly, his hands were on Mateo's chest, balling the younger man's shirt in a fist as he yanked him back up to his feet so that they were nose to nose, his face white with fury, the scalpel millimetres from Mateo's neck.

"You fucked my wife!" he shouted.

Finally – *finally* – Pat sprang into action.

He bounded three huge steps over to the desk, his eyes locked on the big red button hiding on the bottom right-hand corner. He'd bumped it a few times before when he wasn't paying attention. It rarely worked, which he had been thankful for on occasions past – but tonight, Pat mentally crossed every finger and toe that he could, praying that it would do its job.

He hit the button.

Immediately, a shrill alarm blared through the lobby as the soft amber glow vanished, replaced almost instantly with a blinding red light.

Five minutes, Pat.

Eric whipped around, his hands loosening on Mateo's shirt as he pointed at Pat with the blade. Instinctively, Pat whipped his arms up as though someone had a gun trained on him. Mateo crumbled back on the staircase as Eric stormed towards Pat. Under the blood red light, he looked like something out of a horror film.

"You!" he roared. "Haven't you stuck your nose in enough! First you don't do your job properly! Now this? You're going to take this from me as well?!"

Pat hurried away from the desk, crunching through the shards of broken glass, struggling to put some distance between them. The alarm blared again, a single klaxon that rose to a deafening volume before fading back into momentary silence.

"Then you come into my office, drink with me, and have the nerve, the nerve to accuse me of killing my ex-wife!" Eric's eyes were wide and wild as he shouted, his face taut with rage and despair. "Why?!" he roared into the void. "Why would I kill her? I still love her!"

He turned his attention back to Mateo, the red lights of the emergency siren casting eerie shadows over his scrawny figure. "But no! She's busy flirting with Marek, and getting her fill of this guy!"

Mateo's eyes were wild with fear as he cowered, unprotected.

"Yeah, I've made some mistakes! But she was my wife!"

Pat was desperately listening through the din of the alarm, hoping the next sound to assault his ears would be the roar of police sirens. He was still clutching onto his walkie-talkie, thinking that if Eric came close enough, he could hit him with it. His mind was torn between fending for himself, or helping the defenseless Mateo by the stairs.

Four minutes, Pat. They'll be here soon.

"Calm down, Eric!"

Good one, Pat. A+ diplomacy.

The three of them were in a triangle; Pat close to the desk, Eric in the centre of the room and Mateo on the east staircase. Doors had opened upstairs and the late-night crew were flocking to the balconies, gasping as they witnessed the stand-off happening a hundred feet below. Familiar silhouettes craned their necks over the balustrades.

You can do this. Prove them wrong. Prove that you can keep them safe.

"Eric!" Pat bellowed over the alarm. The unhinged man whirled to face him, letter opener still in hand. "It's not worth it, Eric! The police will be here soon. You can't have any more blood on your hands!"

"More blood?!"

Eric finally broke.

The older man sprinted towards Pat, blade raised high, eyes burning with unfettered rage.

Pat took a deep breath.

And then he moved.

He sidestepped forwards as elegantly as he possibly could.

Eric flew past him, knife flailing wildly as Pat swung the walkie-talkie in an arc with all his might, throwing the entire weight of his bulk behind the movement like he was hurling a shotput. Time seemed to slow as the plastic and metal made contact with Eric's cheek, and Pat felt the crunch of bone splintering beneath his fingers. Pat's momentous bulk continued through the swing, sending his head spiraling through a puff of Eric's whisky-breath. The walkie-talkie flew from his and clattered in the centre of the lobby.

Eric dropped like a marionette with his strings cut, and the letter opener sailed through the air, clanging off the tiles by the elevator.

Pat fell to his knees, his ears ringing.

The klaxon blared.

Breathe, Pat. Breathe.

Pat's heartbeat pounded in his ears as he raced to catch his breath.

Am I the hero now?

Pat cast his eyes up to the balcony, where silhouettes were frantically flitting about under the red light. Mateo was still collapsed on the staircase, hyperventilating, his face a sheen of sweat and terror.

Struggling to his feet, Pat shuffled over to the younger man, his heart thumping inside his chest. He offered a hand, and Mateo took it. He pulled the younger man to his feet.

"You alright?" he asked.

Mateo nodded, still shellshocked, his eyes staring past Pat. Pat followed his gaze.

Eric's body was sprawled in the centre of the lobby.

Motionless.

CHAPTER 21

Thankfully, Eric wasn't dead. The police confirmed that just a few minutes later when they careened through the front doors, assault rifles locked and loaded, the red LEDs dancing over Pat and Mateo on the east staircase.

They fanned out in expert fashion, surrounding Eric and kicking the scalpel away from his limp form. Moments later, the red lights were replaced with the soft amber glow, and the klaxon faded into memory.

Pat held his breath as they checked Eric's pulse.

"He's out cold, but alive," one of the cops said, "Call it in."

The next half an hour passed in a blur. Pat called Karen almost immediately. She was wailing over the phone, but he managed to calm her down just in time for Alvarez to appear in the doorway with a face like thunder.

Pat could sense the disappointment in her eyes as she checked on Eric, casting a sour eye over the two of them.

I told her it would be safe. I told her he wasn't here.

She took a statement from them both, her face steely, saying nothing. As expected, there were no discrepancies, and so she flounced off to bag the letter opener and Pat's walkie-talkie, leaving her witnesses sitting on the stairs.

The ambulance pulled up in a roar a few moments later, and paramedics trundled through with a trolley for Eric. Moments later, the wild-eyed widower was promptly cuffed and dumped onto a stretcher, and wheeled out into the night. Pat caught his eye for just a moment as the stretcher clattered through the doors. He looked groggy. Unwell. Drunk.

And then, with a bit more chatter and a few rounds of police tape circuiting the broken glass, they were all gone, and it was just Mateo and Pat again.

But not for much longer. The elevator doors dinged open to reveal a throng of people crowded inside. Others came down the west staircase, seemingly not daring enough to try and push their way past Pat and Mateo on the other side.

All the familiar faces gathered around Pat's desk, arranging themselves precariously amongst the larger shards glass from Eric's bottle. Marek and Luka were at the front, shoulders touching.

Everyone's intentions were clear. They were here for a report.

And you've got to give it.

Pat glanced at Mateo. His eyes were glassy. Pat clambered up a few stairs and rose to his feet.

"There…there was a security incident tonight, folks," he said. His choice of words echoed sorely in his ears.

Another security incident, on your watch.

"Thankfully, nobody was hurt. The perpetrator has been arrested–"

"–was it Eric?" someone shouted from the crowd.

"Was it him?"

"He had a weapon!" someone else called out.

"Well–"

"–he did have a weapon," said Marek. "He was waving it around like a madman. Completely crazy." He broke stance with Luka to wander over to the staircase, and stepped up next to Pat.

Like we're buddies, or something.

"Obviously he was trying to harm some people here. No man – no rational man – does something like this. I'm not saying we should jump to conclusions, but…"

That's exactly what he's saying, thought Pat.

"—well if he did this, I think it's pretty obvious what else he's done," said Gopal. He looked stressed, his dark hair matted and sweaty, small stains forming under his armpits. Amy Morales was lingering to his right, her eyes downcast.

"Didn't he have an alibi?" Monica called out, an open question to the crowd. She was near the back, and Pat could hardly see her, until she shuffled around and caught his eye between the heads of some other onlookers. She smiled nervously and threw him a quick thumbs-up.

Are we good? Is she saying we're good?

Pat didn't know how to respond to that. Eric did indeed have an alibi…but Pat was very much opposed to stirring the pot in a public forum.

Particularly with Marek's hand on my shoulder.

Marek glanced at Pat expectantly.

"Uh…the police are still looking into his alibi, I think," mumbled Pat. "We don't know for sure." The crowd murmured amongst themselves. Pat glanced at Johnny. He had his head bowed.

Making things up doesn't seem so good when you're defending a guilty party, does it now?

"Either way!" Marek continued, "I think it's safe to say that we've found our perpetrator." He paused, as the crowd nodded. "Maybe...maybe now, we might finally be able to return to normal, my friends?"

A smattering of applause echoed through the crowd. Pat scoffed internally. It was only Marek who, in a situation like this, could receive adulations for being a spectator.

Mateo sprung to his feet. "It was all Pat!" he announced, clapping Pat on the shoulder. "He saved me! Who knows what Eric might have done!? He had a knife at my throat!" His hand tightened around Pat as another gentle clap broken out. Pat winced at the attention.

Marek turned to give Pat an oily smile and shook his hand fiercely, before pulling him close.

"Well done," he droned, lips inches from Pat's ear. "See what I mean? If you stop poking around, you do your job really well!" He let go of Pat's hand and vanished past him up the stairs, Luka slinking back to his side.

Everyone else ducked back out to the elevators or the bathrooms, and Mateo disappeared for a moment, retrieving a pair of dustpans and brushes from the cleaning cupboard. He helped Pat sweep up the glass, and then gave him one last thanks before his phone rang.

"My brother's here," he said softly. "Come to pick me up. He...he's been waiting out front a while." Pat nodded. "You should go. Get home safe."

There was no tension between them. Pat figured it was as close of a bonding experience you could have, being caught in a physical fight with someone.

And he didn't doubt Mateo's appreciation.

"Thank God this is all over, right?"

Pat nodded. "Yeah. I guess it's over."

*   *   *

There was a noticeable buzz about Guinness House the following few nights, particularly in the evenings at changeover. Pat was getting congratulations from every angle. Joseph managed to string together a "thank you for your service," and even Lionel made the effort to take note of the happenings.

"Knew you'd figure out which bastard did it," he hummed, spinning his chair out of the way as Pat sat down at changeover. "Well, I knew someone would. Figured it'd be you. Good shit."

Pat was trying to keep to himself, but it was much more difficult than before. Overnight, he had become interesting. People were just short of asking him for autographs, but instead they took to cornering him in the bathroom or digging for gory details on Eric as they made their way out of the front gate. Pat declined to answer most of their questions, instead keeping them at bay by doffing his imaginary cap and maybe saying, 'just part of the job!'

Mostly, though, he tried to say nothing at all. In the quiet moments, everything felt a bit more real…and frankly, a bit more scary. While he was relieved, Pat was still a little bit stunned as to how everything had just…squared itself away. Yes, Eric was the most likely candidate for Nadine's murder. And what with his violent outburst in the lobby, Pat was positive the pathologists would be testing for Nadine's blood on the letter opener.

Maybe that was it.

Maybe this was just a story of love gone awry.

But the anxiety was still peaking.

Pat found himself wondering if his marriage would ever end up the same way as Nadine and Eric's. Karen wasn't exactly the type to split, but Pat's night shifts did mean they weren't spending as much time together as they should. For the few nights that followed, he cut back on his Netflix and called her more than he normally did. He even video chatted her once or twice in the evenings, around the time that he'd normally go up and talk to Monica. He could tell she appreciated it. He didn't want to be like Eric.

And it made him feel less lonely.

The night regulars were still avoiding him. Catherine and Amy practically turned tail and fled if they ever crossed paths in the corridor. Luka still had nothing to say to him, and despite the public display of camaraderie Pat had been offered on the staircase, Marek was definitely keeping him at arm's length.

Pat thought it was odd. If their little clique of college buddies really had nothing to do with Nadine's death, then it was a sad situation to lose a casual acquaintance over the death of a mutual friend.

And so, apart from the phone calls with Karen, Pat spent his evenings alone. One night, contractors came by to fix the door for Microceuticals, and Alvarez came and left to clean up the remnants of the police tape. She didn't say a word to him. It was for the best, as the last few weeks had taken such a toll on Pat that he didn't feel he had the energy to have protracted conversations with anyone.

Except he still had a bone to pick with one person, and was desperate to catch up with an old friend.

A few nights later, the harassment had quietened down and some things were still gnawing at Pat…so he got to work with the former.

Always best to get the hard stuff out of the way.

Johnny continued to lurk in his office. It was just he and Catherine these days; Pat hadn't seen Mateo since Eric's violent outburst. He was probably working from home, Pat could guess.

As Pat knocked on the door, Catherine ducked past him and took off down the hallway, not even returning his cheerful, 'Hi!'.

Pat found Johnny inside the back room. He was flicking through sheafs of paper under dim light, his desk neat and tidy again. The screensaver was the same as last time – Johnny, locked in the embrace of his grandma . Johnny glanced up.

"Hey," he said quietly. He looked a lot more put together than over the last few weeks; he'd shaved, was wearing a clean, ironed shirt, and Pat could no longer smell the lingering aroma of booze.

"Evening. Can we talk?"

"Sure."

Pat pulled up a chair and sat...as a figure slowly faded in from the shadows.

"Mind if I join you?" asked Sal.

As a general rule, Pat was pretty happy to not see too much of Marek's right hand man, aside from their cigarette breaks in the stairwell. He stalked Guinness House with a predatory prowl, his voice low and hushed on phone calls, his eyes lingering just slightly too long if Monica was wearing a short skirt.

But more than anything, Pat felt that Sal looked down on him. More than once, when receiving night deliveries of replacement furniture or door panels, he'd see Sal watching from the upper levels or from the front porch where they smoked together in the summer time. He never offered to help.

As though he liked to see people struggle.

Is Johnny struggling?

"What're you doing here?" Pat asked.

Johnny turned to Sal, who pursed his lips and let the silence hang in the air.

"...Sal and I are working on something together." Johnny finally found his words. "A side project. Personal stuff."

Pat bit his lip. "Well, it'd be good if we could talk in private." Sal didn't move.

"Can personal stuff...wait for a few minutes?" Pat asked them tentatively.

"Not really!" Sal smiled cheerily. He pulled a chair up next to Johnny and clapped him on the leg. "That's okay, though. Whatever you want to ask Johnny about, you can say in front of me. After all, we're mates. We tell each other everything anyway. Isn't that right, John?"

Johnny nodded reluctantly.

Yeah, right.

"What do you need, Pat?" Johnny asked. Pat leaned back in his chair and drummed his fingers on the chair.

"Why did you cover for Eric?" he asked. Johnny hesitated. Sal rubbed his shoulder, affectionately.

"Johnny's a bit nervous, you see," he chuckled. "He's just a bit embarrassed. Go on, Johnny. Tell him what you told me yesterday."

Pat watched his teeth as he spoke. The words flowed effortlessly through white pearls so sharp that it almost looked as though they had been filed to points.

Johnny mumbled something, and Sal slapped him on the shoulder. "Speak up," he said sharply.

Johnny sighed. "I…I covered for Eric because I thought I saw someone else on the fifth floor that night," he said. "I was going for a walk, and I…I saw someone arguing with Nadine."

Pat's blood ran cold. "Who, Johnny? Who was she talking to?"

Johnny mumbled something again. Sal gave him another aggressive nudge.

"I know the cops are going to come asking about this," he continued. "But please, let me explain it to them. I don't want to cause any more drama. And now we know that Eric did it, so it's all a moot point anyway."

"Who did you see, Johnny? Who do you think it was?"

Johnny bit his lip.

"I thought it was you, Pat."

*   *   *

The words felt like a white-hot knife into Pat's heart.

What. The. Fuck.

As he left Collymore & Donovan, with Sal closing the door behind him, he ran through it in his head. Was he on the fifth floor that night? Had he spoken to Nadine? Pat's memory was far from perfect, but he was reasonably confident that the answer to both of those questions was a resounding 'no'.

Johnny had followed up the statement with a ream of reasons as to why he now knew it couldn't be Pat, focusing particularly on the fact that he knew Pat wouldn't do something like that.

But Pat knew one thing for sure – Johnny definitely wasn't telling all he knew. And whether he was covering for someone else by putting Pat in the firing line, or whether he had just drank too much that night and he was genuinely confused, Pat would put money on the fact that Sal was really the one spinning this story.

Sal…or Marek.

Sal had followed up with a brief summary that sounded like plot points to a book, as though he was Johnny's agent. The young lawyer, meanwhile, had stared absently into space.

149

"He covered for Eric because he was so sure that you had done it."

"Johnny was drinking because he was afraid that his caretaker was a murderer."

"He couldn't tell anyone because he didn't have any proof."

"Everything's all okay now. And he's not drinking because he isn't scared anymore."

And so, with Johnny's mysterious drinking problem and convenient false-alibi all tied up in a convenient little bow, Pat could do nothing but leave. As Sal tried to push him out the door, Pat left one last word of warning with Johnny.

"The cops will find out about this. That you lied. Particularly if Eric is guilty."

As Pat took the elevator up to the sixth floor, spiteful thoughts lingered. Yeah, he hoped Eric confessed. He hoped Eric would admit that they were never together.

That'd teach him.

The box of mirrors rocketed up to the sky, a quiet hum in the night. It opened on the sixth floor.

He knocked on the doors of Lafferty Inc, and they flew open almost immediately. Monica was all smiles tonight. Pat's heart leapt more than it had in days. It wasn't the flirty kind of smile, nor the tense polite one that he'd been seeing a lot of recently. It was a proper smile; a 'genuinely happy that you've come by,' smile.

She wrapped him up in a hug, her arms straining to fit around his wide waist.

"I'm sorry," she said softly. "I'm sorry I pushed you away. I'm sorry I said mean things."

"It's fine. I'm okay."

"It's not, though." She broke the hug and held him at arm's length, staring into his eyes. "I said things that were genuinely meant to upset you. I was scared for my safety...and I let that get in the way of our friendship."

"It...it's fine," Pat managed. He could smell her hair – apples? – and was feeling a little more hot under the collar than he should.

"Did you want to come in?" she asked, stepping aside. "We can talk. Catch up?"

"I..." Pat wanted to, but his brain just wasn't finding the words. As the smell of fruit faded from his nostrils, all he could think of was one thing.

Johnny.

Monica cocked her head. "What's on your mind, Patty?"

"Johnny said...Johnny said he saw me on the fifth floor. The night Nadine died."

"Well, that doesn't surprise me."

"Sorry?"

"Well you do rounds, right? You must've been up there at some point."

"I mean, well – I came up to see you, and then I went down…I can't remember. But I know that I didn't go there until…well, until I found her, but…"

"You know," Monica interrupted, "I was wandering around the building that night. Took Kathy with me." She paused for a second. "I didn't tell the police that."

"Why not?"

"Well…firstly, I didn't think it was important, and then…well, I mean, they caught the killer, didn't they? So it's all said and done, right?"

"Yeah…I guess."

"We needed a break," she said. "Just a bit of time to get out of the studio."

For what felt like the fiftieth time that week, Pat was on tenterhooks. She paused, those emerald green eyes hesitant.

Did she see something?

"Monica?" "I saw them arguing," she sighed. "I didn't think it was a big deal at the time. And then, and then the suspicion was on Eric, and then we had the meeting and he looked really upset! And guilty!"

"Who was it, Monica?"

No! It was Eric! Eric did it! He's even got a weapon!

She continued to ramble. "And why would he steal that girl's phone? What does he possibly have to achieve from that?"

"Who, Monica?!"

"Luka!" she hissed.

"She was arguing with Luka, the night she died."

*　　*　　*

Pat headed straight up to Microceuticals and rapped on the door. He couldn't make sense of all the facts together. Eric was indeed wildly violent, but there was still the question of the unanswered break-in…

…with the mystery intruder trying to point towards Microceuticals.

Nobody answered.

Fuck it.

Pat let himself in.

Thankfully, Amy was nowhere to be seen. The foyer was empty and dark, illuminated only by the sterile white light beaming in from the tiny window and under the cracks of the door that led into Microceuticals' private little world. Pat didn't waste any time. He marched over to the door and knocked. No answer. *To hell with your privacy.* Pat pushed through the door, and was met with…

…a laboratory. He could've already guessed that. What with Gopal and

Amy marching around in lab coats and goggles hanging off their necks.

But this lab blew any other one that Pat had seen out of the water.

Racks of test tubes were lined up in the countertops, flanked by plastic packets filled with hundreds of syringes and bags of cotton balls. A huge, white machine – big enough for a person to lay down in – dominated the far corner, and stainless steel benches filled the rest of the space. There were two large doors on adjacent corners of the office, white, with white frames, and big lockable handles that took your whole arm to turn. Pat also saw scalpels – expensive looking surgical weapons that must've had four-inch blades and heavy metal handles – and reusable bags with tubes and needles sticking out of them.

With all the weapons on the walls, it didn't look like a lab. It looked like the beginning of a horror film.

More worrying than the array of large blades, however, were the two people clustered in the far corner of the lab, peering over something on a bench. Pat's mouth instantly dried up. He thought he'd be alone in here.

You're not. So think fast.

"Hey!" he shouted. The moment the words were out of his mouth, one of the doors on the other side of the room swung open – Luka. At that same moment, the pair over the benches whipped around in surprise, flabbergasted at the lone security guard encroaching upon their sanctum.

Luka's mouth was agape.

"What are you even doing in−?!" he started, but Pat was already back out the door. He waited in the foyer, his foot tapping impatiently on the wooden boards. Luka was hot on his heels and looked like he was itching for a fight as he slammed the lab door behind them and advanced on Pat, hand raised like he was about to slap him.

"Did you have an argument with Nadine, on Tuesday?" Pat asked impatiently, taking the wind out of his sails. "The night she died? Did you fight with her?"

For a split second, fear flickered across Luka's face. Then the impetus returned. "Yes, I did!" he spat. "So what? What were you doing in there?!"

"What about?"

Luka stepped forwards, his crooked nose stopping within centimetres of Pat's. "What's this about, huh, Pat? Not satisfied that there wasn't some grand scheme going on?" His breath reeked of garlic and onions. "Yeah, I know you're poking around. For the first time in your life, you've managed to find something interesting going on, and now you're obsessive. Have you no respect?"

The last word was such a quiet hiss it was practically a whisper. Pat wanted to hit him. His fists clenched into fists at his sides. It would be so easy. Just one, decent punch.

"You've got nothing interesting going on, huh, Pat?! Just a miserable fat fuck in a dead-end job. I've seen you downstairs. You watch TV and occasionally trudge up here to try and prove to everyone that you're worth your salary. Well bad news, Patty. You aren't worth shit."

He jabbed Pat in the chest with his finger, and then turned back towards the lab, but whirled around again, obviously not done with his tirade.

"And you know what? Yeah, I did have an argument with Nadine. Over a personal matter. Because we were friends. I know you're not familiar with the concept, you bug-eyed *fuck,* but that doesn't lead to murder. I don't know what sort of fantasy land you live in, but just because I have a fight with someone, doesn't mean I'm going to cut her throat like a dog."

His lip still curling, he backed through the lab door, slamming it behind him with such force that the whole room shook.

You did it, didn't you?

Adrenaline pumping through his veins, and his hands still balled into fists, Pat's mind whirred as he stood, stock still in the foyer of Microceuticals.

And you neglected to mention that little argument in your statement, didn't you?

Pat headed back out and towards the elevator, his big feet slapping on the hard wood as he marched towards the elevators.

Two possibilities. Only two. It was true that this murder could have been a crime of passion. In that case, Eric would surely have the charges brought against him within a matter of days. While Pat had thought that the alternative scenario – that Marek, Malik and Luka were somehow conspiring to bring about Nadine's death – was becoming increasingly less likely, particularly after Eric's violent outburst, Luka's aggression certainly did nothing to dissuade him of this possibility. Possibility number two.

As Pat hit the button for the elevator, he heard footsteps behind him. A hand grabbed at his arm, pulling him around to confront him with a pair of brown eyes, eyes brimming with desperation.

"You've got to be more careful!" Gopal hissed. He was sweaty – like always – a thin sheen of perspiration beading on his upper lip, and more dripping down from his head. He was panting, looking like he'd just sprinted from Microceuticals. "You can't go breaking into the lab like that!"

Pat wrenched his arm free, and tried to muster up whatever authority he had left. "I am security here! I'm not breaking in anywhere, but if there's a safety concern then I will discuss it with whoever I see fit!"

Gopal shook his head. "No, no, no! I know, look, you have a job to do. But this – this! – it's a medical marvel. I don't know how much you know–"

"–you guys say you can cure Huntington's disease," Pat finished for him. "Is that right? Am I on track here?"

Gopal looked slightly surprised. "Yes! Yes, that's what we're working on. And we're so close! But you need to leave us alone while we work!"

"I don't care how close you are," Pat huffed. "If I need to speak to you, and nobody knocks on the door, I'm coming in."

Gopal grabbed at his arm again. "Look," he said, eyes narrow, "I'm not talking about the trials. Hell, you wouldn't know what was going on in there even if we let you see."

Pat ignored the thinly veiled insult.

"I'm talking about Luka," Gopal said. "This isn't about you, or Nadine. This is about him. He's been working on this for years, and if there's a chance that you're going to do anything to jeopardise it..." He trailed off, his mouth a grimace.

"Then what?" Pat asked. "What's he going to do to me?"

Gopal shrugged, and retreated back towards Microceuticals.

"You're playing a very dangerous game here, Patrick," he warned. "With very dangerous people."

CHAPTER 22

Pat wasn't in the mood for warnings anymore. He headed downstairs, grabbed his cigarettes, and ducked into the stairwell. His phone was sweaty in his hands as he fat-fingered through his contact list to find the person who was obligated to listen to his concerns.

"I've just been threatened by Luka Vasilj," he said, not bothering with formalities. "And I'm pretty sure he should be listed as a suspect for Nadine Matthews' murder. He was seen arguing with her that night."

"Did you see them?" Alvarez asked quickly.

"No, but Monica did. Monica Lafferty. I just spoke to her about it."

"Pat," Alvarez sighed. "I won't lie. You've been sort of helpful, these past few weeks...when you aren't a thorn in my side. But we have a primary suspect in custody after he tried to– well, it was you he tried to attack. I'm sure you know how this goes. Jealous ex-husband, all that jazz. And as of right now, all you're really doing is making this a stickier situation than it really should be."

"Well I'm sorry if crime is too complicated for you," Pat sneered. He didn't like being snarky, but there was always a time and a place for it, and in those times, it felt too good to pass up. "You need to be looking at Luka Vasilj. Did you know Nadine was trialing a drug that he's creating?"

Alvarez sighed again. "Pat, we've done more interviews than you'd care to know about over the last week. We're talking to these people day in, day out, over the phone, video chats...everything. Trust me when I say – we've got the right guy."

"What about the break-in?" Silence on the other end of the line. "Detective?"

"We...still haven't found the phone," she admitted sourly. "But...we're working on it."

Pat let Alvarez go. He plopped himself back in his usual position and wrestled with his chip bag, still fuming from his interaction with Luka.

No respect? No respect for Nadine? Hell, I'm the only one bothering to find out who did this to her!

Eventually though, as night wore on, the anger faded a little. The boots came off the desk, Netflix was turned off, and a much calmer Pat made his way upstairs to do a lite-version of his usual rounds.

He stopped by to say hello to Monica, but didn't bother going into any of the usual offices. Sal's eyes met his as he peered nosily through the front window of Mihok & Mihok. PubStunt was deserted as usual. On the second floor, Malik was merrily whistling away as he whirled around the office, loafers dancing across the wood. The evening passed without much incident.

And finally, as dawn broke, Pat went home.

*   *   *

"Frankly, I think you need to let this go," said Karen, pulling on her scrubs as Pat curled up in bed. "They've arrested, what was his name…?"

"Eric," Pat finished. "But I don't know! Something doesn't add up! It doesn't feel finished."

Pat slept fitfully that night, the image of Gopal staring him down in the hallway lurking in his mind's eye. It felt like the most dangerous threat yet. Like Gopal was telling him he really didn't understand what was going on here.

You're in the dark, Pat.

The unanswered question of the break-in rolled around in Pat's head all through the day. He woke in the afternoon, and took a brief walk in the park to try and clear his head, making it back home just in time to take Larry to boxing practice in the afternoon. But even as his son wowed his opponent with flawless footwork, Pat found that he wasn't really watching.

He pulled into Guinness House the next evening feeling defeated. The slush of the leftover snow seeped through his old shoes as he made his way up the front steps, past the police cars…

—the police cars. They were parked askew — not in the parking spaces, maybe twenty feet apart, both pointed at the front gate of Guinness House.

What on earth are the cops back for?

As if to answer his question, Alvarez marched through the front door. She spotted him at the bottom end of the steps and gave him a cursory nod. Three more figures came out after her. Two police officers, and a man in cuffs.

Johnny Ray.

"We found the stolen phone in his office," Alvarez reported as she came level with him, Johnny and the other officers trailing in her wake. She lowered her voice. "Normally, I wouldn't share that with members of the public, but…" she clapped him on the shoulder, "…you did good. You ever think about joining the force?"

Pat nodded absently, watching Johnny stumble down the last of the steps.

Johnny caught his eye. He looked defeated. They bundled him into the back of one of the squad cars.

"Pat?" Alvarez asked again. "You ever think about it?"

"Uh— sorry. No, I guess, not really?" She rummaged in her purse and pulled out a card.

"Well…if it ever crosses your mind…" She scribbled on the card, "…here's my number. It'd be a junior position, of course, but…you never know."

Pat took the card, tentatively. *Sofia Alvarez,* it read, with a number beneath it. She'd drawn a little heart above the 'i'.

"Anyway Pat, I've got some paperwork to do," Alvarez said. "But, keep me posted. And…if you think of anything else, keep me in the loop. I'll take your call." She wandered off, jacket bunched up around her shoulders to protect her ears from the cold, and grouped up with her other officers over a clipboard by the front gate.

Pat wanted to feel valued. He wanted to be able to jump up and down and pump his fists in victory.

But he didn't understand.

He didn't understand why Johnny, of all people, broke into Microceuticals that night.

He didn't understand at all.

Pat waited until he was sure Alvarez's attention was elsewhere, then hurried over to the squad car with Johnny inside. He banged on the window. Johnny turned, and held up his cuffs with an apologetic smile.

"Why?" Pat asked, his face pressed up to the glass. "Why did you steal it?" He could hear his own voice reverberating off the double-glazing, as Johnny cupped his cuffed hands to his ears and mouthed something at him.

"I can't hear you!" "Why did you steal the phone?!" Pat almost shouted, trying his best to open his mouth as wide to help Johnny read his lips.

"I….know….happening," Johnny mouthed back. "Don't….anyone!"

"What?!" Alvarez whirled around and started marching back towards the car, her eyes locked on Pat. His time running out, Pat yanked on the car door handle. Locked, of course.

Johnny was looking more frustrated. "Don't….anybody!"

"It's too thick!" Pat slapped on the glass, frustrated, but then Alvarez was on the other side of the car.

"I'll take it from here, Pat," she said, her eyes narrow. "Get inside. It's cold out." She hopped inside the front seat and started the engine. That wasn't a suggestion.

But Pat wasn't done. "Why did you do it?!" he shouted through the window.

"Keep…looking!" Johnny yelled back, his mouth straining to shape the words. "You were right!"

I was right? But about what? About what?!

"About what?!" Pat shouted, as the car kicked into drive, and a plume of smoke shot out of the exhaust. "What was I right about?"

As the car engine revved, and the tyres gently rolled across the gravel of the front drive, Johnny used every ounce of his breath to scream one last word through the glass.

"Microceuticals!"

*   *   *

Johnny was the thief. Johnny had stolen the phone. But why? Pat traded a few words with Lionel before letting him know he was free to go home, and then settled in. He found his semi-broken walkie-talkie in the second drawer of the desk, so he set about repairing it with duct tape. People milled about in the lobby, waving their goodbyes as the day-staff began to head home for the evening. As the clock ticked past eight, the doors swung open, complete with a winter chill that only seemed to be getting more violent.

Mateo.

He was looking much more put-together than the last time Pat had seem him, but nowhere near as jubilant as normal. Catherine Kim was at his side.

Mateo nodded towards Pat; a silent acknowledgement of their trials together. Catherine, meanwhile, kept her head bowed and ducked towards the elevator, avoiding eye contact.

Amy Morales arrived next. She practically bolted past Pat's desk, shooting him only a fleeting glance as she jumped into the elevator. It was the closest Pat had come to her since their little tussle in the restroom—

—and Pat had an epiphany.

Effectively, you jumped a woman in the restroom. You didn't mean to, but it got to the point where she attacked you…

And she never reported it. Pat fired up his emails. He'd often go days without checking them, but surely if there was a serious accusation, Joseph would call him. *Just come in for a chat,* he'd say. *There's something that needs to be talked about.*

There was nothing. Pat mulled it over. *Whatever's going on here, Eric's arrest isn't the end of the story. Is Amy in on it?*

Frustrations grew as the evening ticked away. Pat felt stagnant. Johnny was in custody. Eric too, most likely. Mateo was back in action, quietly. And Marek, Luka and Malik were all still lounging about in their offices.

What do I have to do to figure this out?

Pat had spoken to everyone he possibly could at this stage. He wasn't going to get anywhere with any more conversations, and snooping around seemed to be out of the question, considering his last surprise encounter had left him with a sizeable welt that still stung.

Luka was standing on the fifth floor balcony, staring down at him.

Could let them come to you, I guess?

"Can I help you?" Pat called up. He was pretty sure it was Luka; too tall to be Gopal, and nobody else would be up there in the evenings. He snatched up his now duct-taped walkie-talkie as though it was a means of defense…

…and then the figure was gone.

Time to do your rounds, Pat.

Gotta keep the building clear. Pat headed into the stairwell first and lit a cigarette. The curls of smoke spiraled lazily up the stairs before fading into the dark, while more of it swam through his lungs and filtered into his bloodstream. The tension melted out of his body.

God, that's good.

He dragged for a minute straight, filling his lungs with the noxious fumes, and just when he would've loved one more puff, he ground the butt into the corner of the stairwell with its friends, and headed upstairs. And he knew exactly where to go.

Luka is way too defensive.

Amy didn't report me.

And Johnny was looking for something.

When he got up to the fifth floor, Pat realised was starting to make a habit of wandering past the spot where Nadine had died; doing a loop around the balcony instead of heading directly to the lab from the elevator. Emotion flooded him like a tidal wave.

Could I have stopped it? Is this what guilt feels like?

He chased the anxious thoughts away. There was nothing he could've done. Whether it was Eric, or Luka, or Marek, or whoever else — it wasn't well planned, and well executed. They'd waited until she was alone, and they'd cut her throat. Not the sort of thing you do if you're trying to steal someone's wallet. It was calculated. Murder in cold blood, in the middle of the night.

Death after dark.

Pat peered through the frosted glass of Microceuticals. He could see Amy at the front desk. She glanced up as his shadow passed over her, and immediately darted off, flying from her chair and into the back room.

Not good, not good.

Pat was too tired for another altercation with Luka. He hustled his way back to the elevators, and worked through the other floors.

Quiet. Normal.

It's not normal!

The frustration was becoming too much to handle. Pat's internal monologue was running wild as he walked Mateo out to the front gates a few hours later. He let him go, waved him off, and stomped back up the front path and back to his desk, the cold biting at his shoulders.

All. Normal.

The night ticked on turgidly. Netflix did its best to entertain Pat, and he called Karen and Larry a few times, just to break up the monotony.

What have Microceuticals done? He borrowed some paper and a well-used ballpoint out of Joseph's office and set about drawing diagrams of connections between people in the building.

You're obsessing, Pat. You do this when you're anxious. He threw the pen down and stomped off to the bathroom.

When Pat came back out to his desk, he had no idea that someone had taken the elevator down to the lobby while he was in the restroom.

Someone who had taken off their shoes so they couldn't be heard as easily.

Someone who had been watching him from the balcony on the fifth floor.

Someone who didn't like how many questions Pat was asking.

Someone who believed in something, and was willing to do whatever it took to protect it.

And so, as Pat fired up Netflix on the tablet for the thousandth time in his life, he didn't realise that it might well be the last.

He didn't hear the footsteps behind him.

And he didn't hear the rush of the bottle as it exploded over the back of his head.

CHAPTER 23

Pain.

Pat woke with a start. It was like someone had jammed a white-hot blade into the back of his head. Instinctively, his hands shot up to clutch at the back of his skull, but they were yanked back down by a sea of cables; taut IVs that had been fed into the top of his hands and wrists, restricting any movement. He felt like he couldn't breathe.

More pain.

Wrenching with all his might, Pat managed to pull himself upright. The movement was like fireworks in his brain, and he collapsed under the weight of his own upper body, falling back into the pillows of the hospital bed.

"Honey, honey!"

Karen bounded over to him. He was in a hospital, there was no doubt about that. The linoleum walls above his head were stark and bare, and the walls were peppered with kids' paintings; flowers mostly. The bed was firm, angled slightly so that Pat was staring firmly at the TV mounted on the top of the wall.

"You're awake! Thank God!"

Pat wailed helplessly as Karen pulled her chair over, rearranging the cables that were ensnaring his arms. She was in her nurses scrubs, mascara stains running down her cheeks, and looked exhausted.

"Wh-where am I?" Pat babbled. "What…what happened?"

"You hit your head, honey", Karen said. "Well….someone hit you, we think. That reminds me…" She refrained from toying with the cables for enough time to whip out her phone and punch in a number.

Pat heard the dial tone ringing.

"The police," she said. "They told me to let them know as soon as you woke up."

"Oh, wait—" Pat groaned, "...just, call this number..."

His jacket was draped over the chair by the door, just within arm's reach, and it had Alvarez's card in the pocket. As he twisted over the rails of his bed, the pain ricocheted from his back up to his neck, and he roared in agony.

"Karen!! Karen get a fucking nurse!!"

Karen shushed his desperate screams for help, hugging him close as his howls eventually became sobs. She mashed the nurse call button, a muted beep under Pat's cries.

"You took a pretty big hit, my love," she whispered. "We were so worried about you. It's been days."

Her words shook him.

"Days?" he asked, still quivering from the pain. "I've been out for days?"

She nodded, somber. "Technically, you were in a coma." She hit the nurse-call button again. "Doctors had no idea when you were going to wake up. It's been almost a week."

A week?! Pat was panicking.

"What about work? Is everything okay? Do I still have my job?"

"Everything's fine, Pat." She stroked his arm. "Larry will be here in a bit to see you. Until then, we just wait, okay? The doctors will want to run some tests. Make sure you don't have a TBI. Make sure you can still walk okay and everything." She must've seen the panic in his eyes. "It's nothing to fret about, my love, okay? Sometimes, people don't wake up for months, so it's all part of routine procedure. Can you still feel your toes?"

Pat tried to take deep breaths, and wiggled his toes. He nodded shakily.

"They're all there."

"Good, that's the first step. Now where is that damn doctor?!"

Eventually, the doc showed up. She was a young girl, blonde and bubbly, and introduced herself as Dr Ford. All too quickly, she ran Pat through what had happened with increasingly incomprehensible language. Finally, she saw his confusion, and tried to start over.

"Essentially," she explained to Pat, as Karen looked on knowingly, "you were hit hard over the back of the head. It fractured your skull, and we had to stitch you up in surgery. We're worried that whoever hit you was really trying to do some damage, so we're going to do some scans just to make sure that everything's working properly."

Pat gave his consent, and the next few hours were a whirlwind. He was stuffed inside a large machine which made thumping sounds as its walls rotated around him.

Thank God I'm not claustrophobic.

After that, they had him walking – ever so slowly – on a treadmill, his hospital gown billowing out behind him as he tried to prove that he could stand on his own two feet.

Fortunately, the good news was worth the wait.

"So, looks like you're pretty much in the clear," grinned Dr Ford as she leaned on the doorway. Pat was sitting on the side of the bed, his head still ringing. Karen looked like she was about to burst with joy.

"You'll have some pain in your head for a few days, but we've got you on codeine for that. It's all covered under the insurance, so if you get a big bill in the mail, don't worry about it for now. If you need something stronger for the pain, let me know. I'd like to get you back in a week for further assessments, and if anything is amiss over the next few days, call me. You can maybe expect some short term memory loss, and some grogginess from the codeine, but other than that I'm not anticipating any significant side effects."

She was right about the memory loss. Pat found he was forgetting Karen's name half the time. She'd noticed straight away, but she told him not to worry about it.

This woman is literally a saint.

"Do you see people like me a lot?" he quizzed her as they strolled their way out to the parking lot, hands shoved in pockets to fight the chill. "Do people normally come out worse than this?"

"Patty, darling." She stopped to face him, and linked her fingers behind his neck. Even that slight pressure gave him a sharp jolt up to the top of his head. "You are a superstar. That's what I've been telling you all these years!"

She stuffed her hand inside his pocket and fell in beside him. Her hand was hot against his.

"Plus, it's probably something to do with that mighty thick skull of yours."

Pat chuckled – the first laugh he had permitted himself since he'd woken up – and ran his free hand over the back of his scalp, checking for damage. Pain flared, he winced. *Best not make a habit of doing that.*

As they strolled underneath the awning and down and around the corner into the hospital car park, Pat did a double take. Karen had brought his car. Its faded green paneling was as much of a comfort to him now as it ever was.

What wasn't comforting, however, was Detective Alvarez, leaning on the hood.

"Time for a conversation, Pat!" she called to him. "I think you and I need to have a little chat."

*   *   *

"A bottle?" Pat asked, incredulous. He was in the same room he'd been in a couple of times now, the interrogation space at the precinct. Karen was waiting outside, as per Pat's request. He didn't want an audience. Alvarez nodded soberly from across the interview table. "Big bottle of booze. Pretty full, from the looks of things. Stank the lobby out. To be honest, the lady who found you – a 'Mrs. Kim' – she actually thought you were just passed out at your desk, and you'd dropped the bottle. The blood everywhere though....well, lucky she put two and two together, frankly."

Someone hit me with a bottle. Pat dug through his memory bank. Did he remember it happening? He was drawing blanks.

Alvarez could see him struggling.

"I don't know if you would've seen them, Pat," she said. "They hit you from behind. Your head was flat on the desk. Honestly, we're analysing the glass at the moment and it seems like it was thin, cheap. You're lucky. We had a guy who got clocked by a bottle of Macallan last year. Let's just say...well, he hasn't woken up yet."

Pat considered himself many things, and lucky was chief among them at this stage. He wiggled his toes inside his shoes. They were cold, but still working.

"So what now?" he probed. "What do we know?"

Alvarez sighed, and flicked her notepad open. "It's tough. You've intersected a lot with the people in the building. Nobody's got a concrete alibi. They were all in their offices working, but we're looking into it. Can you think of anyone who'd want to hurt you?"

Pat closed his eyes and tried to dig. Most things were in there. He could see Johnny's face as clear as day from inside the window of the cop car as they tried to talk through the window. He could even recall the hug from Monica the day before, and Gopal's warning. He also remembered...

"Luka Vasilj," he said. "He was watching me. From the balcony upstairs."

Alvarez scribbled the name down, then leafed backwards through scrawl-covered pages. "He's the one you called me about last week, right?"

"I did?" Alvarez nodded. "Said he threatened you."

Frustration overcame pain for the first time that day. Alvarez could see it on his face.

"He's a pharmacist, right?" she queried.

"What? Uh – yeah, I think so. Why?"

She shrugged. "Well Pat, let's just say pharmacists aren't usually the type to try and hit people with bottles."

"Oh yeah?" Pat shot back. "And in your experience, how many people so far have you met who have been hit over the head with a bottle of whiskey?"

She paused. "Only two."

"Right. So my answer is the same. Luka Vasilj."

She nodded begrudgingly, then underlined it. "Anyone else?"

"Marek Mihok. Malik Wahba. Eric Van De Berg." Pat rattled off the names with confidence, but Alvarez didn't write them down. She sighed, and dropped the pen and pad on the table.

"Pat, I need you to be reasonable here. I know things have been tense in the building, since…you know…"

Pat did know. *Since Nadine had her throat cut.*

"…but you've got to level with me. It can't be at the point where you reasonably think all these people want to kill you."

"But they do!" Pat insisted. "Marek, just earlier in the week, he threatened me! And Luka – well, don't get me started!"

"If I ask you for who you think might want to hurt you, then I don't want to be hearing names of people currently locked up just down the hall," Alvarez said firmly. "Got it?"

Eric's still in custody. That rules him out.

"Got it?" Alvarez repeated.

Pat nodded. "Yes ma'am."

She picked up her pad again. "So, reasonably, who do you think might want to hurt you?"

"Marek Mihok and Luka Vasilj," Pat said firmly.

Alvarez's eyes rolled so far back in their sockets Pat was afraid they'd do a full turn.

"Seriously!"

"You said Marek threatened you?" she asked. "What did he say?"

"He…he told me, uh – not to "put myself in the line of fire," said Pat. "And that someone in the building was capable of murder!"

"Well, we know that," Alvarez scoffed. "You don't think that's good advice?"

"It's the way he said it!" snapped Pat. Her patronising tone was riling him up more than it should. *It's like she doesn't get it!* "It's collusion, Detective!"

She sighed. "And Luka? You said he was watching you?"

"Yep. From the top of the stairs tonight."

"And that's unusual?"

"Definitely."

She scribbled on her pad again. She had a line through Marek's name, but she'd underlined Luka's. He opened his mouth to protest, but she raised her pen to silence him.

"Anything else, Pat? I need to let you go, or your wife's going to have an embolism. I don't want to end up in the bed next door."

"One of Luka's associates," Pat fired back. "Gopal, I think his name is. I can't spell his last name. He said that I was 'playing dangerous games, with dangerous people'."

Alvarez scribbled 'Gopal,' with a few question marks, and then underlined Luka's name one more time.

"Well, you've certainly given me a place to start," she said. "Are you going to be going back to work any time soon?"

Damn fucking right I am.

*   *   *

And go back to work he did. Despite Karen's protests, despite her screams and cries, despite the routinely searing pain in the back of his skull that kept him awake every night, Pat went back to work. He didn't tell Karen about the unusually polite email he'd had from Joseph that had come in a few days earlier, telling him he could take a month off to recover. Instead, he shot a brief message back about how his mortgage wasn't going to pay itself. It wasn't about his mortgage. It wasn't about Larry's college fund. It was about vengeance. Someone who worked there had killed his friend.

And now, they'd tried to kill him too.

Whoever that was – and Pat had a few suspects in mind – he was going to find them. There were a few surprises upon Pat's return to the office, when he finally wrestled through the semi-frozen front door after fumbling with his keycard. A box of cupcakes from a local bakery – his favourite ones! – had been left on his desk. Joseph, who was leaving as Pat came in, even gave him a clap on the shoulder and a slight smile.

But the biggest surprise was the round of applause he received from the crowd in the lobby, awaiting his return. He saw Marek, Luka, Malik. He saw Catherine, Amy, Mateo, all standing there, clapping for him. Even Charlotte Van De Berg was lurking in the back with a slight smile. It was Marek who stepped forward to greet him, beaming.

Genuinely happy to see me?

"Glad to have you back, my friend," he said quietly as the crowd dispersed, amongst shouts of 'Welcome back, Pat!' and 'So good to have you here!'

Marek guided him over to his desk. Pat flopped into his chair as Lionel took advantage of the distraction to vanish out of the front door fifteen minutes early. Marek perched himself on the edge of the desk as the crowd departed.

"Can we let bygones be bygones?" Marek asked wistfully. "I know things have been tense around here, but I'm hoping this is all over now. Eric's locked up, it's all done."

As much as the surprise celebration had caught Pat off guard, that question was what made his jaw drop.

"It's over? Marek, someone attacked me. They put me in a coma. I could have died! What makes you think this is over?"

"Well, I thought that...since I am apologizing..." Pat whirled around to face him. He'd had *enough* of this man. "But you're not apologizing, are you? You're saying, 'lets leave it in the past'. No, 'I'm sorry, Pat'. No, 'I'm sorry for threatening you, Pat'. At the end of the day, you just don't want anymore drama. Good for you, I guess! But you're not the one who just got hit over the back of the head!"

His ire had drawn the gaze of Mateo, who was still lurking at the back of the lobby. He waved at him. "Everything's okay. You can get back to work. Nothing to see here."

Mateo offered a half-thumbs up, and hurried off.

Marek hopped off the desk and straightened himself up. "I'm sorry to hear you feel this way, Pat," he said, his voice a touch sour. "I was really hoping we could get back to being friends, but I guess not."

He vanished up the stairs, leaving Pat alone at his desk.

Was it too much of an overreaction? Should he want to leave this all behind?

Of course he did. But there was no way he was going to be able to do that without figuring out who had attacked him.

The first thing he did was check the security cameras. He raced back five days in the footage, and then sat to watch on double speed to see if anything was amiss. For the most part, the cameras caught his movements. He watched himself duck into the stairwell, fumbling with his cigarettes and then reappearing five minutes later, a little more pep in his stride. A while later, he saw himself go into the elevator.

That's me, going up to do my rounds.

He found himself maybe ten minutes later, on the third floor, and then he was back in the lobby. Then, off to the toilet. Then he saw it. A lone figure, creeping out of the darkness. They'd come down from the stairwell, and were clutching a bottle.

Definitely a man, too small to be a woman.

He watched the bottle in the man's right hand as he tiptoed– almost comically – across the lobby. He couldn't see their face – their back was to the camera, and the quality wasn't good enough to make out any details. And then, they disappeared into the darkness underneath the cameras.

Pat fiddled with the monitor, hoping that by some miracle that would change the angle of the camera, but no luck. He watched helplessly as his former self plopped down at the desk, oblivious to the threat behind him. And no less than ten seconds later, the figure reappeared.... ...and took an almighty swing at the back of Pat's head.

Glass exploded over the lobby. Pat slumped down, instantly unconscious, as a dark liquid started to pool on the desk, slowly dripping onto the floor. The figure vanished back into the stairwell.

In a matter of seconds, it was all over.

Pat rewatched those last ten seconds half a dozen times. He watched the figure creeping away on repeat, back up the stairs.

Is that a clue? Is he from the second floor, or the third? Or does he know there are cameras, and he's just trying to throw me off?

It was almost sickening. Pat watched over and over as his own image collapsed, lifeless, on the desk.

No way am I letting this go.

He clipped the footage using a little video editor that Joseph had shown him how to use, and flicked it off to Alvarez.

Found this on the cameras. Please find this guy!

He didn't want to sound desperate, but he really was. Through the course of the evening, he had subconsciously scooted his chair so far backwards so that he could almost lean his head on the glass of the front windows. After he realised that, he even pulled his desk – his sturdy, oak desk – back to join him. *No sneaking up on me now.*

But nobody did. It was a reasonably quiet night overall, until a few hours later, when Pat spotted something quite unexpected. Sal Whiteman appeared at the stairs, holding a box of personal possessions. It was a classic movie trope, but it happened for a reason – all the offices in the building used those same cardboard boxes, and most of the people who worked here didn't bring enough personal possessions to warrant anything larger. He could've been going away on a company trip, or for a little vacation, but the box was a tell-all that he'd been dismissed.

That, and the fact that Marek was standing at the top of the stairs, watching as Sal traipsed across the lobby and slammed his box of belongings onto the desk. Without a word to Pat, he pulled his ID card and lanyard out from his pocket and tossed it in Pat's direction, then snatched his box back up and shouldered his way through the front doors. Pat hit the button to open the front gate, and then glanced up at Marek. They stared each other down for a moment, until Marek turned on his heel and disappeared back into the dark.

It was unusual, to say the least. From the looks of things, this wasn't a friendly dismissal. Sal and Marek always seemed as close as close could be, so he must've done something serious. *Could it be about the IPO?* Pat wondered. *Has he fucked something up?*

His head still running a repeat analysis on who could have possibly attacked him, Pat went about his rounds a bit more carefully than usual. He stuck his head around corners before he stepped fully into view, and tried to check in on offices from far away before he got too close. The killer could be lurking in any one of them.

Malik was joined by a receptionist inside MedHealth tonight. Pat crossed paths with him twice on his first round. In the corridors outside Mihok &

Mihok, he heard the squeak of the loafers on the wood and caught the scent of a pungent cologne before they almost collided at the corner. On the fifth floor, Pat spotted him again leaving Microceuticals as he was passing by where Nadine had died. He walked quickly, his head down as he tapped away at his phone. When he caught sight of Pat, he waved. Pat didn't wave back.

In Mihok & Mihok, Marek was alone, seated squarely in Nadine's chair at the front desk. Pat caught sight of Catherine Kim and Mateo, working shoulder to shoulder inside Collymore & Donovan, and Monica was upstairs in her office, with a gorgeous young blonde who had arrived minutes after Pat had sat down for his shift. Pat could see the top of Charlotte Van De Berg's shoulders as he peered in closely through the windows of PubStunt...but her father was still nowhere to be seen. Presumably still under lock and key at the precinct...just like the mysterious Johnny Ray.

Would the fact that there had been another attack be a point towards Eric's innocence? Pat hoped so.

But no night could be quiet forever, and a storm was brewing under the illusion of a peaceful workplace. And at eleven o'clock, on his second round of the night, as Pat wandered past where he'd found Nadine almost two weeks ago, all hell broke loose.

CHAPTER 24

The scream came from Microceuticals. A rending, inhuman scream. Pat was, by chance, on the opposite side of the fifth floor, with a glass balcony and a hundred foot drop blocking his path. Could the killer have struck again? He did a quick mental inventory.

What have you got?

He had his taped-up walkie-talkie, his phone, his wallet. Downstairs, he had a very nice red button, providing it worked, and his torch, as well. Could be used as a bat, in a pinch. But he wasn't in the lobby. He was already on the scene.

You've got to move, Pat. This is your job.

He hustled across the parquet flooring, whipping out his phone, heart-rate skyrocketing.

Call Alvarez?

The thought crossed his mind as he glanced at the elevators, still on the ground floor. He'd taken the stairs up. Did he have time to go downstairs and hit the button? Hitting the button was protocol, calling 911 wasn't.

Who gives a fuck about protocol?! Someone's screaming in there!

Pat's body was on autopilot, his hand clammy around the phone and his torch as he raced over to Microceuticals and banged furiously on the frosted glass doors. He shoved his phone back in his pocket, and pulled the walkie-talkie from its clip on his belt. It had served him well just last week – but tonight he had all his fingers crossed that he wouldn't have to use it.

"Security!" he shouted. "Is everything alright in there?"

Nothing. Dead quiet in the night. It was almost eerie, in a way, for such a violent scream to be followed by silence.

It was a woman, right? Amy? But could it have been a man? Do men scream like that?

Pat pulled on the door. It was locked. Only one scream. Somebody could be in danger.

With adrenaline pumping through his body, Pat had a brainwave. He whipped out his phone and pulled up his internet browser. As it loaded, he tried peering through the frosted glass again. Nothing. No movement inside, just the sterile glow of the white light from the back lab.

Pat punched MICROCEUTICALS into the search bar. Their website came up, along with a few phone numbers. He scanned the list. Manhattan Office. He pressed on the number and hit the green button. The rings seemed to last an eternity. Pat rattled the door again in the meantime, praying that some divine power was watching over him and had chosen to unlock it to grant him passage. No dice.

Eventually, the voicemail kicked in. A female voice – not Amy's. "Welcome to Microceuticals, the world's leading Biotech–" Pat rang off. No time for voice messages.

He peered through the window again. Still nothing. The glass was solid, reinforced. Not just the door, but the whole five panels that made up the front of the office. The handle had been repaired since Johnny had broken in, with the middle pane of glass looking brand new, slightly more frosted than the others. They've probably replaced the whole door. He rattled it, looking for a weak point, but nothing stood out.

You've got to go in. It's your job.

He thought of Alvarez again. If he called her, she could be here in five, ten minutes? Or if he went back down to the lobby, the cops could be here in five... ...if the button worked.

Five minutes is a long time.

Pat hurried down the hallway, one goal in mind. He needed something heavy. Something that could break through the glass. And there was exactly one item on this floor, and on every floor, that he could use.

Thanks to Joseph, the fire extinguishers were checked and replaced on schedule; once a year, every year. Pat had never had to use one, but getting it out of the case by the elevators was simple enough. He wrenched the cabinet open, and hefted the large cylinder off the wall. It was a large one, took two hands to carry, and was so heavy it could've been filled with concrete.

He stumbled back down the hallway, puffing breathlessly, and dumped it in front of the frosted glass door.

"Hello?!" he shouted one more time. "I'll have to break the door down!" No answer.

That's their final warning, buddy. You've got to go in.

And so, with all his might, Pat hefted the fire extinguisher up onto his shoulder, took a few steps back, and charged at the front door.

* * *

Pat had aimed for the handle, at waist height. He was hoping he'd be able to break it off the door, then open up and make his way inside, but physics had other ideas. The moment the extinguisher made contact, with its own weight and all of Pat's behind it, the door simply detonated.

Glass exploded in every direction, tiny shards of it flying towards Pat's face. The extinguisher slipping from his hands, Pat closed his eyes and mouth instinctively, raising his arms to cover his face as best he could, but the perilously sharp shards skated through the gaps in his arm and skittered over his nose and cheekbones.

And at that moment, all the lights on the floor went out, plunging his surroundings into darkness.

It was a simple protection system. The electronic circuit breaker would've detected the door shattering, with the general idea being that if there was a hurricane or some other natural disaster like an earthquake, all the power to the floor would off and an alarm would be sounded at Pat's desk. If Pat was around to see it, this was his chance to press the red button and call the police as necessary, or the fire department if it was a natural disaster. Johnny had gotten around that by not actually damaging the door, and just the handle.

Step one. Now get inside and help!

With tiny rivulets of blood streaming down his face, Pat picked his way through the broken glass and stumbled over the fire extinguisher to find himself in the foyer. He hadn't thought about the lights going out, but at least the light of the moon was giving him enough to work with in here. He figured he'd get through to the lab – surely that was where the scream had come from – and take it from there.

But now, in the pitch darkness, he was fumbling his way through the foyer, groping for the reception desk that he could see in his mind's eye. He found it, the marble cold in his hands.

"Hello?" he called again. Thankfully, there was no fancy digital lock on the door to the lab. He'd noticed that last time he'd come in.

That's probably why they're so particular about their privacy.

The glass crunching under his feet, he fumbled for the door handle. It wriggled underneath his fingertips as he tripped over something. A box? A footstool? It could've been anything, but whatever it was, he kicked it out of his way and yanked the door open.

A cold breeze hit him as he entered. The first thing he noticed was the smell. There was obviously a diffuser or something similar in the foyer, because he noticed a distinct lack of it in here. It smelled like plastic and sweat. The door swung shut behind him, and then the light of the moon was no more.

The Microceuticals lab; the sacred space, with a million dollar mystery, was plunged into complete darkness.

Pat wished he had his torch with him.

"Luka?" Pat called out. "Are you here? Amy? Gopal?"

No response. Only silence.

Pat tried to recall what he'd seen when he was in here the other day, tried to visualise the space.

What did it look like?! The big machine, that was in the far corner. Tables – got to watch out for them. *Don't trip over anything.* Scalpels, test tubes, everywhere. Scalpels on the walls. Other than that...

The doors. The two large doors in fact, on adjacent walls. Not quite opposite to where he was now – but if he turned slightly to his right, they'd be dead ahead of him, behind a sea of tables.

Pat started forward, and immediately broke his first rule. His left hand swiped across the plane of a bench as he groped through the darkness, sending something small and metallic clattering across the stainless steel, which was then followed by the sounds of small plastic bouncing off the tiled floor. Taking another tentative step forward, he felt something small – a test tube? – crunch under his feet.

Destroying company property? Tsk, tsk.

He pressed on quicker, crashing into the first table and sending it spinning away from him. More plastic and glass toppled as he pushed past a second one and found a third. Then, his arm was caught in some sort of tubing, and he wrenched it free, sending what sounded like a tower of glass crashing to the ground. He crunched through one, two, three pieces of fallen glassware and his boots sent something metal skittering across the room as he found the wall, and the side of the huge scanning machine.

Okay. Door's on your right.

It surprised him that there was no emergency lighting in here. At this stage, he was hoping that he would end up in a conference room with some lamps, but he couldn't see anything under the doors.

Nonetheless, as he fumbled his way along the wall, he groped up and down, trying desperately to find a light switch. Nothing. He found a handle. The first door. He yanked, but it didn't yield.

Locked. *Fuck.*

Well, onto the next.

And then things took a turn. As Pat stepped forward a little too quickly, his feet hit something slippery on the tiles. Within seconds, as he twirled backwards, his bulk pitched downwards, and in the darkness, he almost couldn't tell which way was up. His walkie-talkie – his only weapon – sailed from his grip. But he landed on his back...

...on something soft. He felt the slick substance on the floor pooling beneath his calves, and as that awful familiar smell crept up his nose, it didn't take a genius to figure out what had broken his fall.

Pat was alone in the darkness.

Cuddling with a dead body.

*   *   *

Fear gripped Pat, fear like he'd never known before. He tried to scramble up, but the blood beneath his feet wouldn't let him get a good footing. Collapsing back onto the body, he gagged violently and rolled himself off it...

...landing on his stomach, in the pool of liquid.

Getting ever more desperate, his hands slick with the blood of an unknown victim, Pat groped wildly for something– –and his fingers found plastic. His walkie-talkie. It brought him back to the moment as he stuck his hands into the warm liquid and pushed himself up to his knees, then struggled to his feet.

The warm liquid.

It's still warm.

This only just happened.

Now Pat really needed his torch. His fight or flight kicked into overdrive, like someone had just switched his Netflix onto high definition. He knew exactly how to get back to the door. Not wasting a minute, he twirled around and beelined for the exit, sliding expertly between the two benches without anymore glass casualties. He found the door and wrenched it open– –to be greeted by a brilliant moonlight.

Pat's mind whirred. Who the fuck is dead on the floor? He looked back into the lab, but it was as black as pitch and he couldn't even see the body behind the tables, let alone make an identification. Meanwhile, blood was coating him, so thick and warm that his shirt was glued to his chest. His hands and knees were coated.

You're in danger.

The anxiety surged again, and Pat found himself frantically ripping at his shirt, just trying to get away, get away from the death.

Okay, so somebody's dead. What now?

Somehow, in the chaos of the last few minutes, Pat's adrenaline-fuelled brain had managed to come up with a plan. He booked it over to the elevators, still tearing at his shirt, tossing it to one side. The air conditioning stung at his chest through his undershirt as he pounded on the elevator button. The longest wait in history. But finally, he was in the lobby, at his desk.

This, this is where I've got control.

First, he hit the red button.

Nothing happened.

He hit it again. And again, and again and again.

Nothing.

He whipped his phone back out and desperately scrolled for Alvarez's number, his blood-stained fingers smearing across the screen. She might be asleep.

But didn't she say she lives just around the corner?

Pat dumped the walkie-talkie on his desk and rummaged through the mounds of paperwork in his desk as the phone rang on speaker, digging desperately for his flashlight. He flicked it on, and the bright beam of light burst across the dim lobby. *Great, still works. Now what?*

"You have reached Detective Sofia Alvarez. If this call is an emergency, please call..." Pat hung up, and dialed 911. No time for voicemails. Phone pressed to his ear, he clipped his walkie-talkie back to his belt and snatched up the torch, bee-lining back for the elevators, heart pounding. His feet were sticky on the tile floor, and he glanced backwards to see that he was leaving a trail of bloody footprints in his wake.

Pick up. Please fucking pick up.

"NYPD dispatch on the line. What's your address?"

"Guinness House, I'm at Guinness House!" Pat cried, stumbling into the elevator. "I– I think that someone– I think someone's been hurt. Please, please get here quickly!"

"Yes, sir, we're going to do our best to help you out here, okay? Can you stay on the line with me?"

The elevator doors closed, and the big metal box shot skywards...

...and Pat could hear only static on the line.

*   *   *

Of all the things that happened that night, the one thing Pat would never admit to anyone but himself was why he didn't call the police back.

Well, I've already called Alvarez.

Well, I gave them my address, they know where I am!

Getting them back on the phone is only going to slow things down!

What if someone else is in trouble?! I need to be there to help?

No, there was another reason that he didn't call 911 for a second time that night. Because this wasn't just about somebody being hurt.

This was deeply personal. They'd rattled him. Marek and Luka, they'd gotten under his skin. Made it look like he couldn't do his job; like he wasn't worth anything. They'd made him feel worthless.

Tonight, I will show them what I'm worth.

On the fifth floor, there was a dead body. The second body on that floor in less than a fortnight. Pat's second dead body in less than a fortnight. If he couldn't stop this, and stop this now, he'd lose his job. He'd lose his income, he'd lose his insurance. He'd probably lose Karen.

All over, red rover.

That's why he had to do it himself. The voicemail Pat had left Alvarez and the address he'd given cops gave him a little comfort, but fear abounded.

However, as the elevator doors opened into Pat's own personal hellscape, focus and determination seemed to take over. Somewhere in his head, a little voice was giggling.

We knew this wasn't over, didn't we?! We fucking knew it!

The torch flickered wildly along the walls as he strode down the corridor, dodging his blood-stained shirt on the floor, pausing for just a moment outside Microceuticals to collect himself. Time to get a win. He stepped inside, the torch in his right hand, the walkie-talkie in his left.

"Hey!" he shouted into the void, his voice surprisingly fierce. "If there's anyone here, show yourselves!"

The only answer he got was a slight echo, not that he'd expected anything more than that. He picked his way through the broken glass and marched into the lab, the recycled air enveloping him once again.

The lab door swung shut, sealing him in, and anxiety threatened to take over.

Calm down, Pat. What can you see? The light of the torch glanced through the darkness. It was too weak to illuminate the whole space, but it was much like he'd remembered it from when he'd let himself in the other day, except for the torrent of destruction Pat had left in his recent wake. Beakers, test tubes and colanders were strewn about on the floor. The tiles were a sea of broken glass, and the desks were askew, with just enough space for his bulk to move between them. More pressingly, as Pat flicked his torch over to near the doors, he could see the ominous dark red pool on the floor. His heart caught in his mouth, and he whipped the torch back in front of him.

For Nadine, Pat.

His breath quickening, Pat picked his way through the beakers he'd shattered and around the desks. Although it was dark, he squinted ahead with half-closed eyes, terrified of what – or who – he might find.

But as he peered over the desk, it wasn't what he could see that racked him with fear. It was what he couldn't. The blood was pooled by the doorways, thick and viscous, seeping under the benches, but the body, the body that Pat had fallen onto…

…the body was gone.

Fear struck Pat like a lightning bolt.

Someone's moved the body.

His eyes – and torch – flicked to the doors, and then back to the blood. There was a huge smear across the floor, and it took Pat moments to piece it together.

The body, the body that he'd fallen on before, had been dragged…

…through the first door.

The door that had been locked when he'd first tried it.

Pat racked his brains. While most of these offices were custom built spaces, the general layout and arrangement of the offices was similar from floor to floor. Right now, for instance, Pat was a few floors above Collymore & Donovan, likely directly above where he'd had his conversation with Johnny, the day after the murder. But, while Collymore & Donovan had a tremendous office space, this lab was a bit smaller. It had been sectioned off, cut in half, in a way.

But why?

Almost certainly, one of the doors was Luka's office. That would make the most sense. Even though he reportedly spent all his time in the lab, he'd have to have a space to do his paperwork, send emails.

Pat flicked his torch over the desks. Just scalpels and test tubes – and broken glass. No laptops out here.

Okay, so one of the doors is his office. And the other one?

Another lab, maybe. Or a conference room or lounge, more likely. They had people up here from time to time. Donors, sponsors, hell – even girlfriends and partners. There had to be a general place where they'd congregate, otherwise there'd be nowhere to bring them.

There was no light from under either of the doors. Pat flicked his torch up from the floor, conscious of the fact that it might be giving away his position if it was reflecting off the trail of blood. He crept over to the first door and pressed his ear up against it. It creaked slightly against his weight.

Nothing. Just the cold paint against the side of his face. Wiping his brow, he crept over to the second door and gently tested the handle. This one didn't spring back like the first one had. Unlocked.

He knew what was behind the first door; it was the end. It had the answers. It would show him who was truly behind this mess, once and for all, and that person would suffer the consequences of his wrath for manipulating him for so long.

But Pat needed a minute. And more than that, he wasn't sure that a torch and a walkie-talkie were going to cut it if it came down to a fistfight…

…particularly if there were two men in that room.

And so, with his heart pounding, he gently cracked the door open to see what was inside.

The lights were off in here as well. The torch showed him a long corridor with a low ceiling, and what looked to be a desk, maybe twenty feet away. Pat stepped through the doorway, peering into the darkness.

The medical smell of the lab almost immediately disappeared, replaced by the aftermath of sweat and cologne. Pat crept down the corridor, leaving the door to the lab open behind him. Plush carpet sank beneath his feet as he ducked beneath a low-hanging ceiling light and moved into the open space.

It was an office. A large mahogany desk dominated the space, swamped under piles upon piles of paperwork, some of them higher than Pat's head. He spotted a lamp, and tried to turn it on, but it didn't work. Priorities, Pat.

You need a weapon.

Pat groped around the desk in the light of his dying torch, ripping open drawers to find something, anything that might be of help.

He felt something cold and metallic, extracted it, and examined it in the light. A staple gun. It was a heavy unit – maybe three pounds – with a little inbuilt handle so as Pat could wrap his whole fist around it. He swapped the torch over to his left hand and weighed up the stapler in his right, swinging a soft punch to get an idea of its weight. It wasn't perfect, but it was heavy, and felt better than his walkie-talkie, so he clipped the latter back onto his belt and edged back down the corridor.

He reversed his grip on the torch so that the light was pointing out the bottom of his fist and lit the path ahead of him. He'd seen that in the movies sometimes. The torch had a heavy handle – heavy enough to hurt – and this way, he could swing it straight down off his shoulder and whoever he hit would get the butt of it.

Pat stepped back into the lab, tiptoed through the spreading pool of blood, and stopped just short of the door. His phone was sweaty against his thigh, a gentle reminder that he could just back out, that he could wait for help.

I'm done waiting.

With the blood creeping up his shoes, he gripped the handle of the first door and tested it again.

Still unlocked.

Pat pulled it open.

Showtime.

*   *   *

The door swung shut behind him, and the latch clicked into place. Pat used his flashlight to track the smear of blood.

This room was like a mirror version of the office – a hallway, opening up into a dark space at the end. He flicked his torch up briefly, and caught sight of half of a large meeting table and a few chairs, the rest of which stretched down around the corner, before realising something.

The light gives me away.

They were in here with him. This was their last refuge. He felt like he was heading into Thunderdome, from Mad Max.

Two men enter, one man leaves.

Pat lingered in the doorway, listening intently. For a split second, his mind flashed to Karen – his love, his life – who was currently unaware of the significant danger that he was in.

God, she's going to kill me.

He crept forward. He could hear the squelch of the blood-soaked carpet under his shoes. He hunched over slightly, as though that would obscure his massive bulk. Beads of sweat trickled down his cheeks, and as his pulse pounded in his ears, he felt the wound on the back of his head prickling. He reached the corner. Jump round it? Charge at them? He knew they were in there, probably lurking down the other end of the room.

Should I say something?

"I know you're in here." His voice trembled slightly. "I know what you've done. The police are on their way." He paused for a second, listening. "I don't know what this is all about, but if it's all gotten out of hand, I can help. There are people who can help. But you need to come forward." Not all of that was strictly true, of course. Yes, there were people who could help them if they did come forward, but Pat wasn't clueless. He knew very well what this was all about. The pieces were all there – it just took a bit of stitching together. But most of it had clicked when he was in the elevator on his way up here.

I know what's going on.

Nadine was purportedly receiving treatment for her disease and getting a referral kick. Except it wasn't a referral kick – it was blackmail. Nadine had been referring people for years, according to Malik. These trials have been going on for eighteen months. When asked about the money, he'd said that she was getting paid from the beginning. But it wasn't paid from the get-go; Karen had said Nadine had only received three lump-sum payments in the last three months. Nadine was bringing them clients, and in return, she thought she was getting the drug.

But she was still getting sick. Bringing them all the business they need, but still getting sick.

She was on the placebo, Malik had said.

Nadine gets mad. Pat could see it now; she wasn't one to back down without getting what she wanted. But they wouldn't give her the drug.

So she insists on money instead.

Blackmail. Or was it extortion? Pat didn't know the difference, but it was immaterial. They give her money, she keeps quiet. Karen had said that she'd been sending that money out the very next day. Two different accounts. Pat would bet his salary that those transfers were going to her family; maybe even Mateo, if they were serious. A nice little tidy sum, to help out the people she loved after she died. Mateo's new watch. *Blood money,* he'd said. Quite literally.

So they'd killed her. Maybe her demands were becoming too expensive, or maybe they didn't like having a sick person front and centre of their new trials. They'd been fighting about it. Nadine, arguing with Luka on the night she died – that's what Monica had said. She had become troublesome.

Best to make her disappear.

With the amount of money hovering around this drug, they'd be trying to tie up every loose end they could.

Now it's time to tie up my loose ends.

Pat took one more step forward, and then Larry's face flashed into his mind's eye. He hesitated. *What if something happens to me? How is he ever going to go to college?*

That moment of hesitation was all it took.

He heard them before he saw them. A rustle to his right, the shorter end of the conference room, then something tore through the space and collided with him at full force! Hands clutched at his face, nails raked at his skin as Pat stumbled backwards, the smell of a woody cologne filling his nostrils as his flashlight flew from his hands in a theatrical whirl. The momentum took them both backwards, with Pat's bulk bouncing off a sharp cabinet as gravity fought to take him and his attacker to the floor. He struggled to right himself, desperately flailing with the staple gun, but his attacker held him tight around the chest and Pat's swings met nothing but air. A fist hit him in the stomach, once– twice– three times – and Pat whirled desperately, drawing his arms tight to his chest to protect himself. Then, a hand grasped at his hair and the pain at the back of his skull burst into life.

Desperate for respite, Pat swung again, staple gun leading the way, and his wrist jolted as the open edge of the gun swept along skin and bone.

"FUCK!"

The attacker stumbled away with a guttural roar, cursing under his breath. His voice was familiar, but Pat couldn't place it.

Marek? Luka? It's got to be one of you.

Just the two of them. *Dancing in the dark.* Pat squared up like a boxer, as light as he could possibly be on his toes, the staple gun his last line of defence as he wheezed for air. His stomach was smarting from the punches, and the back of his head felt like it was on fire, but his adrenaline kept him on his feet.

"Come on!" he bellowed. "You tried to get rid of me, and you fucked it up! Let's try it again!"

He heard the footsteps, and he felt the rush of air as a precursor to full contact. Pat sidestepped, flattening his back against the wall which separated him from the lab, and he could practically smell the fist that swung past his nose.

"Try again!" he bellowed, taking a huge step forward and swinging the staple gun. It scythed through the air, a whoosh in the quiet. He heard heavy breathing, a few feet to his right.

A woody scent passed his nose. The cologne again.

This guy wasn't anticipating a brawl.

Pat squared up again, adrenaline pumping. It was the fight of his life. He knew it, and the other guy knew it. One of them wasn't leaving here alive, and this guy had reason enough to want to bury Pat for good.

But Pat was doing it for Nadine. In the dark, fighting for his life, and her memory.

Then, Pat took a step forward, and it all went wrong. His foot caught on something. Something big, something heavy.

The body.

Pat stumbled forward, but then his other foot caught it as well, and he was careening through space, arms flailing wildly, the staple gun sailing from his grip. His left cheek glanced off something sharp and hard – the corner of the table? – and his neck snapped backwards violently as his back buckled.

For the second time that night, Pat landed flat on his stomach, on top of a dead body.

The wetness oozed through his undershirt. A flurry of movement above him, and a boot thudded into the side of Pat's face. It felt like a thundercrack in his jaw, and Pat felt his teeth rearranging themselves in his mouth as he desperately rolled over, hands reaching towards the sky as the wound in the back of his skull seared as a reminder of the damage he'd already taken.

His attacker fell on top of him and hit him with a heavy hand, square in his nose. Pat felt it crack, felt the warm blood on his face, tasted the metallic edge at the back of his throat…as they hit him again.

Then, they hit him harder, right in the side of the head. Karen and Larry's faces clouded Pat's vision as the blows kept coming, raining down furiously on his skull.

This is the end.

Then Pat's world went black.

CHAPTER 25

Pain, again.

Violent, unrelenting pain, shooting down from the back of his skull as Pat regained consciousness. His left cheek was smarting from where he'd hit it on the table. His neck was stiff, the muscles in spasm. Like a wounded seal, he gasped through his mouth for air, his nose a mess of coagulated blood and broken cartilage.

When he opened his eyes, there was light. Dim light, but light nonetheless. A candle, burning in the middle of the table, illuminating the room. He was sat on a chair – no, he was strapped to a chair – at the conference table. Zip ties were tight around his forearms, anchoring his wrists to the arms of the chair. He tried to stand, but his legs had received the same treatment.

I can't move.

His staplegun had been set on the table in front of him, caked in blood, and the torch – turned off – next to it. And right behind his chair...

...was the body. Fear surging through every pore of his body, Pat craned his neck to see who it was.

Who was their next victim?

In a crisp blue suit, with blood pooling from a gaping wound in his chest, Pat saw the face of possibly the last man he would expect, dead in the conference room.

Marek Mihok.

His eyes – obscured by his old-fashioned spectacles – stared up at the ceiling, frozen in time. His skin looked pallid and cold, and his mouth was open – in shock, maybe?

In a pool of his own blood, he looked just like Nadine. Defenseless. Alone. Pat's instinct was to jump on him, to protect him from any more danger. That was his job, after all; to protect those who couldn't protect themselves. To keep people safe.

A little too late for that.

Pat felt the vomit rise in his throat before he could so much as take a breath, and then, with Marek's dead eyes watching, his chest tightened and he vomited violently across the conference table. Unable to breathe through his nose, Pat gasped for air through the taste of digested Doritos.

The back of his head throbbed relentlessly; another reminder that this guy really, really wanted him dead.

"He's awake."

The voice came from the other end of the conference table. Pat struggled to turn in his seat, straining to see who it was.

And then, through the dim light of the candle, a face faded into view.

A familiar face.

The face of a man that Pat had seen around the building more times than he could count. The face of a man who he thought to be quiet and nonthreatening…but tonight, was covered in blood from his recent brawl.

Gopal Tendulkar was wiping at his face with tissues. The edge of the staple gun had opened half of his face, the deep gash running from his cheekbone down past his lips. Blood dripped persistently onto the pale wood of the desk. They watched each other for a moment, the dim candlelight flickering across Gopal's face. His expression was wrought with fury; eyes narrow, lips thin, nostrils flaring.

And then the man he was talking to stepped out of the shadows. The gentle flame of the candle made him look like a monster. Pat heard that familiar squeak that he'd heard so many times before.

The squeak of expensive loafers.

Malik Wahba stared down Pat with his deep brown eyes, his white coat hanging loosely from his shoulders.

Pat felt like he couldn't breathe. "You...piece of shit."

Malik took a seat opposite him, in front of the television, on the long edge of the conference table. He drummed his fingers on the wood. "I beg your pardon?"

"You're a fucking asshole," Pat hissed. "I should've seen this from the start. I should've seen you were behind this. Only two people can prescribe that drug of yours." He jerked his head at Gopal. "And who's this, your little lapdog?"

Gopal snarled at him. "You're dead, you fat fuck. You've caused way too much trouble for one lifetime." He turned to Malik. "We've got to get rid of him."

Malik held up a hand, shushing him. Gopal fell quiet, tending to his wounds.

"Where are the cops?" asked Malik.

"Gone," Gopal sighed. "Took some convincing, though. I told them I'd made a mistake. Thought someone was in the building. They wanted to come in…can you imagine that?"

"No evidence?"

"Blood in the lab. And the lobby. Wiped up."

Malik sighed with relief. "Did anyone hear the commotion?"

Gopal shook his head. "They've all gone home. I checked." Malik nodded. "Good." He steepled his hands on the table.

"Do you want some ice?" he asked. "For your face?"

What the fuck?

"What, doctor first, murderer second?" Pat spat. The flexicuffs were biting in so deep around his wrists he feared – hoped? – they might just snap.

"Yeah, you know what? Get me some rash cream for my wrists, while you're at it. Oh, and could you untie me? That'd be swell." Malik sighed, and shook his head. Gopal was wearing a triumphant smirk, but the doctor looked worn out.

"It shouldn't have come to this," he sighed. "But….all a means to an end, I guess." Pat stared him down, not daring himself to blink.

"Why, Pat?" Malik asked. He looked genuinely concerned, exasperated. "Why….why wouldn't you just, fuck, off?"

That set Pat off again. He felt the rage building inside his chest.

"YOU KILLED MY FRIEND!" he bellowed, arching forward in his chair, the flexicuffs straining to hold him in place, Malik's face only inches from his own as spittle flew from between his teeth. "YOU KILLED HER! AND THEN YOU KILLED HIM AS WELL!"

Gopal jumped to his feet, about ready to silence him, but Malik waved his hand again as Pat slumped against the back of his chair, the cuffs holding strong. "Nobody can hear us. It's all soundproofed in here."

Whether or not that was true, Pat didn't plan on going quietly.

They might have called the cops off, but someone…someone must know he was here, mustn't they?!

"So where's your boss?" he fired at Gopal. "He's the man behind all of this, isn't he?" He glanced over at Marek's lifeless corpse. "Didn't think he had it in him to kill his best friend, though."

Gopal snorted. "Oh, Pat. You really have no idea what's going on here, do you?"

"Oh, I don't know all the players yet," Pat hissed, "but I know the game. You've invented some fucking wonder-drug, and he−," he jerked his restrained thumb at Malik, "−is going to be the one to sell it. Nadine was meant to be in on the trial, but you gave her the placebo. She's been referring you clients. So what, she threatens to pull them out? Says she won't bring you anyone else? You pay her off so she keeps it quiet, keeps bringing you people. But then she starts asking for more. She has a fight with Luka about it. Only one way to get rid of her at that point."

Gopal scoffed, but Malik was grinning inanely.

"So what then?" he asked, his tone rife with condescension. "What does little Patrick think happened next?"

"You killed her," said Pat. "Either one of you two, or Luka. Can't have anything disrupting the trial, right? That's what you said to me?"

Malik smirked. Pat could tell he was getting a kick out of this.

"So one of us did it?" Malik asked, holding his hands up above his shoulders. "Don't look at me. I've got nothing to hide."

Pat glanced at Gopal. "Then it was you. Or Luka."

"Luka's a fucking moron," Gopal hissed. "And a coward."

"It was you, then."

"No." Another voice, from the corner. "It was me."

Eyes wide, Pat turned.

Amy Morales stepped out from the darkness.

*　　*　　*

She was the one who screamed. She screamed when they killed Marek.

"Be a good time to have a tape recorder, wouldn't it, Pat?" Malik was grinning as Amy ambled over to the table, slumping down in a seat. "You're about to get a signed confession! God, she's been dying to tell someone. Hasn't shut up about it."

Pat gazed into Amy's eyes, full of sorrow…

…and something else.

That's what Pat had seen when she was looking at him the other night. It wasn't fear, or apprehension.

It was regret.

She sat down next to Malik, and dropped a scalpel on the desk in front of him.

"Thanks, darling, but you keep that," Malik cooed, sliding the scalpel to the side. Then to Gopal, "God, it's good having her as an errand girl, isn't it?"

This wasn't the Malik that Pat had seen before. It wasn't the kind, big-hearted, muscly jock that he'd seen floating around the building. This was the next layer, the underneath.

He's insane.

"What….what-?" Pat stammered, his mind completely unable to wrap around what Amy would be doing here. He glanced back at Gopal, and then at Malik, their faces smug masks of knowing something that he didn't.

"Should we let you two talk it out, or…?" Malik asked.

Amy bowed her head, shaking it almost imperceptibly. When she looked up at Pat, he could see tears in her eyes. "I didn't want to do it," she whimpered. "I really didn't. But...she was about to blow the whole thing wide open."

Amy Morales, ladies and gentleman.

Pat was flabbergasted.

"Why? Why, Amy?" "Nadine...Nadine was our test subject," Amy explained. "She was the trial, for Hydroxy. We...we met her by chance. A pure, single stroke of luck that she worked here, and for Marek, too. We saw her most days, in the lab. By the end of it, she was crucial to the success of the project...so we started paying her."

"Story time!" cawed Malik.

Pat ignored him. "Because she brought other patients along?" he asked.

Amy looked confused. She glanced at Gopal – and then at Malik, who chuckled ruefully.

"Ah, I've been meaning to tell you about that", he smiled. "Pat caught me in a tight spot. Had to come up with a tiny, teensy white lie to throw him off the scent." He turned his gaze to Pat, and his voice turned to steel. "That's what happens when you go rifling through people's bank statements, Patrick. You find things you aren't meant to find...things that are much too big for that tiny brain of yours."

I'll put my goddamn torch through your tiny fucking brain, asshole.

Amy shook her head. "There were no friends," she said. "There were never any friends."

Other patients. Where were the other patients?

Pat was frozen in his chair.

If they're doing thousands of clinical trials...why haven't I ever seen a patient?

The money.

The secrecy.

The funding it would cost to run a clinical trial.

It took a moment for Pat...but then it clicked. Malik saw the realisation on his face.

"Look, look!" he shouted, pointing excitedly. "He's getting it!"

Pat ignored him, addressing Amy alone. "There never were any clinical trials, were there?" he said. "You were paying Nadine, because she knew that. You were paying her off to keep her quiet."

"It's a bingo!" roared Malik, hooting with laughter.

Gopal shot him a look of disdain from the corner, shaking his head as he continued to wipe at the gash in his face.

If Malik had been trying to make Pat feel small before, all it took was the truth.

How could I have missed it?

Everything was run out of the building. Malik had even told him that. Clinical trials took months, cost millions of dollars – even Pat knew that much – but more than anything, they required people.

There had to be subjects. And Pat hadn't let in any subjects.

Any at all.

"You faked your paperwork," he said, shaking his head. "You faked it all. The trials. So you could sell the product. She wasn't on a placebo, referring friends. She was everything to you. Your little experiment." He swallowed. "And she was going to go public with that. So you killed her."

Amy swallowed. "We had to."

Not convincing.

"Why?" Gopal spoke up, his voice icy. "Because unfortunately, the pharmaceutical industry doesn't cater to slow breakthroughs, no matter how seismic they may be."

"Our funding is about to run out," Amy continued. "We need the IPO to go through. Without it, we're dust. We didn't have time to conduct a full set of trials. It would've taken years."

"So that's what Luka and Nadine were arguing about, huh?"

The three of them traded glances.

Maybe they didn't know.

And then something else clicked for Pat.

Despite the restraints on his wrists, despite the fact that he was helpless in a soundproof room in an unattended building in the middle of the night, and his final minutes were likely coming…

…he giggled. He'd figured it out. Finally, Pat, you genius. You cracked it! They stared him down as he grinned inanely, his mind piecing it all together.

Nadine was getting sicker.

Their only test subject was getting sicker.

If there are no proper trials, then why would they have someone on a placebo?

"She wasn't threatening to go public with the fact there were no trials," Pat chuckled. "No, that wouldn't bother her, if…if the drug actually worked, right?"

Malik's face was like thunder.

"But it doesn't, does it?" Pat asked. "Your miracle drug doesn't even work!"

*   *   *

Amy seemed to take Pat's realisation as a personal insult.

"How dare you!" she spat, her face knotted up with fury.

"Nadine was getting sicker!" Pat roared back. "That's why she left Eric! Marek noticed it, Eric noticed it! So you promise her a cure, right? She gets close, figures out there hasn't even been any proper trials done. But that doesn't matter, because you've promised her it works! Oh, 'it works, Nadine, it works!' And you pay her a little cash under the table to keep your filthy secrets!"

"It does work!" Amy was face to face with him now. "Every drug has kinks, you halfwit! Kinks that we could push through if someone just hired a few more staff members. I have to work on the fucking front desk!"

Yep. I could see her killing someone.

It wasn't until that moment that Pat realised he was actually looking face to face with the person who had killed his friend. Fury welled up in his chest.

"So what?!" he shouted. "You killed a woman? For this?!"

"No!" she shouted back defensively. Then she glanced at Malik.

Pat understood.

This isn't about money for one. It's about money for two.

"He's going to split it with you!" he shouted, flailing so violently in his chair that he went airborne. "You didn't do this to help people! It's all about the money! Three parts!"

Amy's lips were so thin they were white. She looked like she was about to cry. Pat had hit the nail on the head.

However she wants to sell this, she's in it for the fucking money.

So was Malik. Gopal…he wasn't so sure about.

"What about Luka?" he said. "Where's he in all this?"

They traded glances, as though unsure of how much information to share. Malik shrugged. Gopal rolled his eyes. Finally, Amy spoke up.

"Luka has no part in this," she said, flatly. "But…I think he'd understand why we went to such lengths. He wants this as much as we do."

Pat was flummoxed. "He doesn't know his own drug doesn't work?" he asked, incredulous. Amy shrugged. "We're his research team. We do the hard yards. He takes care of other stuff in the office. Funding, applications, meet and greets. He's the CEO, not a lab rat."

The CEO of what appeared to be the hottest pharmaceutical drug on the planet right now wasn't even aware that his drug didn't work. Pat was shocked, to say the least. But other than that…things were started to make a little more sense.

Pat glanced at Marek's body, then at Malik. "Weren't you all friends? College roommates, or something?"

Malik shrugged. "Yeah?"

Pat couldn't believe his audacity. "You killed your friend?"

"Oh no," Malik replied. "He did it." He jerked his thumb at Gopal, who stiffened.

"Should we really be talking to him about these sorts of things?" Gopal's voice was icy.

"Oh, don't fret," Malik chuckled. "He won't be around to tell anyone."

Pat's blood ran cold.

They're going to kill me.

"Isn't it nice?" Malik continued, his beady eyes glittering in the candlelight, "Isn't it just really nice to have a frank conversation for once?"

Amy looked the opposite of nice. She looked positively horrified.

Pat saw her look down at the scalpel in front of her, and then right into his eyes.

And they're going to want her to do it.

A bell delayed Pat's inevitable execution – his phone buzzing in his pocket. All attention snapped his way.

"Answer it," Gopal barked. Malik shushed him again, and Gopal's expression soured even further – if that was possible.

"I'm the one giving the orders around here," Malik snapped. Then, to Pat; "Answer it."

"I can't," Pat said through gritted teeth.

Gopal abandoned his tissues momentarily and patted Pat down, finally finding the phone in his pocket.

Caller ID: Detective Alvarez.

Pat had saved her number in his phone. Mistake. If he hadn't saved it, maybe they wouldn't have known. Malik's eyes narrowed as Gopal showed him the screen.

"Why's she calling?" he asked. "Did you call her?"

Pat said nothing. The phone rang insistently. Gopal snatched up the scalpel and gesticulated wildly, his breath hot and heavy on Pat's face.

"Answer him!"

"Yeah, okay! I called her. I called her before. When I heard the scream."

Gopal slid his finger across the screen, answering the call, and put it on speaker on the desk in front of Pat. He stood behind him, his hand like a vice on Pat's shoulder. The line crackled as it connected.

"Pat? It's Alvarez."

Malik gestured to get Pat's attention. "You get cute with her, I'll kill your wife, and I'll kill your son as well," he said, just softly enough so that his voice wouldn't carry over the phone. "Make it quick. Tell her everything's okay."

"Pat? Are you there? It's late."

"Detective! Uh, hi," Pat stammered. "Yeah…hi, Pat. What can I do you for? Why'd you call? It's late."

"Oh, uh….I…" "…thought that someone had hurt themselves, but it's all fine now," Gopal cooed into his ear.

"…I…uh, I thought I heard a disturbance, but it's all fine," Pat echoed into the phone.

"Do it for your kid," Malik mouthed at him. "For your kid."

He picked up the scalpel and thumbed the blade, his eyes locked with Pat's.

"Uh…okay?" Alvarez sounded confused. "You couldn't just hit the alarm?"

"It...it didn't work," Pat admitted. "I tried...but it didn't work."

"Uh....." Alvarez sounded half asleep, "...okay? Well, everything's alright now?"

Pat hesitated. Malik flaunted the scalpel. Gopal's fingers pressed urgently into his shoulder.

"Yeah, it's fine. Everything's fine."

"...okay. Goodnight, Pat." She hung up.

*   *   *

As the line disconnected, Malik clapped his hands and whooped gleefully.

"There we go! All sorted. Now you two can stop fretting, yeah?" Gopal nodded tentatively, and – if possible – Amy looked even more downtrodden than before.

"Okay!" Malik continued gleefully. "Now, Pat being here means we have a real chance to get our story straight."

He nodded at Marek's body.

"There's got to be a way to explain that."

"They've been fighting," Amy mumbled.

"Good, good...okay, so..." The conversation faded into the background as Pat's thoughts swum in his head.

"Why didn't the alarm work?" he asked.

Malik whirled around, his eyes alight as though he had a fun fact to share.

"Sal took care of that after he was fired today. A little payoff...makes everyone happy. That said, I think if he knew where it would mean you ended up, he'd have done it for free. What with...you know, botching the job the other day. Bonk!" He mimed hitting someone with something.

Hitting me...with a bottle.

The wound on the back of Pat's scalp prickled in anger. "Sal did this?" he asked. "Sal tried to kill me?"

"We didn't ask him to," Amy said quickly. "He just...thought you were poking around too much. He said he'd 'take care of it'." She paused. "I'm sorry, Pat. I...I always thought you were a nice guy."

It made sense. Sal and his cheap bottles of whiskey.

What did Alvarez say? You're lucky it was a cheap bottle.

"Don't apologise to him!" Gopal yelled. "Look at what he did to my face!"

"Shut up, both of you!" Malik snarled. "You'll have more than enough time to return the favour, but we have to get our story straight. You can't fake a post-mortem, so if we're cutting any fingers off, it has to be done

190

sooner rather than later."

Post-mortem. Cutting fingers off. For a moment, everything felt wonderfully surreal to Pat, like he was living in a movie.

Is this the part where the police burst in, guns blazing, and all the bad guys get shot in the chests?

No. By the sounds of it, Alvarez was already back in dreamland. And the alarm hadn't worked, courtesy of Sal, so Pat was all alone...with the three of them.

Malik and Gopal muttered between themselves in the background, trying to come up with a plan. Pat made another vain attempt to struggle against the flexicuffs. They were getting looser now, grating against the plastic arms of the chair as he dragged them back and forth, but as he pulled his forearms up with all his might, they still held strong.

"Well, it's decided then." Malik clapped his hands together. "Listen up, team; this is how the story goes. Obviously, Pat killed Marek, in here. That means we don't have to move anything."

Gopal nodded. "He already broke in. And he just lied to the police, so that works in our favour."

Pat was astounded. They were talking about him like he wasn't there. Like murder was a spectator sport.

"Right," continued Malik. "But why did he do it?" He jerked his chin in the direction of Marek's body.

"Oh, easy one," sighed Gopal. "There's definitely been some tension. Luka will tell you. Pat's been making wild accusations, I guess...well, it all came to a head tonight? He fell on him, just now. He'll have fibres and whatnot on his clothes."

"He was hiding in the women's restroom a few weeks ago, as well," Amy added meekly. "Kind of...creepy. Catherine – that lawyer, the Asian lady – she saw him. Asked me if I was okay."

That's why Catherine looked so scared earlier.

"Shit, this comes together easily, doesn't it!?" Malik guffawed.

You bunch of fucking psychos.

"Right, so first we've just got to fix this..." Malik produced another scalpel from the table behind him. It was thick with blood. The murder weapon. He waved it triumphantly.

"Same one that Amy used on Nadine!" he chortled, winking at his conspirator. "But Pat makes two for Gopal." He offered the scalpel to his friend across the table. "What should we call you? Head of the leaderboard?"

"I'm not fucking doing it!" Gopal spat. "You do it!"

"I can't do it, I'm a doctor!"

Gopal snorted. "Never one for blood on your hands." He snatched the scalpel and rounded on Amy. "You! You started this whole mess! You can finish it." He pressed the scalpel into her hand and shoved her roughly towards Pat, who was desperately flexing his forearms, praying his bonds would magically break.

Amy advanced on Pat, her face stained with tears, eyes filled with trepidation.

"I'm really sorry, Pat," she whispered. The scalpel glinted in the moonlight.

"Hey! Hold on, hold on!" Gopal jumped forward and caught her wrist. "His…his prints. They need to be on it. And what we were saying before – he needs to have some injuries, or something." He grabbed the scalpel out of her hand and wrenched Pat's wrist backwards, contorting it under the strain of the cuffs. Pressing the weapon into Pat's hands, he squeezed Pat's fingers together around it, then let go. The scalpel clattered to the floor.

"Take it," Gopal ordered. "It can't have my prints on it. Now stab him. In the leg, or something, if you don't want to cut his fingers off."

Amy's eyes brimmed with even more tears. "I don't want to do this," she whispered. "Please…don't make me do this."

"Do it!" Gopal bellowed. "Do it! You fucked this all up from the start, didn't you?! So you're going to fix it!"

Malik steepled his hands on the desk as he watched them intently. He was a picture of calm in the chaos.

Dutifully, Amy bent down and grabbed the scalpel. Tears streamed down her face. "And remember," Gopal continued as he shoved her towards Pat. "You'll be the hero in this story." He patted her on the shoulder.

She turned to him. "I'm sorry, Pat."

Then she stabbed him.

Agony. Unbelievable agony.

The scalpel sank through Pat's leg like a hot knife through butter, and every nerve ending in his thigh screamed simultaneously.

Pat roared like a wounded bull, his teeth clenching so hard together he felt like they were going to shatter. He twisted and turned every way that he could, trying to pull himself free. The zip ties strained under the pressure, even the arms of the chair twisted, but they held strong. Amy wailed again, her face a sheen of tears in the moonlight. She had left the knife embedded in Pat's leg, sticking up vertically like a piece of rebar.

"Do it again!" Gopal ordered.

"I can't!" Amy screeched. "It's inhumane! Don't make me do it, Malik!"

But the doctor said nothing, his expression blank as he watched the chaos unfold in front of him. Gopal advanced on Amy, eyes steely with determination. She backed away, still sobbing uncontrollably, but he grabbed her by the wrist and forced her back towards Pat. "Do it again!"

She's just a puppet. Just a pawn in their game.

Amy tentatively wrapped her hands around the scalpel, and even that set Pat's leg on fire. He tried to kick out at her, but the zip ties around his ankles made that a fruitless effort, although the motion sent his legs ablaze with pain. She yanked out the scalpel and blood poured from Pat's leg in a fountain, and he roared in pain.

"QUIET!" bellowed Malik. Gopal and Amy fell to the side as Malik put a finger to his lips, shushing them. Pat was hyperventilating through gritted teeth as his leg seized up beneath him, the hot blood cascading through his pant leg and running down his ankles.

What about Karen? What about Larry? His three captors paused for a second as Malik cupped his hand to his ear.

Then, Pat heard it as well. A knock on the door. Gopal and Amy looked stunned.

"Check his pockets," Malik whispered as he stood up and strode towards the door, snatching up the second scalpel on his way. "Does he have another phone?"

Gopal obediently patted down his captive, finding nothing but the walkie-talkie. He fiddled with it, revealing static, and set it on the table, shaking his head.

For the first time that night, Malik looked like he wasn't in control.

He doesn't know who's at the door.

Then again, neither did Pat. In his mind, he was praying it was Alvarez; maybe she wasn't convinced by Pat's answers on the phone call and had hotfooted her way over. *Doesn't she live close by? Isn't that how she got here so fast, on the day that Nadine died?*

Malik glanced around the room, and then the knock came again – more insistently this time.

"I know you're in there," came a voice.

Male. Not Alvarez.

Malik whipped towards Pat, and raised his finger to his lips.

"Your wife, and your son," he reminded him. In that hanging moment, Pat felt like his eyes were closing. It was as though someone was wrapping a warm hand around his head and trying to force him to sleep. For a moment, he forgot where he was – he forgot everything except the pain. He forced himself to keep his eyes open.

Whoever's behind that door...that could be your saviour.

Malik paused for a second, then flicked the lock on the door, ready to step out–

–but Pat watched as the figure pushed past him, striding down the corridor and into the conference room.

Luka Vasilj.

CHAPTER 26

Luka stood by the head of the conference table, just inches away from Pat. Marek's body was still on the floor, his toes almost touching Pat's chair.

He must be able to see it!

Pat tried to speak.

"Help me, Luka!"

The words came out as nothing more than a gurgle. His mind was numbing, recognising nothing but pain. He could hardly think, let alone string a sentence together. Luka glanced at Pat briefly, then at Amy – now holding the scalpel, at Gopal – standing next to her, and then back at Malik.

"What the hell is going on?"

"Why are you here?" Gopal spat. "You're never here."

Luka stepped forward, squaring up to the Gopal – who was a good five inches shorter than him.

"This is my business," he hissed, jabbing a finger into Gopal's chest. "And as a result, everything that goes on around here is my business!" He glanced at Pat, again. "So let me ask again, what the hell is going on?! What's he doing here?!"

"He broke in," interjected Malik. "He attacked us. With scalpels he'd stolen from the lab."

Luka paused for a second. He glanced at Amy, who had stopped crying but still looking visibly shaken. "Is this true, Amy?"

"It's true!" shouted Gopal. "Why else would we be here?!"

"I wasn't asking you." Luka rounded on Amy in the corner. "Amy? Is this true?"

Pat watched, helpless.

Tell them the truth, Amy. You're the victim here.

Slowly but surely, she nodded. "He…he broke in and attacked me," she said. "We...we were all in the lab. Dr. Wahba...he got behind him and managed to knock him out, and...and then we tied him up! So he— so he couldn't hurt—."

"We didn't know what else to do," interrupted Gopal, "...so we tied him up. He took the lights out on the way in."

Pat forced his eyes open, and mustered all his energy as it continued to slip away.

"Lu...Luka..." he groaned. "Look....behind..." Swiftly, Luka stepped past Amy and Gopal and knelt in front of Pat. Through the slits of his own eyelids, Pat could see Luka's furrowed brow, staring deep into his own soul. A soft hand touched briefly on Pat's leg, sending pain ricocheting through his entire being—

—but Pat didn't even have the energy to scream anymore.

"He's bleeding out," Luka murmured. "Are the police on their way?"

Malik and Gopal cocked their heads, confused.

"Well you're saying this man broke in and attacked you!" Luka roared. "So did you call the police or not?!"

"No! Oh no – we haven't had a chance to," stammered Gopal. He glanced at Malik, briefly. "I'll take care of it."

He pulled his phone out of his pocket and stepped into the hallway. Luka watched him leave, then turned his attention to the other two.

"Before the police get here, I need to know what really happened," he said quietly. "Why did he break in?"

"We don't know..." said Amy. At least that much is true, thought Pat.

"Luka—" he tried again, but Luka shook his head.

"Don't speak," he said, softly – but firmly. "Don't say anything."

Pat could see the problem. Malik was watching Luka like a lion, ready to strike.

"Amy," Luka repeated. "Why did Pat break in?" Amy's eyes darted back and forth – to Malik, blocking entrance to the corridor – then to Pat, catatonic in the chair – then to Luka.

"He heard me scream," she admitted, unable to come up with another lie. "That's what he said, at least." She paused. "Before he attacked me."

Luka placed a hand under her chin, tilting her head up to look her in the eye. Out of the corner of his eyes, Pat watched Malik take an almost imperceptible step towards them both.

"What happened?" Luka asked. "Tell me the truth."

As Gopal stepped back in the room, tucking his phone back in his pocket, it happened.

Amy broke. It was a waterfall of tears, of guilt, of anguish. She practically collapsed into Luka's arms, and he held her close, stroking her hair softly as the two other men looked on awkwardly from the corridor.

"We....we just wanted everything to work," she sobbed. "...it, it's not our fault – we, we just don't have the funding! We need more time! And…he was asking too many questions, and then Marek found out we were lying, and—"

Luka's eyes flicked around the room and – through his haze of pain – Pat could've sworn that for a split second, they found Marek's feet behind the chair. But he made no mention of it, just held Amy close and shushed her quietly as she let out gut-wrenching sobs into his chest.

Eventually, the moment passed. Luka hugged her tight for a moment longer, and whispered something in Amy's ear, something that Pat didn't quite catch. Then, he stood her up straight, brushed her hair out of her eyes, took the scalpel from her hand, and put it down on the table.

The entire room – Pat included – waited with bated breath.

"He's dead?" he asked quietly. Amy nodded.

"Okay," Luka said. "So our lead investor is—"

"—investments are fine," interjected Malik. "All under control." Luka shot him a look.

Malik shrugged. "We had to do it," he continued. "He found out…he—"

"—he found out that Sal tried – and failed – to kill Pat," Gopal interjected, "and threatened to pull funding."

"Sal has always been number two for Mihok", Malik continued. "Marek fired him, for trying to take care of Pat. That's why he came up here today. But paperwork isn't final yet. Nobody else knows about it. I've already let him know he's still on the team."

Pat tried to piece it all together.

Marek was innocent. An asshole, but he was innocent. Was it just because of Sal? Or did he find out they were faking the trials?

Either way, they killed him for it.

Luka nodded solemnly. "Right…" he murmured. "So…that's the plan? Marek's dead, and what? We just…bring Sal back in, and continue like it never happened? What's the explanation for it? When the police come asking questions?"

"Pat did it," Malik offered. "Pat broke in here, stabbed him with the scalpel before we could stop him."

Luka glanced at Pat.

"It's the only way to protect the product," Malik continued.

Luka bit his lip. He seemed immeasurably calm. "Okay," he said. "That makes sense."

At half speed, Pat's mind whirred.

Is he buying this? Are they telling him that's what happened? Or suggesting that's what they tell the cops?

"Let me get this straight. The four of you were in here – discussing what, exactly?"

"Logistics," Gopal replied, matter of fact. "Distribution," Malik nodded.

"Without me?" Luka asked haughtily. "You're discussing distribution of my product, without me?"

Gopal snorted, and Luka shot him a look that could've burned a man alive.

"Just trying to be efficient," Malik said. "We've got a lot to get through, and I know you went home early. Just because you're not here, doesn't mean things don't need to be done." Disdain lingered in his words.

Luka nodded. Absentmindedly, he twirled the scalpel on the conference room table.

"Alright," he said. "So Pat broke in. I got the alert, by the way; that's why I came down here. He broke in, stabbed Marek, and then you two—" he gestured at Malik and Gopal, "—you two overpowered him and tied him up. Somehow in that mess, he was stabbed in the leg."

"It's not true, Luka!" Pat burbled desperately. "None...none of it's true..."

Luka ignored him. "The cops are on their way," he said, addressing his friends. "Three witnesses to a murder."

"Lock him up and throw away the key," Gopal nodded. "He did it."

Nobody said anything for a minute. The candlelight flickered over all of them; Malik right by the doorway at the end of the corridor, Gopal at the entrance to the hallway, and Luka and Amy standing next to the conference table. Pat eventually broke the silence with a heavy wheeze.

"Let's get you some water in the kitchen," Luka said to Amy, popping an arm around her shoulders and ushering her towards the door. "You look faint."

Even as his mind continued to fade, Pat couldn't quite believe what was happening. Luka paused next to Gopal, pushing Amy ahead of him.

"For the product," he said quietly, and reached out to shake his hand. Gopal's eyes lit up with relief. He gripped Luka's hand in his and shook it fervently.

"It will be worth it," he said. "Once we finish. So many lives to be saved."

And suddenly, everything made sense to Pat.

The scalpel was gone from the table.

*　　*　　*

Faster than anything Pat had ever seen in his life, Luka's left hand shot up from his side, entrenching the scalpel in Gopal's neck. Amy screamed bloody murder. A scarlet fountain erupted, gushing out from Gopal's neck as he staggered backwards, clutching at his throat. Luka swiped at him again, opening a tremendous gash across the side of his face, just under where Pat had hit him with the staple gun.

Gopal's eyes wide with disbelief, he gasped for air as blood cascaded down his chin and chest, his hands failing to stem the torrent of red.

The second attack wasn't necessary.

Gopal was dead before he hit the floor, his face white and ghastly, as Luka shoved Amy violently aside and made for the corridor.

But Malik was gone. The moment Luka had struck, he had wrenched the door open and vanished, white coat flapping in his wake.

Amy shrank up against the wall like a deer in the headlights, her eyes flickering desperately. Luka grabbed her by the scruff of her blouse and pulled her close, nose to nose.

"You move an inch," he hissed, "and you'll get the same." He threw her back up against the wall and rounded on Pat with the scalpel. The blade made short work of the flexicuffs. They burst open and Pat felt the feeling almost instantly rush through to his limbs. Instinctively, he tried to stand, but his wounded leg almost gave out and he collapsed onto Luka. The scalpel clattered to the floor.

"Easy, easy big man," Luka said. "You've got to take a minute."

But Pat didn't have a minute. His eyes were on the door.

You've got to finish this.

The adrenaline of Luka's vicious attack had catapulted his brain back into the land of the living. Blood congealing around his leg, and panting like a wounded bull, Pat snatched up the scalpel from the floor and limped for the exit.

"Pat!" Amy wailed as he passed her, her hands slapping at his shoulders. "Pat! I'm- I'm sorry! They made me do it!"

He shrugged her off, pulling the door back open. A part of him wanted to give her a real piece of his mind, to do to her what she'd done to him with the scalpel. He whipped back around.

"You killed her," he snarled. "You killed Nadine." The scalpel was light in his hand. She looked pathetic as she quivered under his shadow, her throat naked in the candlelight. *Boot's on the other foot now, isn't it?*

"Don't do it, Pat," Luka warned him. "For the moment, as far as I can gather, you're innocent in this."

Pat was so close to her that he could see the beads of sweat forming on her skin. When his voice came out, it was barely more than a whisper, but filled with fury.

"You're done."

And then he was out the door and back in the main lab, his leg roaring at him to slow down, but he pressed on. He crashed past the metal tables, flinging them out of the way as best he could, and they rattled to the side on their wheels. He found the doorway, dipped through the foyer, and rushed to the balcony, hoping to catch Malik in the lobby.

But in the vast empty space below, there was nothing.

He can't be far.

Pat turned on his heel and started limping the short route to the elevators when he saw the light.

A dim light, on the second floor.

The second floor, dominated by the MedHealth office.

Was that on before?

Pat didn't have time to think. He shuffled towards the elevators as fast as his leg would take him and furiously pounded on the button, peering back over the balcony to check if he could see anything inside Malik's office.

Movement. He was in there. The elevator dinged open, and Pat could've almost laughed. This man was so greedy, so insanely unaware of the storm that was about to rain down upon him, that he'd stopped by his office before fleeing the scene.

The elevator shut Pat in, whirring as it plummeted down. Pat inspected his leg. The scalpel had gone in maybe three or four inches, but it felt like it was right the way through. Blood coated his hands and had soaked his pant leg – he must've looked like a victim in a slasher film. He probably should have been a bit more thankful; he'd heard myths that if you were stabbed through a particular artery in your leg, you could bleed out in seven minutes.

But Pat didn't plan on bleeding out. He was just getting started.

The journey down took an eternity, but eventually the doors opened to second, and Pat pressed forward towards MedHealth. The scalpel was hot and wet with his own blood, but he clung onto it. It was his pathway to vengeance.

Yes, Amy had done it. Amy had murdered Nadine. But at her own behest? She was too young, too malleable. He had seen the guilt in her eyes, written all over her face when he'd spotted her at that meeting. Someone had manipulated her into thinking that she was doing this for the greater good.

'You'll be saving lives,' Malik would've said. 'What's one life? Of a woman who already has a death sentence?'

As Pat reached the corner of the landing, the man himself appeared in the doorway to MedHealth. Somewhat fittingly, he'd ditched the white jacket. Even in the disarray, he looked immaculate – loafers, the same linen shirts he always wore, and hardly a drop of sweat. He was clutching a hard leather briefcase, and had a backpack thrown over his shoulder.

They stopped, sizing each other up, separated by maybe forty yards and the atrium that fell the same distance to the lobby. Pat couldn't see his face…but he wanted to.

"You should get that leg checked, Pat," Malik called out to him. "We don't need any more blood spilled tonight." The audacity.

"YOU KILLED HER!" Pat bellowed. "YOU KILLED HER, FOR YOUR STUPID DRUG! FOR MONEY!"

Malik chuckled, the sound booming towards the rooftops as his silhouette grew to monstrous proportions under the lights. It was an eerie sound in the quiet.

Was there no-one else here? Pat thought. *Not one stray, hanging around the building?* He risked a glance upstairs. All quiet.

Malik composed himself and stepped forward a fraction. Pat could see…he was smiling.

"Is that what you think this is about, Pat?" he chuckled. "You think I did this for the money?"

You greedy bastard, of course you did!

"I have enough money, Pat," he continued. "I've got plenty. I did this for the people. And Nadine? The ends justify the means, Pat. One woman dies, and we can finish everything up. Then we save lives. Countless lives, year in, year out. Thousands of people. Hundreds of thousands." He stepped closer still, nostrils flaring, seemingly invigorated by his own words.

Pat looked at the floor, the scalpel hot and ready in his hand. There were maybe ten big strides between them.

But could he make that? With this leg?

"Do you know how many options there are for someone who has Huntington's?" Malik asked coolly. "One. There's one option. You get diagnosed, you ride it out. You make the most of the days you have left. Once you're symptomatic, you die." He scoffed. "And you know what? Nobody's even tried to help. They've studied the disease, but those people have been written off, all their lives! You get it, you die. No, Pat! No! I am here to help people!" His eyes were gleaming, burning with the misplaced passion of a man who truly thought that sacrifice was worth it.

He genuinely believes it.

"She died!" Malik cried. "She died, so that others may live. She was going to die anyway! She had – maybe – four months to go! And you know what? I'm not heartless! I held her hand through her treatments—"

"—her fake treatments!" Pat bellowed. *Take one step closer, you bastard!*

"It's a process, Pat!" Malik bellowed back at him. "That's how research works! You don't start with perfection, you work for it! We test, we try, we re-test, we re-try!"

"But you never tested it!" Pat roared. "And it doesn't work!"

Malik's eyes glinted with fury. "It will work," he hissed. "Because I will make it work!"

He turned away, reaching into his backpack as he made for the stairs…and that's when Pat realized.

He thinks he's just going to walk out of here. He thinks he can get away with what he's done.

Pat charged. His leg surged with renewed pain at every stride as he bounded along the landing like a man possessed, the scalpel tight between his fingers, his eyes locked squarely on the back of the doctor's head. Malik was maybe ten feet from the top of the stairs when Pat lunged for the back of his shirt—

— but his leg gave out, and he staggered—

— and something hit him in the jaw, hard.

Pat saw stars. He'd been hit before, plenty of times. Drunk kids at college bars when he was eighteen and moonlighting as a bouncer on weekends; once when he'd tried to break up a brawl in a restaurant; even when he was a kid and he'd gotten into a fight with a boy in his class on the bus after school.

This was different. He felt like he'd taken a sledgehammer to his face. A simple grunt popped out of his mouth as he dropped to his knees in front of Malik, who was still clutching his briefcase, with his other fist raised like a boxer.

He looks even bigger from this angle.

Malik swapped his briefcase to his right hand and cocked his left fist, determination etched across his face.

"I didn't want to have to do this, Pat. But you really should've fucked off a long time ago."

He swung his fist scything through the still air in a huge haymaker. Pat whipped his hands up to his head, but the doctor swept through his pitiful defences and hit him square in his other cheek.

Pat's eyes whirled backwards in his head as his neck whipped sideways. Something hard – a tooth? – flew down his gullet, and hot blood filled his throat.

Pat was done. He lay in a sorry heap on the ground, coughing up blood, his ears ringing. His teeth were loose in his mouth, and he could feel wetness on the back of his head.

Thankfully, Malik was finished.

"I don't like to hurt people, Pat," he said, nursing his hand. "But you started this. You could've left it all alone. We'd still have lost Nadine, but we'd have lost her anyway. But we lost Marek. And I think we've lost Gopal, too. Amy's done for – she'll go to prison." He paused. "That's all because of you, Pat. Well done."

He turned on his heel, readjusted his backpack, and checked his briefcase.

"Goodbye, Pat."

And he strode away, into the dark.

CHAPTER 27

With all the effort he could muster, Pat finally managed to make it downstairs. The first half was at a crawl, but as he reached the top of the staircase, he swung his legs around and shuffled down on his butt, one step at a time.

He was a mess. His ears were still ringing, blood – both Marek's and his own – coated his pants and undershirt – and more pressingly, his stitches were no longer where they should be. He still couldn't breathe through his nose. On top of that, the exertion of his short sprint before he'd been punched had forced open the clot in his leg, and it was streaming even more blood down his thigh, so much that he could feel it pooling in his shoes. But he had to keep moving forward.

He was sure that Gopal hadn't called the cops. Nobody was coming to help him – he had to make the final stretch to ask.

You need an ambulance. Now.

He reached the front desk on his hands and knees, leaving a trail of blood from his leg across the lobby. His mind foggy, he slapped at the red button, desperate for emergency services.

Sal disabled it, idiot!

Groaning at himself, Pat heaved his bulk up into the chair and groped for the phone.

A hand—covered with blood – slapped down on the receiver.

Wha-?

"Just wait a minute," Luka begged. His eyes were pleading. "Please. I need a favour."

If Pat could've mustered the energy, he would've laughed. "I'm bleeding out on the floor," he wheezed. "Not the best time to be asking for favours."

"I know, I know," Luka said breathlessly, "just – let me ask one thing of you. I'll call the ambulance myself, I'll come with you to the hospital. Just please – please – don't tell anyone about Malik."

His words took the air out of Pat's mouth.

"What...?" Pat gasped.

What–what is he saying?!

"Gopal," Luka insisted. "It was all Gopal. If we turn Malik in, he'll open it up about the fact that we never had appropriate clinical trials...it puts everything in jeopardy. We'd have to restart. Restart, everything. And...I can't do it again." He looked defeated. "Especially without Gopal." In a moment of lucidity, Pat realised the true absurdity of the situation.

"All this?" he gurgled, blood still filling his mouth. "All this? For a damn drug?" Luka nodded.

"All of that," he said, "All of that will have been in vain if we can't finish what we started."

Pat was dumbfounded. He dropped the phone in its cradle and collapsed back in his chair, pain radiating from his leg and the wound on his head awake and alive.

"You do it," he grunted. "Just...ambulance. Please."

Rain started to fall. It gently pattered down on the glass ceiling at the top of the atrium, just loud enough to mask the ringing in Pat's ears from where Malik had hit him.

Luka called an ambulance, before pulling up a chair and sitting next to Pat, who had never been so thankful for anyone's company.

"How's the leg?"

Pat shook his head. "Not great." Despite the wound – and the fact that he felt he couldn't hear or breathe properly – he actually felt okay. Relief, in a certain sense, that this whole mystery had finally come unplugged. Meanwhile, his body was numb and his mind was a slideshow of horror; the scalpel going into Gopal's throat; the terror on Amy's face as she had stabbed him in the leg; the chilling smile on Malik's face; Marek's body, lifeless and cold.

"Marek?" he asked quietly.

Luka shook his head. "He was dead long before you got there."

Pat nodded. Luka obviously knew what he was thinking.

Was there something I could've done to save him?

Pat wasn't the type who typically needed reassurance; despite all the resistance he'd encountered, he'd done his absolute best to figure out what was happening – but it was nice to get some, nonetheless.

"I don't know how to fix this," Luka said quietly, glancing over at Pat. His eyes were empty; not his usual self at all. Gone was the confidence and the dynamism, the determination behind his eyes. He looked shellshocked.

He's just killed a man, of course he's shellshocked.

Gopal. Dead.

Just like Nadine. They sat, side by side, gazing across the empty lobby.

Luka ducked away for a minute, into Joseph's office, and came back with a beer and a bottle of water, the latter of which he handed to Pat. He wedged the tip of his beer on the edge desk and hit down with his palm, taking a small chunk out of the desk and leaving a blood handprint on the wood, and slumped back in the chair. For a moment, Pat forgot that they weren't the only two people in the building.

"What about Amy?" he asked.

Luka didn't say anything. Pat's head throbbed. *How much longer till that damn ambulance?*

"What do we do about Amy?" he asked again. Luka shrugged, and slugged the beer. "Frankly, I have no idea, Pat."

"She killed someone."

"She did. And she'll live with that for the rest of her life."

Is that enough, though? Through the haze of pain and shock, Pat thought he knew what Luka was getting at.

"You don't want to turn her in?" he asked. Luka grimaced. "I don't know," he said. "This…this was all such a mess. She's not malevolent, or evil. She was manipulated. Doesn't she deserve a second chance?"

Pat thought about that one.

Everyone deserves second chances, no matter what they've done.

But the wound in his leg had other ideas.

"You're too forgiving," he grunted through gritted teeth.

"It's up to you," Luka said. "I mean…she stabbed you, as well. If you want to tell the police that, well…I can't stop you. And I won't lie for her."

They fell back into silence. But Pat's mind wasn't quite at rest. He still had questions to be answered; things that didn't quite add up. And Luka was the only person still alive who could answer one of his questions.

"Why were you arguing with Nadine?" he asked. "Monica…Monica told me. You guys were arguing, the night she died."

Luka looked at him, and Pat saw something click.

"You thought I killed her, didn't you?" he asked. There was no resentment in the question, no anger or fury. Just a hint of sadness.

Pat nodded. "I really did."

Luka bit his lip. "I liked Nadine, Pat. I know I can be…officious, I can be protective of my work, but…I'd never hurt someone like that. Not in a million years." His voice cracked slightly. "Not until tonight, at least."

"You were so upset. When Amy's phone was stolen."

"I'm still upset," Luka sniffed. "It was wildly irresponsible. She shouldn't have left her post. You leave your post, you lock the door. She knows that." He breathed a sad sigh. "I guess she had other things on her mind.

"And when I heard Amy screaming, then I definitely thought it was you upstairs. Or Marek. Or both of you."

"Marek? Really?" "In the lobby," Pat mumbled. "When we were all in the lobby, and Eric was arrested. He just...looked so angry. And then the threats..."

Luka huffed. "Well, I'm hardly someone who should tell others how to handle their emotions. Marek, well, he was upset. Really upset. He was close with Nadine, always singing her praises. He was sure it was Eric, and then Johnny got in the way."

"But why did he want the phone back so badly? Why did he send out that email, instead of you? Or Amy?"

"He's an investor, Pat. He might not have been privy to my team's indiscretions, but...he still has a dog in the fight."

It made sense. Finally, it was all making sense.

"And Pat, let me level with you," Luka continued. "I know you were just trying to do your job, but the poking around wasn't doing us any favours. None of us liked it. I'm not trying to excuse his behaviour. He shouldn't have threatened you, but I want you to understand. We're trying to do business, and we've got someone trying to tie us to a dead woman. On two fronts for Marek. I'm not surprised he was trying to get you to back off, but he definitely shouldn't have threatened you."

"Two fronts?" Pat asked.

Luka swigged his beer. "You know – working with her, and being affiliated through the whole..." he meshed his fingers together, "...business-partnership-clusterfuck. Plus, we talked. And I'm sorry to tell you this, but..." he bit his lip, "...we really did think that you'd accidentally let someone into the building by accident. I mean, up until tonight I had no idea that Amy and Malik had ever really even spoken."

Pat scoffed. "You really don't know your own business too well, do you?"

"Yeah, well, that's the price of being CEO. People think you still get your hands dirty, but it's mostly inside the office. Schmoozing. Funding. Phone calls. I'm hardly in the lab with them, anymore. I used to be. Used to be."

"So what were you doing with Nadine, then?" Luka blinked, perplexed. "I never answered your question, did I? Sorry. Uh...she found out what I stood to make off the IPO. She knew it was coming, but I think didn't really understand how much it was going to be. So yeah, she wanted a cut. Thought she was entitled to it." He drained the beer. "I told her no."

Pat said nothing.

"I mean, I think she thought we were friends," he continued. "But she was only ever a test subject to me. We weren't friends." He looked at Pat, somewhat forlorn. "I don't really do, 'friends'. I told her that. She took offence."

The rain was coming down heavier now. An ambulance flew through the front gate, sirens blaring. It screeched to a halt in front of the doors.

Time to go.

The paramedics burst in—

—with Alvarez, right behind them.

"Pat, dear God!" She rushed, her eyes wide with shock. Understandable – Pat hadn't even bothered trying to clean himself up. He waited patiently, sipping on his water as she shoved the desk aside and rushed Luka out of the way to make way for the paramedics.

Then, she saw the blood on Luka's hands. In an instant, her gun was drawn.

"HANDS IN THE AIR, GET ON THE GROUND! GET ON THE GROUND NOW, DO IT!" Pat waved a hand with as much exuberance as he could muster. Alvarez glanced at him quizzically, lowering the gun a fraction.

"It wasn't him," he said. He paused a second, and looked at Luka, who gave him the tiniest of nods.

If you must, he was saying.

"She's still upstairs, I think," he said. "Amy Morales. Try...try the fifth floor."

Alvarez was gone in a whirlwind, not even bothering with the elevators, charging up the stairs like a raging bull. The paramedics rolled in moments later, and with Luka's help, heaved Pat onto a stretcher. They pinched his arm and shoved an IV in there, the same spot where he'd had one just a few days earlier at the hospital. Then, they slipped something around his mouth, and breathing felt much easier.

As the moon dipped behind the clouds, the paramedics rolled Pat out to the front entrance, with Luka following from a distance. As they loaded him gently onto the ambulance, asking him questions he had no energy to answer, Pat felt a cold chill in his arm as the IV started to flow. Luka watched him from the doorway.

"You're a good man, Pat," he said. "I'm sorry, for all of this."

Then the doors closed, and Pat's eyes closed with them.

Time to go.

*   *   *

"Why'd you lie?"

The final question. One of the earlier unanswered questions in this complex affair. And even now, after everything was blown wide open, Pat still had no idea what part Johnny Ray had to play in this whole saga. Perhaps a funeral wasn't the place to ask. But Pat wasn't going back to work any time soon; they'd given him twelve weeks – twelve, all paid! – to recuperate, and he didn't even know if Johnny would still be working in

Guinness House by the time he got back.

So maybe this was the only time he could ask. They were both standing near the back, Pat almost collapsing on his crutches, mingling near the other people from Guinness House. Marek was – of course – absent, as was Sal, who had conspicuously vanished into thin air after the final showdown. Alvarez had shown up on Pat's doorsteps multiple times asking if they had seen him, to which Karen had replied that if he ever showed up around here then he'd never be showing up anywhere else again.

"He threatened my Nan." Johnny kept his voice low so that they could still hear Eric's speech from up the front.

"Why?"

"Because I saw her do it. And Sal...he told me that if I ever said anything, they'd...y'know."

Pat did know. He knew just the sort of threats Sal Whiteman could make, and he didn't doubt for a second that Johnny was lying. But that meant...

"And you still covered for Eric? Even though...?" Johnny nodded. "He was their fall guy. And I fucked it for them."

"Because you couldn't turn them in."

"I had no evidence. Just an accusation. No evidence at all. So...I did what I had to do."

A few mourners glanced at them irritably, and Pat grimaced an apology and did his best to limp away from the group as Eric continued his emotional ramblings. Johnny followed at his side.

"You broke into Microceuticals, didn't you?"

It was hardly a question at this stage, but Johnny gave him the nod anyway.

"Frankly, I'm surprised I got away with it for so long," he said. "Even though I thought I'd timed it well. Catherine left, and I've seen you walk her out to her car. You always disappear for a few minutes after that."

"I was checking the gardens."

Johnny nodded. "Yeah. I thought I had about five minutes. But then they found the phone anyway." He paused, drinking in the fresh air. "I wanted you to see. But I couldn't be the one to tell you."

"Why the phone. though?"

He shrugged. "Thought I might find something on it. Something incriminating. I didn't know who else was in on it until Sal threatened me, and he's too smart. He'd never leave his phone laying around. I thought...I don't know, really. Maybe she'd texted someone about it. Or maybe Sal had texted her to say he had me controlled, I don't know. I just...wanted something I could show the cops. Take them down, you know?"

Pat nodded.

Eric finished up his eulogy, tears welling in his eyes.

"I wanted to tell you," Johnny mumbled. "But I couldn't. If they ever found out we were talking..."

Pat understood.

That's why he ran up and down the staircases. Leading me right to them.

"You showed me," he said. "You showed me as best you could."

Johnny nodded. "I feel bad for Mateo," he said. "I never meant for him to take the heat. I didn't know he was hooking up with Nadine. Just how the chips fall, I guess." He fished a small hip flask out of his jacket pocket and swigged before offering it to Pat.

I guess some things really don't change.

Pat declined and they re-joined the other mourners. The priest presented Eric with an urn and Nadine was scattered into the wind.

It was how she would've wanted to go, Pat knew. Dust in the wind, surrounded by people who cared about her.

And one other person, lurking on the hilltop.

He wasn't wearing his white coat today. He'd traded in the loafers and linen shirt for a black suit. His imposing figure stood stock still on the hill, maybe a hundred yards away.

True to his word, Pat had never turned Malik in. He should've said no when Luka had asked. But, truth be told, there were other reasons. Everything had happened so fast. Amy had been arrested in tears, Gopal and Marek were carted away into the morgue, and he'd been sent home. While Alvarez had been apologetic for his plight, she'd never actually asked him the full story, so he'd never gone out of his way to tell her.

So Pat had kept his promise. Partly because Luka had saved his life, and he felt like he owed him. Partly because a week later, it felt like it was too late to re-open the can of worms. He wanted to put the entire saga behind him.

But mostly because, without Luka to back his story, he wasn't sure if anyone would believe him. Amy was hardly going to turn on her one true love, Marek and Gopal were dead, and Luka seemed desperate to ensure that the remains of his research weren't brought into the limelight yet again.

The man on the hill watched as the priest emptied the urn, and then he was gone.

*   *   *

Over the next few weeks, Pat was effectively a live-in patient at Manhattan General. The rain persisted – sometimes it even snowed – but he was all tucked up in a hospital bed, so it didn't make a blind bit of difference to him. He wasn't up and walking immediately – the doctors told him that it would take at least a month before he was able to walk unassisted, particularly because he was overweight. So Pat put his best foot forward in rehab, with a renewed vow to never taking the elevators again.

He'd dragged himself out of the hospital for Nadine's funeral, but was imprisoned in his room the moment it finished, Karen at his bedside day and night. At least it was a private room with some couches and a chair – courtesy of Guinness House management.

Karen fell asleep with him most evenings, her head resting on a closed fist as she tried desperately to spend every moment with her wounded man. Whenever Pat woke her up, she'd deny having fallen asleep in the first place, and when he insisted she leave and get some rest, she'd beg her bosses for a shift, so that she had any excuse to see him and pump him full of the pain meds that he so greatly appreciated.

The pain got better, but slowly. For the first week, Pat hardly slept unless he was dosed up on a nearly lethal cocktail of medication. They re-did the stitches on his scalp, and a scan told him that he had a fractured cheekbone from where Malik had hit him.

His leg was even worse. They'd told him that when he's been stabbed, the weapon was so sharp that it had snapped his muscle fibres. Karen looked positively horrified at the news, and swept away to bully her subordinates into organising another IV.

But the visitors made the days pass a little faster. Mateo was first up, the day after Pat was admitted.

"I...I heard what happened. And I wanted to say thank you. For everything you did for me." He perched himself precariously on the edge of the bed, almost as if he were too anxious to take a seat properly. But other than that he was polite, asking the right sorts of questions. Nothing too invasive; just enough to keep Pat company.

Unfortunately for Mateo, Pat still had a burning question.

"Nadine gave you money, didn't she?" Mateo smiled wistfully. "Yeah. I...I wasn't too happy about it, to be honest. Not when I found out how she'd gotten it. We...we had a bit of a fight about that."

"Blood money, right?"

Mateo toyed with the clasp of the watch. "Yeah. I just...can't seem to take it off."

"If you really loved her, I don't think she'd want you to."

Mateo's visit was interrupted by Luka, whose knock at the door was the first of many over the next few weeks. He had told Pat that he didn't do friendship, but was already going back on his word. He'd sneak in nasty takeout – even driving down to Philadelphia for Pat's favourite cheesesteak. Karen threatened to throw it away, but she let Pat have his vice.

"Only while you're in the hospital," she cawed. "When you get back home, I've decided that we're both going on a diet."

Pat spent his days watching football – with Luka, or Larry, who came by every day after school, bless his heart – while the nurses and doctors of

Manhattan General ran endless checks. He watched Netflix and read the newspaper when Karen wasn't there.

Alvarez came by – first for a witness statement, and then a few days later with some chocolates.

"The offer still stands," she reminded him. "NYPD could use someone with your...tenacity."

Pat felt like he was being rewarded for being an annoyance. Monica stopped by as well, smothering Pat with kisses and hugs, much to Karen's chagrin. But she let him have his friends over – and even brought some of hers.

Eventually, it was time to go home.

Amy was arrested. Gopal's and Marek's bodies were taken away in black plastic bags. Pat didn't attend their funerals; he didn't think it was right, but there was plenty of coverage of it on the news. Mentions of him cropped up as well – "an unnamed security guard" – and finally the press got a hold of who he was, but he was back at home by that stage, and Karen chased them away repeatedly until they got the message.

Microceuticals itself was blown wide open. All over the papers were snippets of how there were murderers lurking inside a pharmaceuticals company. Their IPO tanked – whether it was the bad press or incomplete research, Pat didn't know. He watched on the news as Luka condemned Gopal's and Amy's actions with a statement.

"What happened in our lab was atrocious," he said in a press conference that was streamed nationwide. "And I want everyone to know that I absolutely do not support the actions of my former employees. I am shocked and appalled that this happened, and the police have my absolute cooperation in this matter. My goal was always to do something good – something great – and they jeopardised that. But that doesn't mean we're giving up."

There was no mention of Malik. His name was not spoken – not by Luka, not even by Pat in his eventual witness statement, as much as it pained him to do so. His dreams were plagued with the vision of that white, gleeful smile.

Every now and then, he woke up sweating.

What if he finds me? What if he finds Karen?

Finally, Pat took a short shift at work. Joseph – out of the kindness of his black heart – moved the rosters around and hired two more security guards, meaning that Lionel and Pat were no longer working twelve hour shifts, and Pat had his weekends back.

He also had his evenings back – they put him on the early day shift – so he could spend his afternoons with Karen...and at doctors' appointments.

His leg healed well. "It'll never be what it was," warned one of the nurses, "but we'll get you there."

Getting him there meant extensive rehab, apparently. Eventually, doctors and nurses stopped showing up as much as they used to, and he ended up spending most of his time at the hospital in a room that would've been better suited to a gym. He had an occupational therapist; Jamie. She was young, innocent. Perhaps a little naïve, but he didn't hold it against her.

"The doctor wants to do a check," she told Pat as she coaxed him off the treadmill and threw him a towel. "Take a seat. He'll be right in." Pat ambled over to a chair and doused himself with what was left of his water bottle. He'd walked for three miles that day and his leg had only given out once – a new record.

Karen would be proud.

He shot her a text.

P: Home soon. Love you.

The door closed quietly.

"Well, Patty. Looks like you've been doing excellent, excellent work."

A chill ran down Pat's spine.

He turned towards the door.

Squeaky loafers.

Linen shirt.

ABOUT THE AUTHOR

Alexander Peel is an English-Australian living on the Sunshine Coast in Queensland, Australia. He enjoys cooking, baking and pretending to go the gym. Professionally he works as an Audiologist, helping underprivileged communities, elderly people and children with hearing issues and communication needs.

Printed in Great Britain
by Amazon

19702357R00129